THE HIGHER JAZZ

The Higher Jazz

BY EDMUND WILSON

EDITED BY NEALE REINITZ

University of Iowa Press Ψ Iowa City

University of Iowa Press, Iowa City 52242

Printed in the United States of America
Design by Richard Hendel
http://www.uiowa.edu/~uipress

Printed on acid-free paper
Library of Congress
Cataloging-in-Publication Data
Wilson, Edmund, 1895–1972
The higher jazz / by Edmund Wilson; edited by Neale Reinitz.
p.   cm.
ISBN 0-87745-653-4, ISBN 0-87745-655-0 (pbk.)
I. Reinitz, Neale, 1923–   . II. Title.
PS3545.I6245H54   1998
813'.52—dc21   98-24436

98 99 00 01 02 C 5 4 3 2 1
98 99 00 01 02 P 5 4 3 2 1

CONTENTS

EDITOR'S PREFACE

My primary aim has been to make *The Higher Jazz* accessible to the general reader, on the basis of a manuscript that was completed but not revised as a whole. I have reproduced Wilson's text from the holograph manuscripts in the Beinecke Library at Yale University, yet in the interest of readability I have made certain changes. I believe that this practice is consistent with Wilson's own statement, cited by Leon Edel in *The Twenties*, that the "handwritten volumes" in his journals ought to be "made as readable as possible." My practice has been closer to Wilson's in his editing of Fitzgerald's *The Last Tycoon* (1941) than to Matthew Bruccoli's in his Cambridge edition of the same novel as *The Love of the Last Tycoon* (1993). I have silently emended errors in spelling and other usages but have retained older forms that Wilson preferred. I have called attention in the notes to his marginalia and revisions when they shed light on the processes of his writing. I have rearranged quoted dialogue in conventional indented form, rather than grouping it in the block paragraphs of the manuscript.

In a more discretionary vein, I have chosen a title for the novel from Wilson's own words, discarding a title that he tired of as it outlived its original purpose. I have divided two of the longer chapters into their natural constituent parts, and I have supplied a title for each chapter (the practice followed by the editors of Wilson's journals). To cite Wilson's review of Hemingway's posthumous *Islands in the Stream*, an editor is not to be censored for "making [the author's] works more coherent if the editing has been done with good judgment" (*The Devils and Canon Barham*, 1973).

The notes have two purposes: first, to bring into focus, where it might be necessary, the world of the 1920s in which Wilson lived; second, and more important, to illustrate the workings of his imagination as he integrated his acquaintances and experiences, his notebooks and his articles into this work of fiction. I have traced this process not simply to ferret out his sources but to show how he "used and reused his materials in so many cunning ways," as Edel puts it in *The Twenties*.

Following the novel and the notes, there are three appendices: corrections of published material on the genesis of the novel, a note on Wilson's use of names, and his essay "The Problem of the Higher Jazz."

I am indebted to a number of people for help in this edition. Steve Jones and the staff of the Beinecke Library of Rare Books and Manuscripts at Yale readily and courteously granted me access to the material in the Wilson collection. The New York Public Library for the Performing Arts at Lincoln Center offered the use of its facilities, while the reference staff of the Charles Leaming Tutt Library at Colorado College provided knowledgeable assistance. Carlton Gamer, Lee Pockriss, Donald Jenkins, and Steve Silverman were generous with their time in reading parts of the manuscript and explaining the musical background. Gale Murray, Fredrick Kaufman, Vivian Perlis, Inna Malyshev, and John Simons answered questions from their expertise. George H. Moss, Jr., graciously introduced me to Edmund Wilson's New Jersey.

On a more personal note: My friend the late Lloyd E. Worner was for many years a sounding board for my interest in Edmund Wilson. My wife, Bev Reinitz, gave me the benefit of her moral support and level-headed criticism. Norman Sams applied his eagle eye and ruthless logic to the text. Lastly and significantly, Lewis M. Dabney provided the encouragement, critical acumen, and insight into Edmund Wilson that were essential to this undertaking.

EDMUND WILSON ON THE ELUSIVE
GLORIES OF THE BOOM ERA

At the time of his death in 1972, Edmund Wilson left among his papers the manuscript of a novel on 207 pages of lined yellow legal sheets. This novel, which he abandoned thirty years earlier, is the first-person narrative of Fritz Dietrich, a young German-American businessman who aspires to compose music that will express the pleasures, the extravagances, and the self-destructive impulses of the Boom Era of the late 1920s. In eighteen months that culminate in the aftermath of the stock-market crash of October 1929, Fritz moves through the world of genteel and popular culture, from an estate on the Hudson to burlesque shows and nightclubs in Manhattan, from cocktail party conversation and the brittle wit of the Algonquin Round Table to a concert of the "League for New Music." The sounds of Debussy, Schoenberg, and Stravinsky echo in Fritz's head as he is driven by the desire both to hear and to create the musical equivalent for the spirit of the times — in Wilson's own words, "the Higher Jazz."

Wilson wrote this novel in 1941 and 1942, when he was able to look back through the years of the Depression at the 1920s. (*I Thought of Daisy*, Wilson's novel set in the Greenwich Village of that time, was completed in 1928, before the decade had ended.) *The Higher Jazz* emerged from his plans for a more ambitious undertaking, a major autobiographical novel, at the midpoint of his career. The time was ripe: in his mid-forties as the 1930s came to an end, he was concluding two decades as a critic of contemporary literature and life. There lay ahead of him thirty years in which he was to explore the classics, the past, and a variety of cultures and traditions.

In the late 1930s he began to write ideas in his journal for what he called the "Red Bank and Moscow Novel." Out of a rambling series of notes he developed a coherent proposal for a novel in three parts, which he had typed up in the fall of 1939. (Leon Edel prints these materials in Wilson's journals of *The Forties*, 1983. I have discussed his treatment in "The Genesis of the Novel: Some Corrections.") Wilson planned a sweeping narrative, *The Story of the Three Wishes*, in which one man was to assume three sequential identities for five years each — as an American stockbroker, a Russian official, and a bohemian writer in Provincetown. These identities reflected in turn the author's excitement as "a man of the twenties"; his radicalism and his visit to Russia in the mid-1930s; and a change he was bringing about: a withdrawal to Cape Cod and the independent writing life.

Wilson never wrote this novel. Some of the reasons were external: it was a time of heavy responsibilities for him. After presenting his original proposal in 1939 — and asking Maxwell Perkins for an advance of $3,000 — he was busy finishing *To the Finland Station* and *The Wound and the Bow* and, for six months, filling in for Malcolm Cowley at the *New Republic*. Soon after Scott Fitzgerald's sudden death at the end of 1940, Wilson was collecting tributes for that magazine (later included in *The Crack-Up*) and editing *The Last Tycoon*, which Fitzgerald had left unfinished. In the early summer of 1941, while Fitzgerald was very much on his mind, he sat down to write the first part of the projected novel. Declaring himself dissatisfied with the fairy-tale title of *The Story of the Three Wishes*, he conceived an entirely different book, and through the summer he kept Perkins informed of his progress on it. It was a story of the 1920s, like the first "wish" of the plan he had conceived, but with a different perspective on those times, from a different kind of hero. He worked on this manuscript well into 1942. Despite certain loose ends and unresolved issues, it would turn out to have a place on the narrow shelf of Wilson's fiction, standing between *I Thought of Daisy* (1929) and *Memoirs of Hecate County* (1946).

A reader of the manuscripts in the Wilson collection of the Beinecke Library at Yale can observe how, after a pause of almost two years, he had turned his original project in a new direction. The departures from the proposal of 1939 gradually become evident. Much as in the proposal, an unnamed narrator takes a train from Manhattan to his home in New Jersey one morning in the summer of 1928; before he arrives at his destination he fulfills Wilson's first wish by hypnotizing himself into the identity of a man who is sitting in the seat across from him, next to an attractive woman. In the character of this man, he gets off with the woman at a station near the shore. He spends the weekend with the woman "at a summer hotel," as Wilson had planned. But the story has begun to change. It becomes clear that Wilson is departing from his previous notion: the man who is now telling the story is not a stockbroker who will become "hipped on Communism" and go to Russia but Fritz Dietrich, the would-be composer. The book that Wilson is writing is no longer the first wish of *The Three Wishes*;

it is the short novel that I have described in the first paragraph, to which I have given the name *The Higher Jazz*.

Early in the novel he disposes of his original, unnamed Wilson-character, who has a mistress in New York and a family in New Jersey. The principal service of this "sometime playwright" is to provide a cold-eyed description of the man whose identity he is unknowingly about to assume. From the outside, Fritz appears "distinctly arrogant" but shows traces of amiability and intelligence. His eyebrows, "in that position which we associate with superciliousness or surprise," gave "his eyes — rather sharp and clear, and brownish green — a perpetual look of the ironic-naive." (Wilson's eyes were described as "dark brown, almost black.") Fritz's physical build supports his arrogance; he is more imposing than the short, stocky Wilson: "He was dark — his skin was quite dark; and he wore a small non-pointed mustache. He was moderately tall, with straight shoulders, and gave the impression of being thick and all in one piece, like a football player without flexibility, with a head closely set on his shoulders, which naturally looked straight ahead."

After the original speaker has become this person, intellectually aggressive and physically formidable, Fritz can tell his own story. At first he is only dimly aware of who he is, like a recovering amnesia victim. When he takes a taxi to the seaside resort, he is at ease in his surroundings and obviously familiar with the woman who accompanies him. The reader learns that he is thirty-one years old, from a reasonably well-to-do German-American family in Pittsburgh, and that music is his chief interest in life, although his means are such that he must otherwise work for a living. Fritz feels that the Germans bore an unjust share of the blame for the War. His German background and his view of life in the 1920s come together in his enthusiasm for Spengler's *Decline of the West*. We learn that he went to "Kendall School" and to Yale, where he did not make Skull and Bones, the senior honor society; that he judges his friends and acquaintances with some severity; but that he is as comfortable among writers, musicians, and composers as with the wealthy and well established.

Who is Fritz Dietrich and how did Wilson come to create him? Although he is not a Wilson clone, the outward appearance of this self-confident, well-built man with the mustache suggests an idealized Wilson, and he is a vehicle for many of Wilson's tastes and passions. His comments and his behavior reveal an appetite for sex, a fondness for drinking, an interest in food, and an awareness of social nuances and political personalities. Like Wilson, who was always short of cash — and thought of himself as a creative writer as much as a critic — Fritz must support himself, in his case by traveling for a drug company, "Payne and Keller." But there are differences, too. Wilson drew some of Fritz's interests, expertise, and situation from his friend Paul Rosenfeld, a gentler, less assertive man. Rosenfeld was a critic who wrote about contemporary music and literature in a number of books and in articles for the *Dial* and the *New Republic*. Although Rosenfeld, unlike Fritz, was Jewish, Wilson used his Germanic background as a point of departure for a portrayal of Fritz as a faintly aristocratic, faintly Junker, Americanized German who is at ease in many circles of society but does not belong to any of them; he is a graduate of Yale who can look critically, with his raised eyebrows, upon the enthusiasms for World War I, the stock market, and his alma mater.

Wilson's choice of Fritz as a protagonist is off-center for him but makes sense, given his long-standing friendship with Rosenfeld. The reason for that choice — the focus on music — is still unusual but even more plausible. Wilson loved music, but this was the only occasion on which he felt confident enough to write about it at length. He listened with pleasure to his collection of records and was frequently in the audience at concerts, ballet, opera, and musical comedy. In the early 1920s he had written a libretto for a ballet by Leo Ornstein, which was never staged. He attended recitals at the International Composers' Guild and its offshoot, the League of Composers. He went to the Berkshire Festival at Tanglewood, Massachusetts, in the 1940s. In the course of his life — and on occasion at Rosenfeld's apartment on Irving Place — he made the acquaintance of a number of composers whose works he knew, among them Aaron Copland, Elliott Carter, and Igor Stravinsky. He respected Rosenfeld as a humanistic, nontechnical critic of music, though much aware of his own lack of musical training. Apart from a memoir of Rosenfeld reprinted in *Classics and Commercials* (1950), he preserved little of his music criticism, notably three reviews from 1925 and 1926 included in *The American Earthquake* (1958). He was convinced, however, of the vigor of "our popular music" — a feeling that pervades his journals and *I Thought of Daisy*— and of the value of the atonal music of Arnold Schoenberg and the other modern composers whose work he knew well. He wrote in 1926 of his hopes for a music that would combine these strains in the spirit of modern America, as Stravinsky (his greatest enthusiasm) had done with Russian folk themes. (According to Wilson, Rosenfeld, who "loathed jazz in all its raw forms . . . could only accept it transmuted by the style of a Stravinsky or a Copland.") In the essay that he was to call "The Problem of the Higher Jazz," Wilson anticipated the principal motive in Fritz Dietrich's search for a musical response to the extravagant pleasures and painful hangover of the 1920s. The novel embodies the central idea of the essay, in this way deserving its present title. Wilson had come a long way from *The Three Wishes*: he was completing only one wish, with a subject he had not planned to write about.

Through Fritz's passion for music, a refracting lens to view the past, Wilson was enabled to revisit the world of the late 1920s, concentrating the action of the novel into eighteen months in 1928–29. The choice of this period suggests a hidden agenda: he was depicting a crisis in Fritz's life in the months that had been a crucial period in his own. As Lewis Dabney has pointed out in his biographical essay in *Edmund Wilson: Centennial Reflections* (Princeton UP, 1997), the eighteen months beginning with Wilson's relatively tranquil existence when he was finishing *I Thought of Daisy* in California included a complete breakdown in which, unable to work and to decide whether to get married, he was confined to a sanitarium. Fritz's exhilarating yet disappointing struggles are parallel in time to Wilson's ordeal, but to recall the events of this period in his own life was too painful for the author. (He wrote nothing about his breakdown until the posthumous journal of *The Twenties*, 1975.) In *The Higher Jazz* he chose to fill the eighteen months with experiences drawn from other times. What happens to Fritz in 1928–29 comes out of Wilson's mid-1920s (a promising time for him) and early 1930s, as well as a mixture of trips outside New York and visits to friends.

Wilson fused and reshaped the myriad incidents of his life with skill, perhaps not quite as seamlessly as he had molded the raw materials from his literary quarries in *I Thought of Daisy*, and would mold them again in *Memoirs of Hecate County*. The notes and drafts for *The Higher Jazz* show that as his memory came into play, he thumbed through his notebooks, his loose notes, and his published articles — for conversations, sexual interludes, visits to country houses, evenings at a burlesque show or a recital. As he wrote, and sometimes revised, he molded the impressions he had acquired, to fit his time-scheme and his story. The opinions Wilson had about the 1920s, the places he knew, and the people he remembered found their way into the novel for a variety of purposes. Many of the characters in *The Higher Jazz* were based upon discernible models or constructed as composites, in the manner of Professor Grosbeake of *I Thought of Daisy*, a combination of Alfred North Whitehead and Christian Gauss. (Wilson vigorously decried the practice of identifying fictional characters with their originals, but at times could be led into making identifications of his own.)

Caroline Stokes, the woman whose "well tailored blue back" and "round little rump" Fritz follows as they step off the train, is created from an intensely remembered part of Wilson's personal life in the late 1920s and early 1930s. After a sensual but emotionally precarious weekend at a seaside hotel early in the novel, Fritz and Caro-

line are married. Their growing incompatibility accen-
tuates Fritz's inner tension: she does not appreciate music, and she chooses her friends from a "cocktail set" that
Fritz regards as representative of all that's most hollow in
the society of the time. The creation of Caroline was Wilson's first attempt to recall in fiction the vicissitudes of his
life with his second wife, Margaret Canby, who in 1932
died tragically by falling down a flight of stairs in Santa
Barbara. (She lived there with her young son for some
months each year, while Wilson was in the East.) Later in
the 1940s he made her the model for the "Western girl"
Jo Gates, a fairly minor character in *Memoirs of Hecate
County*. Wilson was to dream about Margaret for the
rest of his life, but the literal details of their love and their
conflicts did not appear in print until the posthumous
publication of his journals, notably *The Thirties* (1980),
which included his extended memoir of their marriage.

Through Caroline, Wilson attempted to memorialize
Margaret, while at the same time, for the purposes of the
novel, exaggerating her philistinism and the tension between her and Fritz. Caroline is more petulant and con-
tentious than Margaret, who had a lighter touch, but her
personal circumstances are close to Margaret's. She too
is not an intellectual; she too has a life away from New
York — in New Orleans; she too divorces a drunken
husband. Like Margaret, she takes her new husband to
visit an eccentric, wealthy elderly relative who lives in
Philadelphia. Wilson derived his descriptions of Caroline
from passages in his notebooks and the memoir of Margaret that he wrote shortly after her death. Like Margaret,
Caroline has a "cunning, little thick body," like a turtle's,
with "little arms and legs"; she makes love with her eyes

open; and she has a Scotch Canadian habit of combining "British coolness" with a certain "rakishness."

Caroline, cool and reserved on the surface, is at once a foil and a confidante to a very different woman, who appeals to the intellectual side of Fritz, and who comes out of Wilson's professional life in the 1920s. Kay Burke is a brittle, undisciplined person with "round black eyes," black hair, and a "windblown bob." Through the novel, Kay keeps a bright running commentary as she falls in love, is neglected, disguises an abortion, and cuts her wrists — but manages to survive — in the manner of her original, Dorothy Parker. Kay Burke looks, speaks, and acts like Parker; the Parker puns recorded in Wilson's notebooks come out of her mouth ("Hiawatha nice girl till I met you"; "Paroxysm best city in the world"). Kay writes drama reviews for a magazine whose name is said (mistakenly, Fritz points out) to be *Manhattan*, just as Parker did at times for *Vanity Fair* and the *New Yorker*. She is generally esteemed for her sophistication.

Parker's place in Wilson's life — professional, intellectual, witty — was exactly the opposite of Margaret's. She had helped him to his first job in New York, on *Vanity Fair* in 1921; he liked her and respected her, and they drank and gossiped together. But her presence in the novel is another surprise, for although he knew her for many years, he was never emotionally involved with her and could view her with some detachment. Although he quoted her frequently in his notebooks, she appears nowhere else in his fiction. At the time that he was working on this manuscript, he was married to Mary McCarthy, who had little in common with Dorothy Parker. It is interesting that during this stormy marriage Wilson should model his principal female characters on two other women. (To an interviewer in the 1980s, McCarthy professed to have no knowledge of Wilson's work on the manuscript.) Some traces of McCarthy can be found in the vulnerable, mercurial Kay Burke: Wilson tried out "Myra" before he settled on a name for her. As "Kay Burke," she is "partly Irish," her "Irish aggressiveness" mixed in with a "masochistic" Scandinavian side.

Kay Burke and her friends form a circle of mordant wits who sparkle at Fritz's parties and at country week-ends, in lively, if for Fritz nervous, contrast to his staid family and Caroline's idle socialites. Fritz realizes that this group epitomizes the self-destructive 1920s in their disordered private lives, but he cannot help but be drawn into their self-lacerating wisecracks and word games. Kay's friends are loosely derived from other members of the Algonquin Round Table, a circle that Wilson found, apart from Parker, superficial and "rather tiresome." Nick Carter, her faithful companion, who combines acerbic wit, nagging insecurity, and a strange evangelical streak, has his origin in Robert Benchley. It was Wilson's pleasure to endow this character, who resembles the Harvard-educated Benchley in his platonic attachment to Kay and his untiring comic routines, with the moral earnestness that the Princetonian Wilson considered en-demic in right-thinking, clean-living Yale men. Kay's dis-astrous affair with Bill Shippen, an unemployed arche-ologist "who had briefly tried a brokerage office," blends Parker's feckless attachments to the writer Charles Mac-Arthur and a businessman named John Garrett.

A giddier side of the 1920s appears in the characters of Phil Stewart and Irving Freeman, Caroline's old friends from the "cocktail set," whose vacuity and superficial wit bore Fritz even more egregiously than Kay, Nick, and their circle put Caroline ill at ease. Fritz's own friends show their inner emptiness in two episodes in a country house toward the end of the novel, as the clouds of the Crash begin to gather. Wilson's notebook entries for the early spring of 1933, made six months after Margaret's death, provide the material for a scene in a house, which, as Wilson wrote in the margin of his manuscript, was like "Scott's house in Baltimore." Fritz, Caroline, and their friends drink, play tennis, swim, and talk as guests of a pipe-smoking host in golf pants and his languid patrician wife. The host couple inherit some of the mannerisms of Scott and Zelda Fitzgerald, overlaid with a few spare hints of Gerald and Sara Murphy (whom Wilson knew only indirectly at the time but whom Dorothy Parker adored). Wilson's notebook furnished the physical details of the house, with its newel posts and varnished wood, and realistic suggestions for the people in it. In the same chapter of the novel, Fritz observes Kay Burke, her friend Nick, and her lover Bill working up a self-destructive fantasy in which they act out the parts of mad, eccentric members of a family called the "Ratsbys." Wilson had a predilection for rats (he wrote about them more than once), but the association with "Gatsby" is inevitable where there are reminders of Fitzgerald.

The spirit of the age is captured more broadly in other ways. Fritz and Caroline conduct an entourage to an evening at Dixie McCann's nightclub, where a narcissistic comedian perfects the art of self-deprecation, and drunken businessmen snatch ostrich plumes from the scanty costumes of showgirls. Fritz is fascinated and repelled by this frantic interplay of ego, money, and power. The character of Dixie McCann is adapted from Wilson's published sketch of Texas Guinan, hostess laureate of Prohibition, but the dynamics of the scene are his own invention. As a running background to the novel, the public events of the late 1920s, scattered in Wilson's journals, are crammed into these eighteen months. Fritz hears references to the speculation in Florida real estate, Lindbergh's flight to Paris, and Al Smith's defeat at the hands of Herbert Hoover, whom Fritz calls "an illiterate engineer who writes with his mouth full of pancakes."

These portraits of the Jazz Age, with its accompanying Babbitry, are boldly contrasted with the Edwardian world of Fritz's family. Julie, Fritz's sister, is married to the urbane, middle-aged Henry Powell, who presides over a baronial establishment on the Hudson and takes part in New York state politics with *noblesse oblige*, not condescending to the gaucheries of Smith, then governor. For the scene at his sister's house, where Fritz breaks the news of his intended marriage, Wilson adapts — sometimes word-for-word — his notebook account of a 1936 visit to the estate of his Princeton classmate Bill Osborn. The portrait of Henry, Fritz's brother-in-law, is based on William Church Osborn, Bill's public-spirited father.

Fritz is hoping to perceive, understand — and perhaps re-create — the dynamics of this world through music. Here Wilson departs further from his notebooks: imagination plays a prominent part in Fritz's pursuit of the rhythms of jazz and the new atonalities of classical music. He listens to the work of a variety of modern composers, admires a charismatic Jewish violinist with hints of George Gershwin, and despises a smart-aleck night-club singer and songwriter in a vulgarized image of Cole Porter. In solitary moments Fritz sits down at the piano to improvise the quality of a New York sunset or the "careless and regular shyness" of the ephemeral hostess who glides down the stairs of her country house. He begins to see the commonality between the popular and the classical when on successive evenings he and Caroline attend a burlesque show and a concert of the League for New Music. The cruel humor of Schoenberg's *Sprechstimme* (speech-song) *Pierrot Lunaire* brings to Fritz's mind the violent horseplay at the burlesque show of the night before. (Caroline is simply shocked at the burlesque and bored at the recital.) The raucous details of striptease, slapstick, and a parody of *Antony and Cleopatra* come out of Wilson's *New Republic* articles on burlesque from 1925 and 1926; but the concert of the League for New Music is a satiric sequence of avant garde performances before an odd and intense audience, rising in parody out of Wilson's review of a composers' group.

The outcome of Fritz's search is revealed to him as the novel comes to an end with a recital he arranges in his old-fashioned Fifth Avenue apartment in December 1929, two months after the Crash. Fritz has invited Edgar Rockland, the elderly, eccentric New England composer who has become a major repository of his hopes for the achievement of American music, to perform a series of "New Hampshire pastorals." Rockland is an energetic, charismatic crackpot, whose personality and music are exaggerated versions of Charles Ives and his compositions. Although Wilson had not declared an interest in Ives at this time, his work was coming into public notice.

Paul Rosenfeld had written about him, and Copland had played his music, since the 1920s, when he was relatively unknown. Fritz turns the pages for Rockland as he pounds out the "pastorals" that begin with thunderstorms in the mountains and are loaded with quotations from "Onward Christian Soldiers," "How Dry I Am," and "By the Light of the Silvery Moon." In his reaction to Rockland, Fritz must decide whether his quest for an American music, combining the popular and the classical, has been fulfilled. At a climactic moment, Kay Burke, the Dorothy Parker character, arrives on the scene in emotional turmoil. Her remorseful wit surrenders to the idiosyncratic composer-philosopher in a highly charged scene in which Rockland utilizes economic panaceas, Indian myths, and hypnotism to offer a verdict on the moral condition and the music of the era of Boom and Bust: "We're all bleeding to death. . . . we're bled of our emotion and we're bled of our money — and our music is bleeding away."

The novel was not so much unfinished as unresolved when Wilson ceased work on it, apparently in the early summer of 1942. In the last chapter, Fritz's musical quest and the prosperity of the 1920s come to an end at the same time, but the stories are not effectively interwoven. Wilson wrote out a three-page summary on the effects of the Crash — the storm-cloud that finally burst over the 1920s — as a guide for the conclusion but could not work its essence into Fritz's musical search. Nor did he carry through the dissolution of Fritz's marriage (despite repeated self-promptings in his marginal notes) or integrate it with the Crash and Fritz's disappointment in Edgar Rockland. Once he had set aside the manuscript, he did not go back to it in any serious way: he seemed unable to resolve these issues.

Even as he was writing *The Higher Jazz*, Wilson seems to have been attracted to another idea, which better suited his mood of the early 1940s, a time when he was uncertain about his marriage to McCarthy and felt isolated from many of his contemporaries, by his opposition to World War II and because the generation of the 1920s was now fading. The notion of a society inhabited by the devil and ruled by the goddess of witchcraft was emerging in the stories that would make up *Memoirs of Hecate County*. In December 1941 he wrote Maxwell Perkins that he was dividing his efforts between his novel and the new stories. By the fall of 1942 he had dropped *The Higher Jazz* and was giving his principal attention to *Hecate County*, which had "turned into much more of a project than I had contemplated." It was evidently easier for him to develop a new book from a series of tales with a central motif (two of which he had written in 1941) than to prepare for publication a work that needed the effort of significant revision. He had already gratified his impulse to explore the subtleties of musical composition in the story "Ellen Terhune," which was to become a part of *Hecate County*. Like the earlier motivation for *The Story of the Three Wishes*, the struggles of Fritz Dietrich lost their appeal.

There was another reason for Wilson's abandonment of this hero. Although attracted to the 1920s as a literary subject, he was ambivalent about his ability to write in fiction about those times. Fitzgerald's death and his own editing of Fitzgerald's work had taken his thoughts back to the earlier decade after his absorption in the events of the 1930s. When he came to the end of *The Higher Jazz*, however, he was subject to a backlash. One can surmise that he felt as he had in 1929, when he compared the page proofs of *I Thought of Daisy* with *The Great Gatsby*: that his own work was markedly inferior to Scott's in "prose and dramatic sense" and "vividness and excitement." Giving up on this book, Wilson did not give up on the 1920s. In the 1950s he went back to the articles, short stories, reviews, and notebooks he had used in his manuscript, revising them for retrospectives of the period. The sources of scenes in *The Higher Jazz*, such as those from Minsky's burlesque, football weekends at Yale, Texas Guinan's nightclub, and the Algonquin Round Table, peek through the collected essays of *The Shores of Light* (1952) and *The American Earthquake*, as well as the journals of *The Twenties*. He felt confident to exhibit outside of fiction the pleasures and malaise of the times that Fitzgerald had revealed so well in *Gatsby* many years before.

Certainly the boom and bust of the 1920s and the guilt-tinged rehearsing of Wilson's second marriage provide much of the historical and personal interest in *The Higher Jazz*. For Wilson as a writer, however, the intrinsic importance lies in the parallel between Fritz's search for an American music and the issues at the center of his other two novels. *The Higher Jazz* qualifies as the second volume, rather than the first, of a trilogy that the author would eventually complete in lieu of *The Story of the Three Wishes*. This new trilogy is devoted to the search for a truly American culture, neither exclusively high nor low. Like the men in *The Three Wishes*, for whom the "modern world" had "presented the same problems," the heroes of *I Thought of Daisy*, *The Higher Jazz*, and *Memoirs of Hecate County* seek answers to a single question, in their various concerns with poetry, music, and painting: How can the artistic intellect comprehend the meaning of America? The time line of the three novels taken together, running from 1920 to the early 1940s, roughly resembles the fifteen-year span allotted to the *Three Wishes*.

Instead of a stockbroker, a Soviet bureaucrat, and a bohemian writer ("the same man all along") the men of *I Thought of Daisy*, *The Higher Jazz*, and *Memoirs of Hecate County* are upper-class college graduates with modest inheritances. The nameless character in *Daisy* is a writer; the narrator of the *Memoirs*, also nameless, is an art critic. Wilson has given Fritz more distance from himself than he gave the other two, through his name and the accompanying Germanic traits. The protagonists of all three novels, like Wilson, are at home in the traditional arts but have a taste for popular culture; they seek a reconciliation that will focus their sense of America. This cultural dilemma is accentuated by the contrast between the pairs of women in each novel: the rarefied poet Rita versus the unselfconscious Daisy; the witty, brittle Kay versus the sensual, irritable Caroline; and, in *Hecate County*, the effete "Princess" Imogen versus the working-class Anna. Wilson confronts the tension between high and low culture — a perennial problem for him — in his essay on "Gilbert Seldes and the Popular Arts" in *The Shores of Light*, originally written in two articles a quarter-century apart.

Although Wilson did not choose to make the revisions that would effectively integrate Fritz's musical search into his own life of the 1920s and the tragedy of his marriage, *The Higher Jazz* stands as an example of his methods and purposes. It shows how he refashioned his experiences and his observations, his notebooks and his articles, into a novel driven by an idea. It offers a bonus of eccentricities, such as the climactic meeting of a Dorothy Parker and a Charles Ives, which extend beyond his rigorous plans for *The Story of the Three Wishes*. Readers deserve access to this short novel, just as Wilson, as a critic, accepted the posthumous publication of Hemingway's *Islands in the Stream*, commenting that it is no disservice to publish an "uncompleted book," if it reveals truths about the nature of the author and the quality of his talent.

THE HIGHER JAZZ

PRELUDE

JUNE 1928

I came to realize late Friday afternoon that I was contending against a stubborn aversion to going down to see my family in the country.

I had stayed on so long in my office in conversation with others who had also stopped work, saying poised and intelligent things and smiling repeatedly and pointlessly, that I had left myself too little time to make the last train before dinner. I called up and told them at home that I would be down on the midnight train; then went to my college club, had two highballs, and dined alone.

There was nothing to keep me in the city. It was getting toward the end of June, and New York was abandoned and hot. I could not go to Lucille's that night, because it was one of the rare week-ends in summer when her friend Mr. Filsinger was staying in town. I was disgusted, besides, with the whole thing. She told me — and it wasn't incredible — that Mr. Filsinger was so old and so queer that all he wanted was to touch her breasts; she

1

even told me she paid her own rent, but I knew she could not live on her modelling.

After dinner, I went to the Follies, still alone, and there fell in with a publicity man, with whom I afterwards went to a speakeasy and had a long uninteresting conversation over a series of bad little bootleg brandies, in the course of which I listened with friendly attention to his account of his producer's play and made quick and keen observations which showed my grasp of the subject. On the brandies, I called up Lucille. I wanted to on the assumption that it was true, as she had told me, that Mr. F. never spent the night and that he invariably went away early; yet I had always on such occasions been afraid I might compromise her. It turned out that Mr. Filsinger had been suffering extremely from the heat and had gone out the same night to Stamford.

I called up Monmouthbury and told them I wouldn't be down till the next morning, then I went over to West Fifty-Seventh Street. I found her rather upset: the old man had had a kind of collapse. "I was really scared," she told me. We drank some Old Overholt he had brought her — in those days bottled in bond — and her apartment began to look more amusing, even a little romantic. I could almost feel the appeal of the big bronze Chinese jar that diffused a subdued lighting, of the electric-lighted goldfish aquarium with its nude figures of sprawling china sea-maidens; of the enormous Empire bed, with its lettuce-green canopy, its apple-green sheets, its pink bed-lamp, and Lucille's pink silk nightgown. As I slipped the nightgown down from one of her breasts, I was able to feel gratification that a figure sufficiently elegant to give her at least partial employment at one of the fashionable dressmakers' should willingly lie in my arms. I wondered but did not ask whether the collapse of Mr. Filsinger had occurred at the moment of touching her breast.

She was tired and wanted to go to sleep, but I went into the other room and finished the rye and played some phonograph records; and I passed into a tranquil rapture as I relished the rich sensuality, the blue unhappy beautiful longings, of American popular music.

I did not get off the next day till noon, and got on the train with the most dismal kind of hangover. It seemed to be hotter than ever. I tried to get the window up as soon as we were out of the tunnel; but it was hopelessly stuck, and all my effort only made a great throb of pain in my head, like the dynamo of the city turning over when I wanted things to be quiet, and left me feeling coerced and cooped-in. There they were: the rank befouled green wilderness of the salt marshes, the big brick home for alcoholics, the giant dumps for tin cans and rubbish, and — reaching me even from a window far ahead — the horrible smell of the pig-pens where the pigs were fed on the refuse. Already the thick air of the summer gave the sky — neither gray nor blue — a look that was both dull and glaring. I had taken a seat at the end of the car in the hope of being able to put my feet up on the permanently facing seat; but at Newark a young man and woman insisted on sitting down opposite me.

The man said, "Is this seat taken?" with a coolness and assurance which I thought had a touch of arrogance.

I thought at first he was being perverse; but then it occurred to me that they had wanted to be together and

preferred this to separate seats, which were no doubt all
that was left in the car, even though these would be more
comfortable and faced in the right direction. When I had
pulled in my legs and readjusted my position, I closed
my eyes in an attempt to relax again and found myself
alone in the dark with a fresh and intense pressure of
pain. Then the glimpse I had had of them seemed vividly
to have been thrust back into my mind independently of
my interest or will. I saw them as they had looked when
they sat down after the man had put up in the baggage-
rack an old suitcase with straps of his own and a small
smooth light brown suitcase of hers with stickers of
French hotels. He had asked her something which, in my
stunned condition and with the noise of the train's starting, I hadn't overheard — I suppose, whether she wanted
anything out of her bag — and she had answered definitely and quickly; and now I saw his lifted eyebrows
as he had looked down at her and her brief inaudible
reply made without looking at him and hardly moving
her lips.

I opened my eyes again and glanced at them sitting
there, then found when I had shut my eyes that I had
photographed them and could study the picture of them
as if it had been a still from a movie. The man's face *was*
distinctly arrogant, but it was not entirely unamiable, or
rather perhaps it was not unintelligent: I saw that his
eyebrows, which I had remembered him as lifting, were
actually situated in that position which we associate with
superciliousness or surprise — up at the ends over the
nose and drawn down on the other side — in such a way
as to give his eyes — rather sharp and clear, and brownish green — a perpetual look of the ironic-naive. He was

dark — his skin was quite dark; and he wore a small non-pointed mustache. He was moderately tall, with straight shoulders, and gave the impression of being thick and all in one piece, like a football player without flexibility, with a head closely set on his shoulders, which naturally looked straight ahead. He was wearing the conventional Brooks suit of my generation at college — a greenish gray herringbone that went with his hazel eyes. Though he had assumed the straw hat of June in place of the derby which was unquestionably habitual with him, he was still wearing his cheviot vest, with the last button correctly unbuttoned. On the other hand, he had gone in for one of those colored silk shirts that fastened with a gold pin under the tie — a brown one with a dark green spotted necktie — which my own conservative taste still shrunk from. The woman was small with regular features; I did not think her pretty or plain, and did not at first get as complete an idea of her: I only noted that she was quietly and smartly dressed, with a blue cloche hat on blond indeterminate hair and a travelling dress that matched. She had a glossy dark blue purse, which she had plucked from under her arm and put in her lap. When I had opened my eyes again, she had leaned her elbow on the window-sill and looked out. I saw that her hand was tiny. The man looked straight before him.

The vision began getting obsessive, as had happened to me sometimes with those images that come to you between sleeping and waking and that the psychologists call *hypnogogic*. I felt a compulsion to scrutinize their features, to note eyelashes, nostrils, wrinkles, and I opened my eyes to shake it off. I gazed out at the suburbs of Newark: old yellow and brown wooden houses, with black

Ford cars parked by the curb, boys playing baseball in
the summer dusk. I had seen them so many times — I
had been taking that trip all my life.

The man opposite turned to his companion in his im-
perfectly flexible way and said something about "these
tacky New Jersey cities," to which she replied something
I couldn't hear, looking down at the purse in her lap,
which she first nervously pulled up with both hands,
then thrust on to the seat between them.

It was true enough, I thought; but this calling of one's
attention to the discordant character of the landscape
gave it the power to twinge my bad head: I had been looking out the window for repose.

Where there were fields was a little better. We presently passed a big square old house, with French windows on the bottom floor and a mansard roof with a
cupola on top, which had undoubtedly once been the
mansion of some well-to-do local family but was now
stranded in an industrial region only a little way from a
long factory that made steel tubing. There was no longer
any fence or any grounds, and what had once been a
lawn with terraces simply merged with the bare littered
waste that a factory spreads around it. Yet it seemed to
be partially inhabited: though some of the blinds were
closed, there was a baby-carriage at the top of the terraces and one of the double front-doors was open. A
poor workers' family, I imagined, who found the barnlike rooms habitable in summer. But the old drab and
dead and important house represented to me disheart-
eningly today my own family to whom I was returning.
The home of our childhood remains for us the time of
our childhood, too; and I always seemed to reenter at

Monmouthbury the anxiety and depression of school years and to breathe the thicker air of an era, before radios and automobiles, when people kept more to their houses, did not even travel often beyond their towns, and so generated a closer atmosphere.

I was about to plunge back into that under circumstances that peculiarly irked me. The situation of my parents itself was gloomy enough at this time. My father had not long before had a stroke and was in that most heartbreaking condition of the blasted paralytic who is learning to move and to speak and hopes soon to be back at work. My mother was getting queerer and queerer. She was sure that my father would never be able to work again. There was, of course, money enough to last them, but it was true that my father, successful though he had been, had never been interested in money making for its own sake, and had tended to take to foreign travel or simply to sitting at home and reading when he had accumulated a comfortable balance. He had been one of the first to invest in Florida, but he had cashed in to a considerable extent before the big Florida boom began. And now my mother worried continually for fear she should be left with nothing and be unable to help the sisters and nieces who with time had become dependent on my father. Furthermore, since I was an only son, she worried inordinately about me. And this darkened my spirit with feelings of guilt whenever I approached the house at Monmouthbury. I was not getting along fast in New York; I was just turning my thirty-first year and for five years I had not had a raise. None of the men of my mother's family had been quite so inconspicuous or unambitious; and it was plain that, if the values in Florida continued to drop as they had begun to do that spring, I should be unable to help out in such a way that they could keep up the big old place.

Furthermore, I was not yet married. I had even ceased to go out very much, and my life outside the office had now lapsed into a kind of routine between my club, my small apartment, and Lucille's apartment — of which of course my mother did not know but of which she had in some way caught a whiff. She had the sense that I was no longer striving to make myself a place in society, and she had been cherishing a plan for the solution of my problem which caused me the most extreme embarrassment. I had a cousin — a second cousin once removed — who had inspired the first and longest of my series of childhood crushes. Her father had been a painter and had seemed to me in his early phases one of the most sympathetic members of the family; but he had turned into an alcoholic and had ended in an institution, where my father paid for most of his board. I always thought he had fallen a victim to the womenfolk of the early nineteen hundreds, who did not yet drink. The purple-faced saturation and the disastrous periodic "sprees" of Cousin Fred's generation had been partly produced by the tragic looks, the pathetically pleading voices, and the ominous hushings-up which were calculated to demoralize the drinker even more than the effects of alcohol. Cousin Lydia, Cousin Fred's wife — a perfectly conventional woman, who had originally painted a little, too — had endured a good deal of poverty and some painful humiliation, and had at last, with the putting-away of Cousin Fred, taken a job in one of those big New York galleries that sells all kinds of valuable things.

The arrangement was that her daughter, Cousin Elly, should come to live with my parents, and Cousin Elly had just arrived. The girl had suffered extremely from the collapse of her father, which had occurred in her late teens. It had been only the subsidies of her relatives which had made it possible for her to go away to school, and she had never been able to come out at all; and the effect had been to drive her over to the side of these better-off relatives, who made security seem bound up with conformity. With a childhood among artists behind her, she had come to have a serious respect for money and an earnest desire to demonstrate that she herself was absolutely correct.

This aspect of Elly terribly chilled me — and especially when it had become apparent that at this point in her life — she was twenty-six and had never had the right kind of beaux — our family figured for her as the only dependable connection with the correctitude and money she craved. With me she evinced an interest in the theater, because she knew I fooled around with writing plays, but I had come to put this down to an instinct to play in with my mother's idea that she and I ought to marry. I was all the more suspicious of her, and I am afraid rather superior and sharp with her because I had always found her attractive. She had red hair and a round body, and there was something rather jolly about her that made you forget her limitations. I half-liked her; and I shrank from the whole situation — Elly had come to live with my parents since I had been down there last — of the family's turning in on itself. That our obsolete place in New Jersey, in a region where the original county society, pre–Civil War and semi-rural, had died leaving scarcely a vestige and had long been abandoned by the fashionable world that had flocked there in the racing days; that our pretentious house, built in the seventies and at once too barnlike and too fancy in its efforts to appear palatial, where my parents lived both winter and summer, preoccupied with the unenlightened notions and surrounded by the cluttering objects that had been esteemed at the beginning of the century; that this should count now for poor Elly as the highest possibility she could hope for and that she should associate me with Monmouthbury; that she and I and my parents should all roll up in the old place together, with Cousin Fred in the alcoholic ward: all this was intensifying the depression of my hangover as it had brought on the night of drinking that had caused it. At least my life of visits backstage and to boudoirs in the West Fifties had been an attempt to get away from Monmouthbury. . . .

The people in the opposite seat had taken to examining a time-table, and the man was being sarcastic about the train, which he said stopped at every wayside hamlet.

"We get off at Mayport, do we?" said the woman, swallowing both ends of her sentence.

They established that it was the third stop now. Since they were taking that absurd train that ran at noon, they had evidently slept late like me, and they could hardly be expected for a midday meal. They must just be going somewhere together. They did not seem to me precisely married, yet they were used to one another. I liked the woman: she had small gray eyes, set rather wide apart, a straight nose and mouth, and a compact little figure that was broad in relation to her small hands and feet. With her broad and clear brow, she combined the candor of a

child with the dignity of a serious lady, and there was
something both definite and appealing about her little
sudden movements.

Since I was sitting away from the window in order to
avoid the sun, I was, however, directly opposite the man,
and I found when I again closed my eyes, trying to make
my mind a blank against the difficulties toward which I
was headed, that I was under the impression that my own
legs, in a position now similar to his, were clad in greenish gray herringbone trousers. This was a kind of thing
that I recognized as having happened to me several times
before — when I had involuntarily identified myself with
someone with whom I had been talking or whose presence I had for some reason impinged on me in a subway,
a bus, or a shop. It was not merely that I saw things for a
moment from the other man's point of view, but that I
seemed actually to have taken over the other's appearance and dress. I had once gone around for half a day
under the illusion that I had claimed the body of a very
unprepossessing young man who had come to my office
to ask about a job. His legs had been disproportionately
short, so that his overcoat, which was somewhat too big
for him, had come almost down to his ankles; and I had
been ridden by the disconcerting sensation that a great
tuck had been taken in my legs, and was driven to un-
button my double-breasted ulster after I had gone out
into the street in order to dissipate the impression that I
was enveloped in an immense hollow case. When I had
spoken to people, I had been conscious of smiling with a
fatuous assurance. Now the symptoms were beginning
again, and I opened my eyes to dispel them. My trousers,
rather out of press, were the same very light gray that I

had left them. The phenomenon had a little alarmed me. You did not simply seem to mirror the other person: you felt that he had substituted himself for you, so that you had ceased to exist as an entity. But now that I could see the other man there, looking out through the windows across the aisle, I could be sure of myself again.

But I followed his gaze out the window. We were out of the industrial region and skirting a little backwater bay: smooth blue and edged with light green marsh-grass and a narrow margin of sand; there were a sailboat and a bather or two. Further on there were worn motor-launches moored in a little inlet among the rank green river-reeds. Then the old red roads between rye fields or meadows, marked off with gray rail-fences, the fields of rich red earth planted across with green asparagus rows. The train passed beside a high green privet hedge interwoven with pink wild roses and with some kind of climbing white flower; I could just see through slits and thinnings a pond, round and dark with slime and weedy with water-plants, the sort of pond that belongs to a family, and beyond it a rather fine white house with a verandah of thin square wooden columns. We had once known the people who had lived there, but I did not remember to have seen them since my childhood; it was removed from me now as by the screen of the hedge, and I could get only an indistinct glimpse of it as it sped back among the foliage and field that the train was leaving behind. Low peach orchards and apple orchards now paraded past; and then the buff and blond soft fur of a rye field that, smoothed down and tinged with shine by a breeze, reminded me of the border of maribou around the neck of Lucille's negligee — which seemed to be the only charm that, half-shamefacedly, half-defiantly, I was bringing to Monmouthbury to guard against its vapors.

In this countryside the train suddenly stopped. I looked out: there was no station in sight. I was used to these delays on that road, and at first simply closed my eyes with the intention of resuming my stupor.

Then I heard, after a moment, the woman say nervously, "I wonder what's the matter"; and felt the man get up and look out the window.

I came to and leaned out myself. The brakeman and the conductor were walking around outside. I decided to get out, too, and inquire; I would come back and tell the attractive little woman. As I started down the aisle — the car was closed at our end — I had the sensation again, and even more completely than before, of having become embodied in the man whom I should have just left behind me in the seat. I carried myself like him with the short neck and broad shoulders, from which I diminished toward the waist, so that my whole physique was rather wedgelike; and I looked over people's heads with an impassive self-confidence and irony; I was aware that my well-pressed herringbone and my brand-new wide-brimmed straw hat — the one that I had gotten on the train with had been cleaned from the season before — were superior to those of the other men. I climbed down — feeling vague and unreal: I was moving for the first time in an hour — and asked the conductor what the trouble was. There had been a motor-accident, it seemed, at the grade crossing down the line, and they were clearing away the wreckage.

I went back. The young man was gone; but it was as if I hardly noticed his absence. I sat down across from the girl, and told her what the conductor had said.

"Was it a serious accident?" she asked, swallowing the first three words; she took me for granted so readily that it was almost as if she knew me, but I hardly felt it strange.

"They say not; but they'd probably say that anyway. They're always having accidents on this line. They don't have any gates at a lot of these crossings, and nobody has ever been able to induce the railroad, with its directors all millionaires, to spend a few dollars to put them up."

It did seem to me for a moment a little queer that at the time I had been talking to the conductor, these ideas had not been present to my mind. Had I known about this? Yes, of course: I was dim perhaps about the facts upon which my conviction was based; but the conviction was probably familiar: it was a part of my mental equipment.

"People don't always stop to see whether a train's coming," she replied as if to fend off my indignation, in a way that seemed also familiar. It checked me as if she were calling in question, not my statement, but my right to make it.

Yet the memory grew distinct, undeniable, of journeys on the trains of that road, not in a lifelong relation to New Jersey, but in travelling to Philadelphia, and then, a good deal farther back, to Pittsburgh. There had been people who had told me about that — I would have them now in a moment: some kind of liberal lawyer.

"It's the cars that need protection from the trains rather than the trains that need protection from the cars," I replied with what I heard as a shade of shock at an accent of bland arrogance.

The train started. She looked out the window with an intentness which made me feel a little scornfully that she wanted to escape the conversation. I didn't like being so nervous.

"Ours is the next station, isn't it?" she said.

I drew up to the window and looked out. There was a new concrete bridge with a line of cars going across it, over an expanse of broad brackish water, where people were fishing in rowboats, and on the bank toward which we were going, the junky-looking boathouses and dock, the wooden crates of rundown middle-class houses and the department-store stucco hotels of one of those common New Jersey towns, all raw in the mid-day light. We slowed up, and I saw the station platform with MAY-PORT sliding by on a sign. I got down our two bags, and we waited inside the door, I behind her looking down at her well-tailored blue back so erect above her round little rump.

The train stopped; I helped her out. She was silent — self-conscious, I could feel, as I got us into the nearest taxi and told the driver to take us to Sea Bright.

I

A WEEKEND AT THE SHORE

There was a film of familiarity about the shopping blocks, with their bright movie posters and displays of vegetables and fruits, with open summer roadsters and station-wagons drawn up in the serried ranks of Saturday afternoon errands; but I put it down to some actual memory of the place from the visits of my college days — I had always gone by the shore-line before; and all these towns, when the summer people were in them, looked pretty much alike. Yes, and there was always a gilded elk in front of a BPOE building.

"I can smell 1916 already," I said.

But the only response I got to this remark was, "I hope we don't meet Adela Perry or anybody."

"I thought you said she was married in New York."

"Yes, but people come down here for week-ends. I suppose her family still spend their summers here."

"The only people I ever knew well here" — I tried to reassure her — "were Bud Taylor and Archie Graves, and Archie was killed in the War and Bud Taylor lives at the

Yale Club and has been drunk ever since the demobi-
lization — his family were only down here a couple of
summers."

I tried again:

"There's something rich and wonderful about the
American summer, you know. It's a sort of never-never
land where everything's always humming, and you just
loll around and lose the sense of time. That time I first
met you down here is like something that never really
happened in the actual chronology of my life. I can't
remember when it was in the summer or how long I
stayed down here or anything about it except dances and
drinks — and our romance out behind the Beach Club."

"I wonder whether the Beach Club is there just the
same," she said.

I felt that, in view of the occasion, she was being almost perversely prosaic, and I remembered my inability
to melt her by sentimental appeals at the time of our
original estrangement when we were only kids.

The taxi was on a concrete motor-road that ran along
the same body of water, with large plutocratic estates, full
of greenhouses and travelled drives, between the road
and the water, and on the other side, cheap little new
bungalows with those obnoxious light green umbrella-
trees that indicate so unabashedly a certain level of
taste — prosaic enough, I thought: I had perhaps made
a mistake to bring her back here. But further on we began passing enclosures where for some incomprehen-
sible reason the landscape-gardening plutocrats had left
tracts of a kind of tangled wildwood, where the fences
were laden down with honeysuckle that saturated the
moisture-heavy air, and she remarked that it smelt sweet.

Near the shore there was a little more naturalness about the lawns of the big summer cottages; the afternoon sun, which the moisture had thickened to an almost palpable yellow, spread its gold on the luxuriant green.

"You see what I mean," I showed her: "You could cut it with a knife. Everything looks *velouté*, as they say in the French novels."

She agreed, and I took her gloved hand; she answered my affectionate squeeze in her firm and frank way.

"Nobody comes down here much any more," I said; but in a moment we were confronted by the tennis club, where some of the principal matches were played and where a dozen or more courts were bounding with white pants.

Not only was the Beach Club still there, it was right next-door to the hotel; but I wrote a bogus name in the register with a nonchalance I hoped would sustain her. Fortunately the real season hadn't begun yet, and the hotel was relatively empty.

The bellboy led us up and down flights of stairs that were soundless with red carpets and down corridors that stretched on and on with the interminableness of boardwalks — both the silence and remoteness were welcome — till we were let into a fine corner room that looked out two ways on the ocean and that had twin white iron beds, furniture with that slightly bleached look that everything gets beside the sea, and a glass pitcher with inverted tumblers sitting on a glass tray. I sent the pitcher away for ice. We had both brought liquor in our bags.

A drink made the situation much better. It was pleasant to be alone at the end of the long wing with only the sound of the surf outside. I dramatized our being back there as lovers after almost exactly twelve years — after our break, the War, the marriage, her life in the South, her other lovers, my various love-affairs, at least two of them passionate and enchanting, with girls I did not care to marry. It may be I overdid a little the power that our first passages at Sea Bright had over me during the interval: the fact was that I had not thought of her often and that I had not at first felt any very keen interest in her when I had met her again at a cocktail party; but it was true that the idea of sand in summer, especially sand at night, had always since our petting-parties been full for me of sexual suggestion. She told me, what I dare say I had known but in the course of the years had forgotten, that I had been the first boy she had ever gone quite that far with. She said that her own erotic ideas were connected with New Jersey on my account and because, when she had been a kid, they had gone to Lakewood one winter and she had gotten her first strong inkling of sex from hearing about a friend's French nurse who had gotten into trouble and been fired for going to the coachman's room. The coachman's room had been over the stable, and it had given her a queer thrill to think of the pink-cheeked and smiling woman, who had always seemed so disciplined and neat, doing something with the coachman in leather leggins over the stable with its horse manure smell. I saw, as she bubbled up in her spasmodic half-articulate way like water coming out of a bottle, that the trip was meaning more to her than I had thought from her impervious behavior in the taxi. She then went on irrelevantly to tell me that her sister's straw hat had once been eaten up by a horse when they were crossing on the Jersey ferry.

But it made her a flapper again, a flapper of 1916, and the talk about sex had excited me. I wanted to have the flapper that I had never had then, and that I had never really had, though I had been her lover now for two months. We made love without any clothes, and she was obviously gratified and pleased; but, no doubt just because she was, it wasn't like having the little girl that had only let me go just so far. It didn't seem that it ought to have been so easy.

Yet it was fun. We wanted to do some beach lounging before it got too late, so we got up. I embraced her, still nude, after we had wiped off the perspiration, standing in the middle of the room. She was solid and very warm, and had a certain old-fashioned female amplitude in the spots that the women of the period were trying so hard to keep down. She was the shortest girl I had ever had: with her shoes off, she hardly came up to my chest. She had tiny small-boned feet, which I found I was stepping on. She was with me on our holiday now; she had entirely forgotten her constraint. And when I shot up the shades, we looked over on the whole of the blue Atlantic, and the highballs put a beautiful bloom on the blazing summer sun.

We walked down the white companionways of a series of little decks on which our room opened directly; and we leapt into the surf at once. The swimming in that part of Jersey is usually pretty foul because there is practically no beach and the water is all bilge; but we were exhilarated enough to disregard the rotten oranges and vegetables that had been thrown overboard from ships, and the shredded seaweed, like spinach, that stuck to us in green translucent flakes. We let the waves bang us around and inhaled the smell like dry salty dust shaken out of the breaking crests that reminded me of the sultry night when we had sat out behind the Beach Club. I swam out beyond the lines, where the water is level and deep, while Caroline did a little paddling, frequently clinging onto the ropes and floating on her stomach with her head up: I told her she looked like a turtle.

Then we lay on the sand, smoked and talked and watched the four or five other people. There was a girl that I thought at first was a boy, but whom I presently recognized as a girl by the way she held her cigarette. She had glossy black hair, boyish-bobbed and wore a white swimming shirt tucked inside a pair of black boy's trunks. When she came close to us later, playing ball with one of those big balloonlike beach balls, melon-striped in white and blue, which she would throw from between her slim spread-out legs, standing with her toes turned in, I saw that she was definitely cute. She was at that time the fashionable type and the type I had been going in for. Caroline's breasts — she was lying on her back — flattened and broadened out under her bathing suit in a way that seemed almost gelatinous. Yet she was appetizing, too, in her plumpness; and she was, after all, a lady as none of my fast little girls had quite been. She was in fact the only available lady that it would be at all possible for me to live with.

I lay on my stomach with my face on my hand, and I saw us as a most attractive couple, going to concerts together — it was a good thing she at least knew the rudiments of music; appearing at various kinds of parties:

social parties and musicians' parties and parties that were merely amusing, where you met the town characters and wits. We should ourselves give incomparable parties — of a smartness that the professional smart people couldn't manage, at which the tone would be set by my sardonic ease, by my understanding of the interests of the purely social people, and by my serious concern, as a cultivated man, for those achievements and aims of the arts which I understood, also, so much better than most of the figures in the social world; and by Caroline's piquant combination of dignity with childlike jollity, of rakishness with the British coolness that is the only thing perhaps in the long run that makes rakishness in women tolerable. And she always dressed so well: her smallness made her dressing seem more precious. I could see her in her short little black velvet jacket and her long pleated white skirt that reached to her feet, tempting people with one of those trays of anchovies wound around stuffed olives and little frankfurters spitted on toothpicks. They would not be on a very big scale, these parties; we didn't have very much money between us. But one of the good things about her was that she knew how to get along without spending very much money and that she even found it amusing to do her own work.

We talked about people we knew, and while we were talking, I sorted them out from the point of view of whether we should ask them to our parties.

It began to be a little chill. We looked up and saw that the sun had dulled and the waves were turning dark with that look of mid-ocean water that is so different from the white curling crests and the gleaming blues and

green that we like to see in the surf; so we got up, took a
final dip, and went back to our room. It was almost six
o'clock. We and the slim girl and her boy-friend had been
the last to stay, and while we were walking up to our
deck, I turned to look at the sky and saw her put her ball
under her arm and disappear on the other side. A sudden sadness like the darkening of the sky came down on
me as I looked back from the platform on the beach
where she had just been playing and where we had been
dozing in the sun.

Inside, we swabbed ourselves with towels, then embraced naked again. It was wonderful to feel her cool
flesh just fresh from the sea and to taste the salt on her
shoulder when I kissed her. Her shoulders and arms were
brown from earlier swimming that summer, and where
the bathing-suit stopped, so white that now the softness
of her breasts seemed delicious. We lay down on the bed
and soon made love. There is something profoundly satisfactory after the immersion of the body in the ocean,
about feeling at the vital points of sex, the steady heat of
the man and the warm and oily liquids of woman, awake
through the coating of cold, the effect on our human
organisms of the chill and this inhuman water, against
which we reassert ourselves. I told her about a friend of
mine in Paris who, in describing his erotic experiments,
had rather recommended making love in the water: "*Ça
empêche un peu*." It was a part of the British side of her
that she had a certain hearty love of pornography.

But when we went down to dinner, we met with a
contretemps. I had gone down first to call up New York,
and, coming out of the telephone booth, had been confronted by a college class-mate — a man that we called

Nick Carter — who was also a fraternity brother. He had with him a large and gay mixed party, all pretty far gone in liquor. Nick Carter had at one time been a pal of mine: he was the class's most accomplished comedian, and we had used to work together till the iron laws of life at Yale had inexorably separated us. We had been sidesplittingly funny in our sophomore year in a series of vaudeville acts at the time when Nick had also thought it funny to stand on Chapel Street the night of a big game and hand out toilet paper to the passersby; but his room-mate had been headed for Bones and had succeeded in carrying Nick along with him by dint of making him give up his drinking and go in for Dwight Hall and the track team. I had never had any capacity for becoming a big man at college, so our act was eventually broken up. But now I had run into him in the company of what was evidently the Broadway type of people who were entertaining themselves with acts of their own — he was pretending to give an illustrated lecture, which had been suggested by a billiard-cue he had found — and he insisted that I should introduce him as the exploiter of a trained seal. I explained that I had to be somewhere for dinner, and ascertained that they were not spending the night. Caroline had come down behind me and had stopped and turned her back and pretended to look at the old copies of *Vogue* that were lying on a table. I didn't want to go to her direct and hung around for several moments as if etherized by the atmosphere of nonsensical fantasy, a kind of thing I rather liked, while Nick went back to his lecture to explain how he had caught his seal on an ice-floe — a man who was not as clever as the others, but who was laughing even louder and more constantly, said, "That's why you call her Flo!"— and to imitate their mating cries. I couldn't stand his froglike face on its neck that was too slight, and turned, perhaps rather sharply, away.

I went out and stood on the verandah, thinking what to do; but in a moment Caroline joined me. I couldn't help feeling guilty.

"We'll go to the other place," I said.

"Are you sure they're having dinner here?"

"Yes, of course they are," I answered.

"Was that Kay Burke?" she asked.

"Yes. Do you know her?"

"I met her once."

The other place was one of those restaurants where they specialize in shore dinners. It was quiet and rather dark, and we had an unusually rich clam chowder and slabs of sole with wedges of lemon and little gravy boats of tartar sauce, along with overgrown tasteless corn.

I wished she were a little more flexible. It would not have created any scandal even if she had to meet those people; but she steered away from the subject in a way that made me feel that she felt the whole thing had been dreadful. We heard somebody playing the piano in a room which did not open into ours — it began with fairly lively jazz, then became troubled and desultory, till it seemed about to break off altogether; and the sadness of the fading of the afternoon sun came back on me with the lapsing of the music: something that, though I did have Caroline, I didn't have and had never had. Now the pianist picked up again, and rather had finally found herself — she must have been a woman —

in a soft strain of contented revery: MacDowell's "From an Indian Wigwam."

That was the only American music — that flimsy nostalgic stuff. How I wished I could bang out the real music, with a head that could make the mechanical rhythms speak for living people and hands that were strong and exact on their craft! I tried to tell her about it, and I thought she was bored because she listened mostly in silence and said things that seemed to me stupid, such as, "I don't see how you could play telephone-bells the way you do regular musical instruments."

"You could have them in octaves," I explained. "You could play them exactly like chimes. You could have people whistling a motif that had been written for telephone bells just the way they do the bells in *Parsifal* or the bird in *Siegfried*."

But her objection made me irritable because I wasn't sure myself it could be done — though of course there was always Stravinsky; and at the moment I was really being acted on by the lady who played MacDowell and to whom I felt closer at the moment than I did to Caroline. I should have liked to go in and talk to her and sit down and pound out some college Wagner, which was the only thing at which I was really proficient; but I know that it would embarrass Caroline by calling attention to our presence and because she didn't like making the acquaintance of people she hadn't met in the proper way.

She was also embarrassed to go back to the hotel till I reminded her of the fact that our room could be reached from the outside of the building. We walked around, giving the place a wide birth. The tide was now in, and there was nobody on the sand. We walked along the strip where it was dry all the way to the end of the beach, where a breakwater walled it off from the club. The club was entirely dark, and I suggested climbing over the rocks to find the place where we had sat that summer. I knew that this would worry her, too, but I wouldn't let her spoil our romance by inhibitions about being caught by night-watchmen.

The place, which had been a sort of alcove in a bank overgrown by beach-grass, was no longer exactly there because the bank had been leveled down and there was now a bathing pavilion on the other side of the club; but we sat down in the shadow of the big board wall that shut the pavilion off from the club. She slipped off her high-heeled shoes, I produced the magic flask, and we each had a scorching gulp, and we became quite happy again. I felt now that she liked to have me tell her about how romantic it had been.

"I used to have dreams about you," she said. "In fact, I dreamed once you were a coachman — "

"And we went to bed in the stable?"

"Something like that was going to happen."

"I don't know whether I like that. You certainly let me down at the time of the War."

"No, I didn't."

"I thought you got afraid to go around with me because I had a German name and you suspected I was a German sympathizer, because I wouldn't go to a training camp."

"No, I didn't. You went away."

I knew that she had all the same: it was the old Canadian British blood that made her conclude instinctively that any kind of unpopular position means that you're not playing the game.

"I confess that I ran away from the obloquy."

"But afterwards you enlisted."

"In the Naval Reserve. As a matter of fact, I did sympathize with the Germans at least as much as anybody else; and they had a hell of a rotten deal when France and England finally got them down."

"They started it, though," she said.

I tried to explain that it was not so simple.

"Yes, the German children were starving," she remembered, though with indirect relevance, toward the end of my exposition. Her insistence was subsiding; I kissed her, and she was just like a girl again, with no issue of the War between us. But I continued to hammer my point:

"It was Syd Lefanu's uniform."

"Maybe it was partly," she said.

We lay looking up at the stars, which were obscured as by a fine dust of sand. The night was damp and thick, and the shore-smells soggy and rank, and as the stimulus of the drink wore off, we found ourselves tense and shivery, and decided to go up to the room.

The next day was gray and wet, and we both had a pretty severe hangover, as we had done some more drinking in the room. After breakfast, we went out on the porch and looked at the expanse of gray gravel which had in the center an ornamental bed of cockroach-brown calla-lilies. The railroad tracks ran right beside the hotel, between it and the business street; and we felt as if we had got ourselves imprisoned.

We tried to go for a walk, but we found it practically

impossible to get away into anything like the country, because the whole place consisted of estates and then was nothing but landscape-gardening. Yet I thought as I saw her in her gray plaid cape and with her hair a little beaded by the mist that she would look well in a more attractive kind of country life such as my sister's up in Dutchess County. With all possible contempt for the pomps of the textile and utilities kings that reign along the Jersey coast, it is always a little galling to walk along the road in such places. And I felt Caroline growing tense again. In the hope of getting away from the main road, I had turned off down one of the cross streets, and it presently came to light that she was afraid that it was the street where her friend Adela Perry lived. It was characteristic of her, I recognized, that she wouldn't have told me before we turned in, but should have accepted my suggestion and then allowed it to spoil our walk. I told her that Adela Perry wouldn't be likely to know her again if it had been seven or eight years since they had seen one another.

"Yes, I suppose I'm an old hag now," she said.

I laughed at her and tried to reassure her, but I knew that she couldn't help feeling that it was somehow an evidence that she was aging and that she was allowing herself to be cheapened that she had come down here like this with me. It was the tennis club, the beach club, the big houses — it had not been the place for an escapade.

It was with a touch of exasperation that I turned off down a hedged dirt lane. We both became acutely silent, and I began to be tortured by a feeling that she thought the big white house we were passing was the house of the people she had visited and that they were about to come out of the drive. What did come out of the drive was a shining garnet roadster with the top open that nearly ran us down. A chauffeur was driving two immense floor-lamps that were leaning on the back seat: they seemed to be made of some kind of purple velvet and had fringes of golden beads.

"You don't suppose he can be taking them back?" I speculated.

"No: they're giving them to a son who's just married."

When we emerged from the network of lanes, we found ourselves upon another of the main arteries. The road was a smooth white concrete with a strip of tar down the middle; there was no footpath, so we had to take the road itself, with the Sunday motor traffic tearing past us. About every ten yards we were confronted by a dead animal that had been crushed by a car. There were a couple of birds and a turtle that had become so flattened out that they were no longer even gruesome: they looked like patches on old tires; and finally we came to a cat that had been laid out like a tiger-rug as a slab of blood and fur and of which the only recognizable feature was a series of small ribs.

I realized that the only thing to do was to get back and have a drink before lunch, and at the prospect, from the moment when we turned and were frankly headed back toward the hotel, my own tension was relieved, and I loved her. She was cheerful and friendly again by the time we got back to the room and she had a drink in her hand.

But just as we were about to go into the dining-room, we were waylaid by Nick Carter again. We had walked right up to him without being aware of him because he was concealed by a Sunday paper, and when he lowered it and we were face to face, it seemed to me less compromising to stop and introduce Caroline than to go on without speaking to him. It turned out they had all spent the night.

"You walked out on me last night," he cried. "I saw you turn on your heel. But you mustn't think I haven't got my serious side. I want you to explain to Mrs. Lefanu that I've got my more serious side."

He had been laughing in such a way as to make a joke of every line: it was the patter of the parlor humorist which had been becoming, since he had been in New York, more and more automatic and professional; but now he wanted to become more serious in the spirit of service to Yale.

"Honest, I'm writing a darn good play, Fritz: it has the brilliance of Shaw and the mysticism of Maeterlinck. It's really good. All this isn't enough" — he meant the people with whom he had been going — "Underneath is the human soul, and every one of us has one whether we like it or not. I don't like it myself " — he made it a joke, an evangelical joke.

"Have you tried a bromide?" I suggested.

"You'll see," he said. "My play's going to be good — and you'll be sorry you turned on your heel. Honest, Fritz: there's going to be a new religion. There's going to be a new Christ, and he's coming out of America."

His habitual lightness and brightness kept it always in the vein of the line which had originally been developed to carry him triumphantly through debutante dances; but he was serious with that awful off-key seriousness that had used to come with his hangovers at Yale when his room-mate had been persuading him that he ought to go out for Dwight Hall.

"And all these," he went on, with a gesture that indicated his late companions, still at that moment in bed, "all these will be touched with the light. And you'll know it — you'll be one of those that knows it, Fritz. And Mrs. Lefanu will know it, too."

"Well, shall we go back to the fish place?" I suggested, when we had detached ourselves from Nick.

"We might as well eat here," she said — she was now floated on a swell of self-assurance. "If we're in for it, we're in for it."

At least we could laugh about Nick as we dealt with a Sunday dinner that involved cold storage turkey and cranberry sauce and dressing that must both have come out of cans.

Nick and Kay Burke and another man presently seated themselves at a table not far from ours, and the others gradually trickled in. Each arrival was greeted by a salvo of quips, and Nick, disregarding for the moment the advent of the new American Christ, began to pick up his audience with more and more hilarious results. Each of his cracks, always followed by his own short laugh, now set off the laughter of the others, and when the man in the green shirt had joined them — he had been the last to appear and was received with special fireworks — his laughter shook the room.

"People like that get on my nerves," said Caroline, whose drink was expiring. "It would simply drive me crazy to have to listen to his jokes with a hangover."

I said that he could be awfully funny and that Kay Burke was positively brilliant. Caroline and Kay Burke had looked at one another without speaking. Presently Nick Carter came over and, standing and bending down to us with a hand on the back of either chair, asked us whether we had heard "Kay's Hiawatha": "Hiawatha nice girl till I met you."

We declined to join them, but stopped a moment when we had finished and were going out.

We went up and lay on the bed and read the Sunday papers. Then we fell into a doze under the influence of the overcast day and of the surf banging the beach outside. She pulled her little legs with their tiny feet up under her big hips. I was behind her and had my arms around her. She had already learned to turn over when I did and would put her arms around me when we lay the other way; we had found out how to fit together. When we woke up, the gray was dissolving and the sun was breaking through, but it was late in the afternoon. We had a drink and decided to go in before we had another (I had checked up, by calling the desk, on the fact that Nick and his party had left). It was fun to be alone on the beach with the fog and the reviving light; we lost all our inhibitions in the mess that the sea had become. I did an Australian crawl, sprawling in the rough water that tried to drive me against a formidable-looking breakwater. When I stood up, feeling the gravel sucked back about my feet, I saw her figure, dark and clear, a girl with bare feet at the seashore, against the background of mist, where a bright sun was setting dimly. She looked lovely; and now she was mine.

At the hotel there were only four hotel women quietly playing bridge in the long deserted sun-room. After dinner, we returned to bed. She sat bolt upright on the side of the bed smoking a cigarette in a blue bed-jacket that brought out blue in her gray eyes, and gold mules on her smart little feet that hardly touched the floor. She had just washed her face, and her skin was smooth and clear with the powder off, but I could see how the strain of recent years had actually made creases between her brows. I put my arm around her waist; she felt warm. I had just had a very stiff drink.

"Why don't we get married?" I said.

She was always shy and rather indirect: there was the tightening that always pulled in her emotion. "There's nobody I'd rather marry," she said — almost as if she didn't believe I wanted her, as if it were a hypothetical proposition.

"It's too much of a bore," I continued, "going on like this. There's nobody *I'd* rather marry — there never has been anybody." I asked myself for a second whether this were quite true, then decided that it really was, since the girls I had found more exciting were out of the question from other points of view.

"I'll have my divorce in September," she said.

I winced a little at this, but women always go straight to the practical aspect of such matters.

"Is it all right then?"

"I hope so," she said, looking up at me and smiling. I kissed her and made her lie down. She was the warmest woman I had ever known — I don't mean the most passionate, but physically the warmest: her whole body seemed to get pink. And she was passionate, too, in her way — though, instead of saying things or uttering cries as other enthusiastic women do, she would make a kind of grunting noise.

When we were quietly lying afterwards with our arms around one another, she said: "We could live in my house."

"You mean I could commute from New Orleans?"

She became a little flustered and inarticulate as she answered, "Would you want to live in New York all the time."

"I've got to hold down my job."

"I thought you didn't like your job."

"I don't like it especially, but I can't throw it up."

"We'd save money by living in my house — and you could do some music," she blurted, more indistinct still. A slight touch of terror chilled me.

"I'm not a composer," I said, "and I'm not a trained musician. I can't just sit around and study music."

"You want to compose, don't you?"

"If it should work out that way. It isn't anything I can count on though."

There was a silence. I didn't think about the future. My mind became an utter blank. I listened to the steady surf, which could become rather monotonous and boring: the sudden abrupt stop, then the crescendo boiling and swish — an indefatigable recurrent insistence on dashing down the hissing brine on the shore.

"New York is where we will live," I said. "We can go to Biloxi sometimes for vacation." The life of the fashionable Southern resort began to unroll before me.

"So long as we don't end up in Florida!" I added.

"Don't you like Florida?" she asked.

"Florida is vulgar."

"I don't see why you say that. I loved it when I was there."

"It's all right to go there in somebody's yacht, but not just to camp in an expensive hotel and *dolce far niente*."

She was silent; this evidently puzzled her. Her father had never done anything, and her husband had never done anything; and it was difficult for me to explain why I resisted the idea of Florida when I confessed I wasn't interested in my work. The truth was I very much enjoyed visiting the very rich, and I clearly saw us lounging at the doors of beach cabanas, in the beach robes and straw espadrilles that I regarded as a little effeminate for men, with long gin drinks in our hands, commenting — I in my caustic vein — on the various celebrities of the season.

I pulled myself up with the thought that it was out of the question for me to live on Caroline's income.

"I don't really like the cocktail set," I went on. "That is, I don't like them unless they're clever or can do something or other. For example, I like Irving Freeman, because he can at least compose funny songs; but I don't like Phil Dewitt, because he can't do anything but drink and gossip in a tiresome way."

"I like Phil," she said.

I thought that it was difficult for her to grasp an objection to anyone like Phil, who was an accepted social institution; and I was unexpectedly gratified when she said:

"I know he's just a drunken waster — he and all that crowd!" It was the Scotch Presbyterian of her mother's family, upright Canadian bankers, that had suddenly asserted itself.

"There are some of them that I don't mind much," I continued with more positive force, "but I think we ought to pick our people. Don't let in the whole ribald rout. I want to see something of the musical people. We could give some damn interesting parties — the kind of parties that almost nobody is giving."

"I never could give decent parties with Lefanu," she said. "He always got himself into such a mess."

"I always thought you were a fine person," she said so softly and indistinctly that I had difficulty in realizing at first that she had made a remark so unlike her; and she turned and lay over on me, putting her arm around me. It was something she had done before, a gesture impossible to resist — for it implies a complete confidence, a childlike dependence.

We talked about our plans till we decided to go to sleep. Before I dropped off, I listened to the surf, and I heard that the tide was receding: at the end of the long movement of incessant aggressive crashing, the lapses were beginning to abate to the expirations of breathing — these lapses themselves were longer and the stoppages less abrupt — relenting, letting up, boiling and insisting less emphatically, gathering longer to boil — a mere churning of the night, almost drowsy, which eventually put us to sleep — asserting itself only enough now so that we should not forget its personality — the invincible personality of the sea.

II

AN ESTATE ON THE HUDSON

"Well, Countess!" I greeted my sister — it was a relic of the days of our childhood, when we had lived in Pittsburgh and gone to Europe in summer, and I suppose I was trying to make sure of our intimacy at the moment of telling her about Caroline.

She was looking particularly smart in a dazzlingly white linen dress with a crisply pleated skirt that set off her olive skin, now deepened by summer sunburn. She had the absolutely spic-and-span cleanness that comes after playing tennis and then taking a bath in the late afternoon. I bent down to kiss her and felt the piquancy of a very freshly clean woman, the feminine smell of whose skin still contrasts with the starched and washed costume. They get themselves up more appetizingly than we do and at the same time seem closer to the animals, so that the whole thing is a triumph of civilization that always evokes wonder.

"Hello, Fritz," she said. "I don't like that tie: I think you're too old for those enormous stripes."

She had the power of making my customary sangfroid
fade out into an innocent boyishness that made one feel
confusion. We passed through the house with its pleasant smell of cut flowers, chintz coverings, clean wood,
its splatter of light paint by Monet that at least looked
rather decorative from a distance, its clear-eyed children
by Mary Cassatt.

My brother-in-law Henry was out on the porch, reading the morning paper. He was dressed with the usual
elegance that became his tall and still slender figure in a
light brown country suit, of which the trousers had no
cuffs but came down rather low over his heels, hanging
always at precisely the right height. It was one of the details of his appearance that went back to the dandyism of
the end of the century. He was almost twenty years older
than Julie. His mustache was also an ornament from the
nineties, the mustache of Guy de Maupassant, Theodore
Roosevelt, and William Travers Jerome, though a little
bit thinned by time and a little trimmed at the ends: no
doubt his infallible taste had never let it become extravagant. They had cocktails on my account: they never had
them, they used to tell me, for themselves; and there
was something incongruous about seeing them served
from a silver cocktail shaker which had been shaken in
the kitchen and seemed chastened by the quiet old Swiss
butler.

Henry's being there made it impossible for me to talk
about Caroline to Julie, because I really did not know
him well enough. I had always found a peculiar embarrassment — though she was only three years older than
I — in talking about my love affairs with my sister, and I
should have to have her alone. Not that I doubted she

would be delighted: it all fitted into the picture and was just what our mother would have wanted.

It was pleasant on the porch. It had no roof, and the floor was level with the lawn. There were red tiles, green summer chairs, and two earth-colored bowls of white flowers set on a low stone wall. A light green birdcage which my sister had hung outside the living-room intensified the general effect of the bright July colors and brought out the almost fantastic quaintness of the old Hudson River house: The triple arch of its three sections matched the arches of the long ogival windows; the variegated finches went vividly with the dark peacock-blue blinds; and on the straw-colored sides of the house the canary looked a deeper yellow. Julie was a little like a bird herself — she had always had this predilection for finches. Unlike me, she was small and slight, and she had a small aquiline nose, small black eyes and a recessive chin. She sat up straight, with her legs crossed and the toe of the lifted foot rather sharply sticking out.

Henry laid his paper on his knee and talked to us about New York politics with the definiteness and lack of emphasis that were characteristic of him. He had once been Republican state chairman, and he seemed still to wield a certain discreet influence in the ancient "silk stocking" tradition. He liked to back schemes of civic betterment and to work for charitable organizations — though he picked them with scrupulous care and always knew precisely what he was doing.

I asked him whether he had heard the story of Mrs. Al Smith's reply to some compliment by Queen Marie of Roumania: "You said a mouthful, Queen!"

"I've heard it," he said, "but I don't believe it's true. I

imagine it was invented by some wit. Mrs. Smith isn't a particularly polished person, but I don't know whether she'd say anything so grotesque as that."

He addressed me with his round brown eyes, which, though the movements of the lids and the eyebrows responded perfectly to the demands of civility, maintained a perpetual blandness of irony; but his irony did not seem to correspond to the ridicule of the ordinary rich person — I had been indulging in it myself at this moment — who had been cherishing a story about Mrs. Smith: it rather was at the expense of the people, including possibly myself, who had accepted a cheap comic-weekly joke as something that had actually happened. I admired the justice of his perceptions; and asked him about Al Smith himself.

"He's a very able man — he's not educated, but he's been doing a very good job as governor — along the lines that he's interested in and understands."

Yes, Henry was a genuinely superior fellow: he was far above the level of the idiots whose opinions followed party lines, and his ideal of responsible public service prevented him from being snobbish about the Smiths.

It was always a satisfaction to come here, and the slight strain of apprehension I had felt when I greeted Julie had now been relieved by two cocktails. I looked out over the smooth lawn that had been left to its natural unevenness and that easily but at the same time daringly heaved up further on into a hillside; there was a gravel path lined with a mixture of hollyhocks, columbines, and zinnias, which seemed to have been planted at random and yet gave an attractive effect, that led up to the vegetable garden, the greenhouse and the tennis-court. In a meadow below were some sheep.

"I'm going to have to trim that tulip-tree," said Henry to my sister. "It's a pity to spoil its symmetry, but it's making the dining-room too dark." He turned to me:

"It was planted by my grandfather, who didn't foresee how big it was going to grow in seventy years. That's why I put the oaks so far from the house — so that they wouldn't be a nuisance later on."

It was pleasant to think that my nephew, now in the boarding-school stage, would get the benefit of Henry's foresight when he was growing old in the Powell place — that the family solidarity, the regard for the convenience of one's descendants, extended to such details. Our childhood, Julie's and mine, had been spent in such impermanent habitations. The dark old hollow house where we had originally lived in Pittsburgh, maintaining our Germanic patrician caste amidst the cinders and grime of the mill-town, had been turned into a Y.M.C.A. in a section that had ceased to be fashionable; and, as we were always getting away from Pittsburgh, we had spent a great deal of time in hotels and European pensions and cottages rented for the summer. Our mother, after Father's death, had lived almost entirely in hotels.

"I wonder," said Henry to Julie, "what kind of job Fred Lagrange has been doing picking up the field."

"I don't know: I haven't been up there today."

"I'll have to go up and see. Fred," he explained to me, "is the town drunk. He owes me several days work, and I'm having him clean up the field where we had the horse show. You can never be sure he's going to turn up."

"But he's very good-looking," said Julie.

"If you shaved him," Henry continued, "and put him into decent clothes, he could pass for a foreign noble-man. He must have some very good French blood."

"I thought they were all Dutch around here."

"No: The Dutch migration didn't come here. They went along the other side of the river and up the Mo-hawk Valley. We have a number of French families in the village. They came down originally from Canada — very poor: they hardly got through the winter."

Henry would have given them food, and they would work it out in odd jobs: the whole thing was very feudal. I gazed up the wooded hill at the castle with a pointed red tower and a long red roof like a gingerbread house that had been built by Henry's grandfather in the fifties: one window had caught the sun and was shining as bright as a lighthouse against the solid piled-up clouds, whose edges showed as sharply on the blue as the clouds in a Maxfield Parrish picture. Yes — the cocktails were making me romantic — the grand old Rhine and the grand old Hudson! There was a difference — the Ameri-can *Gemütlichkeit*, or rather the American homeliness, made the surface of things more democratic. It was a part even of Henry's aristocratic quality that he culti-vated this kind of homeliness — which was not alto-gether insincere. If there was much of the landlord and tenant about his relation with people like the Lagranges, there was also something of the friendly understanding of men who have been boys together in the same small American town. They would have gone shooting in the autumn woods, swum in the ponds together. Henry had even sent my nephew for a year or two to the local school so that he should establish good relations with the visitors. I believed I should do the same thing: that was the way to handle it. A more arrogant and provocative personality than Henry — that was the German manner — I could not do better in certain things than follow his distinguished example. Already I was seeing myself on the Hudson as a kind of American baron of modest means but superior taste, the patron of tolerated musicians, who composed, and not badly, himself. All that part of the river seemed to be populated for miles by the Powells, and they had innumerable houses of all sizes. It seemed to me a notion worth playing with that Caroline and I should live in one.

Henry excused himself and walked away up the path. I felt quite equal to making the announcement, but, while Henry was getting out of earshot, I found myself concentrating rather dazedly on the obtruded toe of Julie's white sandal, and remembering how years ago, it must have been when I was a freshman at college, I had seen her with white summer shoes and the new fashion of dark gun-metal and smoke-blue stockings; and how the contrasting stockings had given me for the first time about her a conscious erotic feeling which embarrassed me: I had seen her as desirable to other men in the same provocative way that other girls were getting to be to me.

"Well, I'm going to get married," I said.

"Who to? Caroline Stokes?" She looked at me quickly. I was surprised that she should have guessed.

"Yes: she'll have her final decree in September, and we're going to be married then." I paused, but Julie looked at me in silence. "I've always been in love with her," I said, "from the days when I first knew her before the War. You remember how hard hit I was then."

Julie was still silent. I went on: "We get along wonderfully together. And she's developed a lot since I first knew her."

She spoke finally — she had become rather rigid, sitting up straight in the chair: "Well, I shouldn't have thought Caroline Stokes was the right woman for you, Fritz."

"Why not? You don't know her. You haven't seen her since she was in her teens." When Karl came out at this moment to ask whether she wanted more cocktails, she replied that she did not.

"I know that she's been knocking around for years with the international drinking set. And frankly, Fritz, I don't see how that sort of thing can be very good for you. You've been drifting along for years without getting any real hold on yourself, and I don't see how a girl like Caroline Stokes can be anything but a demoralizing influence. She seems to have made a mess of her first marriage. I understand that her husband is a complete drunkard."

I saw that she had been making inquiries.

"*Lefanu* is a mess. He never did anything but drink. Also treated her with considerable brutality."

"You know that there are always two sides to such things. She hadn't been living with her husband half the time for years. She used to go abroad for months and leave him alone in New Orleans."

"She hadn't been living with him at all for years. She had a house of her own down there."

"Well, I think you ought to think very seriously before

you do anything definite. I don't think" — she went back to what I had said at the beginning — "that your first flirtation with Caroline was anything more than a kiddish crush. You got over it easily enough when you began to go round with Evelyn Manning."

"I had to go around with somebody. That didn't mean I didn't love Caroline."

She made me feel lumpish: I was lying back in my chair while she was sitting forward. I had a cocktail in one hand, and my other hand was petting a red setter. The dog had come up while we were talking, and, combining with the red tiles, the earth-colored urns with white flowers, and my sister's tanned forearms and V at her neck, filled out a composition from which I with my too wide-striped blue tie was now to be excluded — since Caroline and I were not to live there.

"I think you're still rather adolescent in certain ways, Fritz. Mother always used to say that she thought you were too young for your age. You oughtn't to get married on the same sort of basis that you used to sit out dances at the country club in the days before the War."

Poor Julie, through only three years, belonged to another generation: she had never quite understood how the innocent sitting-out of dances in the days when she had been a deb, had turned into the kind of petting that had made our evenings at Sea Bright memorable.

"Do you really think," she went on, "that Caroline wants to live with you? I'm conventional enough to believe that when you marry a person, you ought to live with them. And Caroline's record isn't very reassuring. I don't think she even treated you very well back when you were first interested in her. However, you must make your own decisions. But do try to make them like a grown-up person."

"Well, Julie," I replied, recovering and finding my own voice again, "I couldn't lead your kind of life — though I admire it and I'm sure it's right of you. All the people who go to cocktail parties aren't worthless wastrels, you know; and there is a lot going on in the world that you people living out here haven't got the faintest idea of. All that's gorgeous and exciting and bitter in the life and art of to-day simply seems to you disorderly conduct."

Sometimes she listened quietly when I became exuberant and brilliant and would let me go on for some time; but now she drew into herself as if she were offended by it. I could feel it, but I plunged on:

"There are things that are terrible and things that are glorious and things that are very strange, and it is something to feel those things, and maybe to give them expression. I feel them and Caroline feels them, and together we feel them even more excitingly — and that's the test of the validity of a relationship, the test of sensibility. The life out here is beautiful, and, as I say, it's right for you, I know, but the whole Hudson River Valley is just about half asleep all the time!"

Henry had come back through the house. "I agree with you, Fritz," he said as he opened the screen door. "The Hudson River Valley is the most somnambulistic place in the world — and one of its most confirmed somnambulists is Mr. Fred Lagrange, who is probably away playing ten-pins with the goblins in the mountains, for he certainly hasn't been doing anything for me."

"Dinner is in twenty minutes," said Julie to me, sitting up. She was something more than chilly — she seemed silenced; and I felt that I had asserted myself and justified my point of view.

Julie, it turned out later, had told Henry about Caroline and me while I was up getting ready for dinner, but nothing further was said about it then. At dinner we talked about music. Julie, who played the piano, had gotten up an amateur orchestra; which, with the assistance of a few paid professionals, had been rehearsing the Jupiter Symphony for some kind charity benefit.

"Why," I asked, "don't you play something a little more modern than Mozart?"

"I can't bear modern music, Fritz, if you mean Schoenberg and Stravinsky and such people."

She had definitely shut down, I could see, on our lines of communication: I had taken her, in the course of the winter, to several concerts of the League for New Music, and she had listened with friendly attention while I explained to her what the moderns were up to.

"You used to talk just the same way, Julie, about Debussy and Strauss before they were accepted by the concert halls. I remember an argument we had about *Heldenleben* in 1912, it must have been, the year I got out of school."

"There's nothing in Strauss or Debussy like these songs of Schoenberg's we heard," Julie answered with the dignity that had been growing on her since our mother's death the winter before. "There's no key — and no form of any kind. There are just a lot of disagreeable sounds."

There's bitonalism in Strauss, I insisted. "*Also Sprach Zarathustra* ends in two different keys, and in the finale of *Salomé* there's a chord in F on top of a chord in C. It's perfectly logical to go from bitonalism to atonalism the way Schoenberg did. The course of modern music had been tending in that direction since Beethoven. *Wenn man A sagt, man müss B sagen.*"

"I'll never like Schoenberg, Fritz — so there's no use in arguing about it."

At this point, Henry, according to his custom, firmly took over the conversation. "Isn't it true, Fritz," he said, "that Schoenberg had thoroughly mastered the accepted theory of music before he made his innovations?"

"Of course: he teaches music in Berlin; he's written a textbook on music. He's probably the world's greatest master of musical theory."

Henry went on with his line of thought: "It's a very different matter to work in the established tradition and to carry it out to further developments than to begin by kicking over the traces and trying to go it entirely by yourself like some of the wild men of modern art. It's so in painting: men like Monet and Renoir were thoroughly grounded in the traditional technique."

"Yes," I agreed readily, grateful to Henry's intelligence. "And Picasso has been doing in painting very much the same sort of thing that Schoenberg has been doing in music."

"There's too much of the smartaleck about Picasso," said Henry. "The whole French school since the War seems to me essentially a smartaleck affair."

"Oh, some of it is great stuff!" I felt now that they were both against me. "Distortion is normal to art. It was the photographic nineteenth century in painting that violated the real tradition and made deliberate distortion necessary in order to see the world again the way the artist ought to see it — the way Schoenberg or Picasso sees it. What Julie doesn't understand about Schoenberg is that he's only bringing out certain things —"

"I'm hopefully old-fashioned, Fritz: I think that art ought to make things beautiful."

"But Schoenberg *is* beautiful. Good God! he's heart-breakingly beautiful. You liked *Verklärte Nacht*— and what you have in his later work is the tragedy of a beautiful soul that is continually getting kicked in the pants. It's romanticism after it's been knocked cockeyed by the traffic of the modern world. Schoenberg picks up the pieces."

"You have two arguments there, Fritz," said Henry, as we were about to get up from the table. "The argument that the distinctions of modern art are bringing things back to a norm, and the argument that they represent the abnormal process of the artists being knocked to pieces."

We had coffee in the living-room, and Henry changed the subject. Then Julie had to go to her rehearsal and Henry returned to his paper, and I went into the octagonal library, where I isolated myself in a large leather chair with a lamp and attempted to read Spengler, but brooded about marrying Caroline.

Presently Henry came in and addressed himself to the subject *sans ambages*.

"Julie tells me," he began, sitting down, "that you're about to take an important step."

"Yes. I'm going to marry Caroline Stokes," I said, smiling to deprecate the "important step," but, as I felt, perhaps a little boyishly.

"I knew her uncle very well," said Henry, "and her father, too — though not so well. They were rather an unpleasant family. Fred Stokes was a great man about town, and he finally married a chorus-girl, one of the girls in the Floradora Sextette. He died of syphilis, and he used to be a sight, because his face turned blue from taking mercury — they used to treat it with mercury in those days. I don't think it was hereditary: I think he'd picked it up in the course of his riotous living."

"Yes, Caroline's told me about her uncle."

"Pete Stokes, Caroline's father, also died under something of a cloud. He drank very heavily and I think his wife left him."

"Yes, she took Caroline and her sister to Canada."

"Pete spent most of the last part of his life in a cure for alcoholics. He died from taking an overdose of some sort of narcotic they were giving him. I don't know that he committed suicide. It's rather hard to tell in such cases. I never saw so much of Pete because he lived in Philadelphia — though I knew them both at college."

He talked on with such quietness and courtesy — sitting relaxed in an old morris-chair, his long legs stretched out before him and his hands resting finely on the ends of the arms of the chair or raised and clasped in front of him while he rested on the arms with his elbows — that it was impossible to resent his assumption that I had not learned from Caroline herself a great deal more about her parents than he was in a position to have learned from his slight acquaintance with her father.

"Fred Stokes when he was young," he went on, "was one of the most attractive chaps I've ever known. He had a charm that was irresistible, and I can understand Caroline's being attractive. Fred's charm made it fatally easy for him to be popular without doing anything to deserve it, and it was one of the things that led to his eventual deterioration. The qualities that make young people attractive before they have gotten out into the world and had to assume responsibilities are sometimes precisely the things that get them into trouble nowadays."

"Caroline has plenty of character" — I decided to take a stand.

"I hope so. I suppose that the fact that she's divorced her husband doesn't necessarily mean anything nowadays."

"Her husband was a hopeless proposition. He was one of these Deep-Southern souses. He used to threaten her, and she got to be afraid of him. Caroline really doesn't fit in at all, Henry, with this horrendous picture you're giving me. Her mother was a Scotch Canadian — and a Scotch Presbyterian. I can assure you that she's a perfectly sound character."

"I didn't mean to give you a horrendous picture" — Henry's sense of proportion was much too just for that — "But I think you ought to take your bearings before you set out on a voyage that's supposed to be for life. Of course, when a fellow's in love" — he smiled with his brown eyes and with a movement of his responsive eyebrows, but his use of the word *fellow* in this way, which marked him as of another generation, emphasized the difference between us — "when a fellow's in love, he's in love, and what other people say is irrelevant. But have you thought about the problem of marriage from the financial point of view? A fellow can live on a small salary as you've been doing and have the run of the town, because all he needs is a couple of business suits and a couple of sets of evening clothes and a few other things; but a married man has to buy clothes for his wife and he has to entertain and he has to provide for his children. Do you think you're in a position to do that? I don't think there can be very much left of the family fortunes of the Stokeses."

"Caroline's used to getting along on very little. She even cooks her own meals sometimes. We'll be able to get along in an apartment. It'll be cheaper because we'll only have one instead of two as we have now." It was on my tongue to tell him that it was different from the way it had been in his day, when getting married had meant founding an establishment: that it was all right for young couples to camp out; but I was checked by the ghost of a hope that from his own sense of how things ought to be done he might be disposed to come to our rescue by setting us up in one of the Powell houses.

"Well," he went on, "I think if I were you that I'd take advantage of the occasion to ask your boss for a raise." I was silent, as I had of course thought of this and was by no means sure that I'd be able to get it.

He got up and stood above me, with his hands in his trousers pockets, and turned his head to see the title of my book. "There's a horrendous picture, if you like," he said. "Do you think we're as badly off as that?"

"These tables he's got are pretty impressive."

"The Germanic mind"—he did not let me finish, though his method of interrupting made the interruption hardly perceptible—"The Germanic mind is always impressive if you're impressed by an accumulation of data. But it seems to me that all German thought suffers from a fundamental lack of realism. They bring up their heavy artillery, as they did when they started the War, but in the long run they fail to attain their objectives, because they haven't any accurate idea of what the world outside of Germany is like."

"Well," I interrupted, "if we live, we'll have a chance to see whether these ominous blanks of his are filled in the way he expects them to be."

"I'm afraid," he went on imperturbably, "that there's a good deal of special pleading in Spengler — he wants to show that, since Germany was defeated, the whole of Western civilization is finished."

When Julie came back, she was more cordial. I think she had depended on Henry to throw the fear of God into my heart. Henry had to go to town the next day, and Julie and I arranged to have a ride the next afternoon. Henry kept himself in excellent shape and always went everywhere and did everything with Julie. But she would have liked to go out more than he did, and there were places to which it was more fun to go with someone nearer her own age, like myself. There were neighbors, a young couple who had known Henry as a member of their parents' generation and toward whom Henry, for all his incomparable grace, could not help behaving a shade paternally; and Julie and I used to enjoy calling on them, as only happened, however rarely, without him. I foresaw that we should end up the next day in the Burnets' swimming-pool, that we should have cocktails which would get us higher than the cocktails at Henry's did, and that Julie and Sam Burnet would indulge in the little flirtation, very light and amusing and correct, that had been going on between them for years. Julie was always animated in her rapid and emphatic Germanic way, but what she needed was the enlivened and smiling eye which Sam Burnet was able to inspire or the girlish friendliness that came out when she was alone with me. I was the only man she had besides Henry, and I supposed she was a little jealous at the prospect of my getting married. Still, I would have to have it out with her the next day at the risk of spoiling our ride.

I collected myself and forced the situation as we sat in the cool screened living-room, eating cherries and apples, which Karl had brought in a bowl with plates and little fruit knives. Henry talked about the different kinds of cherries while with masterly simplicity and dignity he slowly devoured one after the other and dropped the pits on his plate.

In my room, still staring at Spengler, I reaffirmed to myself my intention of marrying Caroline. I was still a little hurt and sulky. I wondered about Henry and Julie in bed. I imagined him performing the operation in the same way that he had eaten the cherries — though he would put into it just the right amount of tenderness. He would pride himself on having mastered this important department of activity as he had done so many others. If his tactful and well-calculated efforts did not produce the desired results, he would know how to instruct his partner. I couldn't believe that Julie had ever had so good a time with Henry as Caroline had with me. That was what people like that were unable to understand: that

there were other things worth living for and paying for
besides a well-ordered family life and a beautiful house
in the country. Could Henry appreciate passion? Was he
even, fundamentally, intelligent? He had lived much in
Paris in the eighties and nineties. He had enough taste or
acumen to buy the Impressionist painters. To be sure, he
seemed to assume that Monet was a painter on the same
plane as Renoir; but perhaps for that generation that
was a natural thing to think: after all, Monet had been
Renoir's master.

There, among the eighteenth-century watercolors which
somebody had brought back from Italy, the delight-
ful smell and feel of the sheets and the light summer
blankets, the air from the rich valley darkness coming
in through the copper screens, I wondered whether it
could possibly be true that Caroline was unreliable. She
seemed so loyal and so perfectly sincere. But she did have
these evasions and these silences; it was hard to get at
her directly and to establish an explicit understanding.
There had been once during the winter when I had
found myself confronted with an unexplained obstruc-
tion and had found out that she had been going around
with another man — whom, however, she had certainly
dropped when I had a showdown with her about it and
with whom I didn't believe she had ever slept. She hadn't
believed I had really cared about her — that had been
the trouble; I had only to convince her that I did. She
couldn't have demoralized Lefanu: he had never had any
morale. If he had gone so completely to pieces when he
was married to her, it was because she was stronger than

he. And wasn't I stronger than she? I knew that she had some kind of respect for me that she had never had for Lefanu. And I was strong enough to marry her and make a go of it where that poor soak from New Orleans had failed and in spite of the fact that she and I didn't fit into Henry and Julie's picture.

III

THE FIRST PARTY

We got married in the vestry of what Nick Carter called the Church of the Holy Zebra, that striped affair on Lexington Avenue. Nick was there, and Julie, and Caroline's friend Martha Gannett. Nick and Caroline and I had all had a good deal to drink, which it cost us a certain amount of effort to conceal from Julie and the minister. Afterwards, we had a wedding lunch, to which a few other friends had been invited, in a private room at the Meadowbrook restaurant. Nick Carter made one of his best speeches, which began by introducing me as an old Kendall boy who had made good in the missionary field in China, went on to announce my election as captain of next year's football team and to praise me as a quiet plugger upon whom the school had learned to count, and ended with one of those sentimental outpourings, wishing me success and happiness, which seem to be characteristic of humorists. I thought that Julie relaxed a little and entered into the spirit of the occasion.

We got away for two weeks to Florida, going first to

Key West, where we went fishing, wore old clothes and did not see anybody we knew, and only went on to Miami the second week.

We gave our first party in September, the time of excitement in New York. But it was not so successful as we had hoped.

We had taken an apartment on lower Fifth Avenue in one of those old places that had once been fashionable that had not yet been done over. It was in fact the last to survive. It had broad stairways covered with carpets and large, slow and carpeted elevators that were run by quiet Negroes. The rooms were enormously high and the windows were long and low; there were great built-in wardrobes and chests of drawers. Kitchen facilities of the kind that one invariably has in even the smaller new city apartment were almost impossible here: they were forbidden by the fire laws, and, besides, there would have been no place for them. We had most of our meals, when we took them at home, brought up from the dining-room downstairs, and they appeared under great half-melon covers that must have been protecting roast-beef and chops ever since the Civil War. The apartments were almost all occupied by old people who had been living there for countless years but who were beginning at last to drop off, so that an attempt was being made to bring in a younger clientèle.

Caroline had shied away from the place — which had the Anglophile name of the Tavistock — because it seemed to her so far away from her friends uptown; but I found that I shied away from the places that one paid a lot more for in order to give the appearance of fashion-

able addresses — and not only on this account but because I wanted to entrench myself with the ideal of living I had precisely against Caroline's friends. Down there
I had them more under control. So Caroline draped the
windows with splendid red brocade curtains, caught
up with bright brass chains that she had salvaged from
her previous household, and set out various ornamental
mahoganies or objects of silver and glass that had been
inherited by one or the other of us. The living-room,
with its marble mantelpiece surmounted by an immense
gold-framed mirror, which had already an impressive
spaciousness, acquired thus even a certain sumptuous-
ness, and I loved to stand against the mantel when I had
just come back from work at five, while Caroline in her
chartreuse dress was serving her perfect rum cocktails in
glasses with iced and sugared rims, and talk to people
about the season's concerts and our friends as they came
and went between New York and other places.

We had been merging our respective groups of
friends, and in the process they seemed to have mul-
tiplied, as, with the exception of certain of Caroline's
beaux who had been giving her a rush in her walk-up,
more people will call on a couple than would ever come
to see them living singly. Our first party, a cocktail party,
was to blend the best of both sets. We had invited two
first-rate celebrities — a young Russian-Jewish violinist,
whose evenings in the West Fifties I had somewhat fre-
quented, and a man named Eddie Frink, whom I had
known very slightly at college but who was a great friend
of Caroline's drinking friends, an immensely clever fellow who had a great vogue at a night club singing ribald
and partially improvised songs and who that fall had

made a kind of hit with his first musical comedy score. I had tried to carry out a resolution not to have anyone actually stupid; but Caroline had insisted, when I had narrowed it down, that that was not enough people to ask, as there would always be some who wouldn't come, so I passed a few of Caroline's pals whom I regarded as congenitally defective and whom, as they went everywhere with the rest of their group, it would anyway, as Caroline pointed out, be useless to try to exclude, as they would be certain to show up just the same.

The first arrival was Martha Gannett, who had come early to rally round Caroline. Caroline, it turned out to my surprise and a little to my impatience, was frightened at the prospect of my friends, about whom, in talking about them, I had somehow given her the impression that they were tremendous social and musical highbrows. With all her rather varied social experience, she still remained strangely shy. I knew that she did not yet like my sister, whose positiveness and precision disconcerted her, and that her feeling about Henry — who set off in her old reactions toward what she regarded as the stuffier type of Philadelphian — was a mixture of imitation and awe; and I saw now that she actually shuddered at the prospect of trying to keep afloat with the professional musical world. Martha Gannett was just the person to keep her up — though I rather resented Martha's role, as I wanted this to be our party and Caroline to depend on me. She was rather a tall girl who just missed being handsome. She was, in fact, the inevitable wife's friend who always provides a subject of controversy because one's wife insists that she *is* handsome. She came from Philadelphia, too, from some kind of pretty good

family, and had one of those hard accents with spine-
chilling r's that only the best people are permitted up
there. She had it in common with Caroline that they had
both been let down by the family money: Martha worked
in a big antique store and practically ran it, though it belonged to someone else. She was tall and had black eyes.
Caroline was always hoping that she would meet someone at one of our parties.

The next to arrive were Phil Dewitt and his crew, who,
since they arrived shouting, "Are we early enough?" I
found out, again rather to my annoyance, Caroline had
asked to try to get there first in order to give her support.
They were all, as was usually the case, recovering from a
heavy night. "For me," said Phil, "it was a fresh advice-
filling evening — I advised people about buying cars,
about keeping dogs, about everything — I advised one
old lady about the market. Oh, God! — and there was
nobody there to advise me not to take those last nine
drinks!"

"I advised you," said Claire, his wife.

"You did like hell!" retorted Phil. "You were guzzling
champagne cocktails at that bar, showing me your beautiful back."

"I wanted to go at one point, but you didn't want to."

"The person who really needed advice," said Ann,
"was poor Joe Lovett."

"Yes," said Phil, eagerly taking it up. "Joe woke up this
morning and told Katy that he'd have to apologize to his
hostess. 'Yes,' Katy said. 'Maybe you ought to.' Joe went
on to say that he didn't think anything was ruder than to
go to somebody's party and leave without saying good-
by. 'What do you mean,' said Katy, 'leave without saying

good-by? You overdid saying good-by.' Joe insisted he hadn't said a word of good-by — hadn't even seen Bertha Runkel. Then Katy broke the news that when he had come to say good night, he had leapt upon Bertha with a bearlike embrace, given her many resounding kisses, and finally slipped on the rug and fallen on his face."

Phil had learned a technique of carrying a conversation like an actor carrying a scene; he had acquired it in his role of eternal guest whom people liked to have around because he could be so completely depended on; and you could see him going at it even when he was tired. He was plugging it particularly now in order to hold up Caroline's party, and with very slender material he was getting his laughs as steadily as any professional comedian. When he laughed himself, he opened his mouth very wide and there was a wild hilarious light in his eye that excited other people to hilarity. He was rather a pleasant-looking fellow: he played enough tennis in the course of his visits to the country so that he kept in pretty good shape, though there was more of booze than of sun in his excessively red face.

"And another thing I gave advice about was the use of contraceptives. Mary Stopes in person! I ought to start a clinic! I explained all the different devices."

"With illustrations?"

"With illustrations!"

"Who were you explaining to?"

"To somebody I'd never seen before. He looked like a freshman at Yale."

"At Princeton more likely," I said.

"At any rate he had the idea that condoms were difficult to get —"

At this moment Henry and Julie arrived. It was just what I had been dreading. Phil had too much social sense ever to take a wrong line with people — it was another of the reasons for his success in getting himself asked around; but their appearance put a quietus on the usual gaiety of the group, and I became acutely aware of the shoddiness of Phil and Irving and their women. Phil, though a professional parasite, had come from a good family in St. Louis; but he married a professional model. Claire was almost incredibly pretty in her blond and willowy way, and she made a good appearance socially just as she did when she was modelling; but there was something underbred about her way of making a good appearance. She was also abysmally stupid. With Irving and Ellis, it was the other way round: Ellis was the better of the two. Her mother was old New York and her father an extremely rich broker, and her reason for marrying Irving and her apparent continued devotion to him had always remained rather mysterious. She was a little bit stolid and plain, had probably never had very many admirers, and Irving must have convinced her that he really wanted very much to marry her. And I suppose he was genuinely devoted to her, not for romantic reasons, but because he knew she was the real thing. Irving was a phoney of a very peculiar kind. His origins and career were obscure, though he constantly talked about them. Everything he said about himself sounded completely untrue, though he may really have done all the things he said he had just as he had really married Ellis. He appeared to have been highly successful in promoting a jewelry business — he certainly made a lot of money; but one always had the feeling that his company might at any moment fold up. He was broad-shouldered and well set-up, and his features were clean-cut and good; but his good looks had the unreality that one would feel about one of the idealized young men in the cereal and motor ads if he were able to come to life: Irving should only have existed on paper. He did not drink so much as the others, but Ellis drank prodigiously. In company she was always tight and she was always tight when she arrived, perhaps because she was ashamed of Irving and every appearance with him in public was an ordeal. She and Irving and Phil and Claire had somehow become very close — no doubt because the elements in each couple, though differently distributed between husband and wife, were more or less the same.

It did not take Irving long to let Henry know that he had just played squash at the Racquet Club, where he had gotten some valuable dope on the market from his opponent, and to show his intimate familiarity with leading personalities of Tammany Hall from the moment when he discovered that Henry thought Al Smith was doing a good job:

"Yes, by Jove," he remarked with an excessive quietness and ease which was habitual with him and undercut even Henry's, though in a definitely vulgar way, "you can say what you please about the crookedness of Tammany, but they at least deliver the goods to their constituents. I just saw Joe Flannigan the other day, and he was on his way down to some place on Second Avenue to bring a chicken dinner to the wife of some man in one of those lower East Side wards, who was sick. He had it in a hamper and he was taking it down himself in his limousine. He took it in himself instead of getting the

chauffeur to do it. I know, because I was riding downtown with him and I waited while he took it in. When he
came out, he talked about her illness as if she'd been his
own sister. Allowing for the sentimentality of the Irish,
you have to admit that Tammany has a real sense of
responsibility. Naturally they're not taking any dinners
to people who don't vote for their candidates — but
Al Smith has gone farther than that and shown a sense
of responsibility to the community as a whole. When
I saw Mrs. Moskowitz last, she told me that she thought
he had grown faster than any man in public life since
Lincoln."

We couldn't have had a worse beginning. Henry with-
drew from the conversation and turned his attention to
Caroline and Julie, who were discussing the arrangement of the room. He always seemed to make a point of
listening to all the conversations that were going on
around him, and he loved to intervene with a quiet but
authoritative word.

"You've made a charming room," he said. "These old
places are likely to be cavernous. An aunt of mine stayed
here once, and I used to think it extremely gloomy. But
you've made it quite bright and gay."

I couldn't be absolutely sure that there wasn't an ironic
nuance at the expense of Caroline's frivolity in brighten-
ing up a place once inhabited by his aunt. But no: it was
true that she did have a touch that made things bright
and gave them style. I looked about with pride at the
sumptuous brocade, the polished mahogany surfaces,
and the glittering silver and glassware, the black shiny
baby grand piano with a red cover like the curtains
across it and the white pages with their beautiful little

notes open on the rack, that combined to such happy effect, not with the impressiveness of prearrangement, but with the freshness of good taste.

At this moment Nick Carter and Kay Burke appeared. Nick's entrance, which he had obviously thought out as he came up, was a nonsensical burst of humor about the old-fashioned elevator.

"What became of the rope?" said Nick. "I was afraid that we'd fall because they'd forgotten the rope. I suppose it doesn't know that the rope is gone and just keeps on going up and down — it's in its dotage now. It's getting slower. Some day it will realize that the rope is gone and it will drop off with a dying sob."

He laughed after each one of his jokes, and thus got other people laughing, too. I observed that Phil Dewitt was watching his routine with interest.

"I loved the red-plush seat," said Kay, who had a distinctly developed social sense and apprehended the presence of elements with whom she could not begin by clowning.

"I love sitting down in the elevator. I wanted to ride up and down." The professional glibness of Nick Carter a little abashed Phil, who, though expert, was entirely an amateur. These two elements of New York gaiety did not get on so well as I had somehow imagined they would. When you got them out in ordinary society, you saw how much of the *cabotin* there was about them, in spite of Kay's intensive efforts to do and say the right thing. Besides, her characteristic humor turned out to be too intellectual for people like Phil and Claire. I encouraged Nick to play their game of embodying words in sentences, and they produced some masterpieces of the *genre* such as "Paroxysm marvellous city" and "Embezzle woman in the world"; but Phil's laughter and "That is wonderful!" were forced: he didn't really see it as funny. Ellis was the only one to whom punning was a familiar form of humor, but she just thought these were stupidly bad puns.

Irving finally blocked and obliterated the whole course of the conversation by telling some joke of Irvin S. Cobb's, which desolated Nick and Kay, and going on to tell about a lunch with Cobb which he claimed to have had at the Players' Club and at which Cobb "with his marvellous drawl" had kept them all in stitches. Finally, the colored waiter, who was serving the *sole marguery*, couldn't control himself and burst out laughing and dished the sole right into Cobb's lap. Cobb simply picked it up and put it on his plate, and said, "I'd like a little more of the sauce, please. You can put it in my vest-pocket."

I had been once to the Players' Club, and it seemed to me that the waiters were white, but it was characteristic of Irving's stories that you were never able quite to check up on them.

In the meantime, the musical element had come and were engaging Henry and Julie. Jehuda Janowitz was a handsome and very Hebraic dark young Jew, who, at the age of twenty-seven, had succeeded in playing the violin with miraculous technical proficiency and compelling nervous force. He was personally friendly but a little aloof, and I never could help feeling a little in awe of him. Though he was so young, he was clearly surrounded by a whole *cénacle* of Jewish admirers, who with an inborn instinct of discipleship had singled him out as a master. The trouble about knowing Jehuda was that you always had to see him in this circle. Off the platform and outside practice, he seemed to spend all his time in a large and rather gorgeous apartment west of Central Park, where his admirers played the piano with him and turned pages for him, flattered, entertained, advised, and nursed him, and offered newcomers drinks. When he went out, he was always accompanied by his chief disciple and general factotum, a little man with a pince-nez, who threw out his hands like flippers and was likely to become rather embarrassing by telling you about Jehuda's love affairs. He regarded it as a part of his duty to celebrate the prowess of the master, and seemed to act as more or less of a pimp for him. I had heard that he arrived every morning and put the ladies out so that Jehuda would start practicing on time.

"Well, how is Jehuda?" I asked Furstmann, the disciple. Jehuda himself was talking to Julie. (She had been very much impressed by hearing him, and I was glad to think that she was at least getting this out of our party: the fact that she was a musician herself gave her a reverence for all accomplished violinists.) Besides, you never asked Jehuda how he was: you always asked Furstmann.

"Not so well," said the disciple, dropping his voice and shaking his head as he proceeded: "These concerts are a very heavy strain on him. He doesn't complain but one can see it. So we mustn't stay very long."

Eddie Frink was, of course, quite different. He was a hollow-eyed and pale little man, who looked like one of those puny and tender and almost transparent tree-toads. He was dressed in a green shirt with the collar secured by a gold pin, and all the chic of the Riviera and the Duke of Westminster's yacht under the influence of Noel Coward and the Prince of Wales. I had known him only slightly at college, as he was a couple of years ahead of me; but Caroline had known him in Paris. I began by asking him about men who had been to Yale in our time — in most of whom he made it obvious that he took not the faintest interest; and I then went to what I considered it was the kind of thing for us to try to do at our parties. Eddie was really a clever musician with a certain amount of musical cultivation. One of the features of his night club songs had been parodies of the classical composers which were usually over the heads of his audience. I complimented him on his musical comedy score and asked him why he did not take himself more seriously; I urged on him the importance of contributing to a modern American music.

"I can't do Schoenbergle and Stravinsk," he replied. "Wouldn't want to, if I could. Schoenbergle is a bore, if you ask me, and Stravinsky is *assommant* in the literal sense of the word: He knocks you on the head and leaves you helpless."

I reminded him of Auric and Honegger and the rest.

"You can't have that kind of thing over here," he said, "and why should you want to, if you could? We've got half a dozen writers of jazz that are twice as good as Auric and Honegger.

"I've been working on a sonata," he said.

"Good work! I'd like to hear it."

"Be glad to play it for you when it's finished. I never get any time to work with three performances of these goddamn songs every night. Frank wants me to go on again at four, but I'll be goddamned if I'll do it. They don't listen at the two o'clock performance, so to hell with them!"

"They don't get a lot of your jokes," I said.

"They don't even hear the songs any more. All they know is they've paid money to laugh and then say they've heard Eddie Frink. They get cockeyed, and they all laugh in unison — always in the wrong places. It's getting on my nerves so that some night — one of these nights when they roar in the wrong places — I'm going to stop suddenly and bow and say, 'Thank you, ladies and gentlemen, for your intelligent appreciation of my efforts. I want to pass among you and thank each one of you personally,' and I'm going to grab a decanter, and go along the table and boppo! boppo! boppo! — and crown buyers and their tarts on the head till they drag me away to the nut-farm!"

The bell rang, and when I went to the door, I found Lefanu, obviously very drunk, his thin blond hair tousled about his flaming liquor soaked face. With him was Elizabeth Danziger, the large and somber Jewess from New Orleans, who had loved him all his life and who had finally, at least for the time being, been able to take him over when he and Caroline had broken up. He had heard about our party from someone and, calling up Caroline the day before, as he tended to do when he was drunk, on the pretext of locating some possession of his own or of restoring something of hers, he had asked her if he might come, and she, not taking him seriously, had said, "Certainly."

I did not know this at the time, as she had never thought to mention it to me, and I resented his appearance all the more; but I received him with the cordial politeness one can afford with a discarded husband.

He on his part seemed to know how to behave with a minimum of social friction, as all New Orleanseans do — though his smooth Louisiana charm seemed to me to be becoming pretty buttery and even a bit rancid when he started in with "Ho 'bout ye?" on the Freeman-Dewitt contingent and began telling them his amusing stories. It reminded you that his father had not been one of the real people but only a cotton broker. Lefanu had made such a mess of the Law that he had lately gone in with a man from Shreveport for speculating in Florida real estate. He had a whole new repertoire of anecdotes. He had taken a trip to Florida and gone around as a prospect to see how the thing was being handled:

"They take them down there on a special train — and when they get off all they can see is a great barren waste with a little shack with a crude board building that's just been thrown together — hasn't even been painted — and they take you in and give you a miserable lunch. And then all of a sudden there erupts into the room the man who's going to sell you. He's a reg'lar evangelist — he used to be a Baptist minister, he tol' me. He gives them hell-fire sales-talk — jus' like an ol'time sermon. He tells them that there are three cardinal sins for a prospective real-estate buyer: Fear, Caution, and Delay — and he preaches them a reg'lar sermon under those three heads:

Fear, Caution, and Delay. And he winds up: 'An' if Jesus Christ was alive and among us today, he'd buy a lot in Florida right here where we're standin'!'"

"Did the people buy the lots?" asked Ellis.

"Several people bought lots just as soon as he'd finished — just like they'd got religion. I went up to the preacher afterwards and congratulated him — I said 'That's a great line of bunk you've got there.' He was mopping his brow — he'd worked hard. 'Coordination shows,' he said, 'that I sell a bigger percentage of prospects than anybody else engaged in the same line of work in Florida — and what I'm getting for it is the merest pittance.'"

"I hope you signed him up right away," said Irving.

"I wanted to, but somehow I couldn't: I didn't want to sell real estate by those methods — and that's why I'll never be a success as a real-tor."

He lighted a cigarette. I could see that the whole thing embarrassed him, and that he had to make fun of it all the time in order not to be ashamed. He had to make an effort to control his trembling hands in order to strike the match on the box, and then he dropped it into a vase, not being able to locate the ashtray.

Elizabeth Danziger sat on the side, smoking and smiling in the right places with more animation or expression than genuine feeling for humor. Her large green eyes were bright and hypnotic; they had behind them the Jewish force of soul and the Jewish solemnity of intellect. They really had nothing in common with anything that Lefanu was and yet they saw something in him; they had at once projected something into him and appropriated him as their own. Or was there some moral principle in Lefanu — say, rather, some striving for distinction, which had, for example, made it impossible for him to exploit the evangelist-salesman?

"I don't think Lefanu is cut out for a real estate man," she said.

It was all making Caroline fearfully nervous. She kept offering people new drinks and not paying attention to what they said to her. I was actually conscious that Henry and Julie must be aghast at the arrival of Lefanu, which would confirm their worst suspicions of Caroline — though at the moment they were talking to Jehuda, Henry, I noted as I paused there, exhibiting his knowledge of the techniques of playing various musical instruments and of the functions they performed in the orchestra. Eddie Frink had been wandering around in his rather sad and frog-eyed way; but he now connected with Kay and Nick, and they were obviously exchanging wisecracks, at which Nick was laughing loudly — I feared, at the expense of the sour notes being presented on all hands by the party. But I joined them and brought in Martha Gannett, who was delighted by all their jokes. She told them a dirty story, which I felt didn't go quite right — either because it was too flatfooted for them or because they were imbued with the idea that nobody could tell stories but themselves.

Other people came in; I lost track of Lefanu. The first intimation that I had that something was definitely slipping came when Ben Furstmann presented himself to me in the role of Jehuda's gentleman-in-waiting and explained that Jehuda was tired and that they would have to go home now.

"Such parties are too much of a strain," he said.

"These mixed contacts put a tax on his nerves that he can't afford when he's playing." I felt that there was a distinct reproach implied.

"Thank you so much," said Jehuda. He was always polite and pleasant, but reserved — he had a certain inscrutability. I saw that Lefanu was standing by, and that he had reverted, under the influence of whiskey, to the crumpled and sore-headed little boy who seemed to be at the bottom of his character. He had become tousle-headed and round-shouldered; he stood with one hand in his pocket and the other holding his glass.

"I hope I didn't tread on the toes of your Jewish friend," he said.

I asked him what had happened.

"I simply said in the course of conversation that I thought the Jews were better as interpreters than they were as creative artists, and your violinist's little friend began to tell me that Wagner was a Jew. I expressed my opinion of Wagner's music — I never could bear it — all this swooning sensuousness, fornicating mysticism, or mystic fornication, or whatever you choose to call it — I'm sure it must be Jewish."

I wondered whether this didn't apply to his relations with Elizabeth Danziger.

"— and I guess that offended their sensibilities. I hope you don't mind my comin' here, Fritz," he said, suddenly changing the subject and, as he did so, slipping down to a level of more obvious drunkenness, "but I'll always be fond of Caroline and wish her well — I want her to have any kind of happiness that's possible for her. Maybe we aren't all capable of happiness. 'It is not long the singing and the laughter — Hope and desire and hate.' I'm thirty-three — Caroline's twenty-nine — you're how old? . . . Thirty-one. We get old fast nowadays. My mother is still a beauty — she don't tell her age, but she must be over sixty. She looks younger than Caroline right now."

"You manage to remain youthful," I said.

"Yes: in a way," he replied. Then, after a moment's pause: "I don't know whether you mean anything by that. Caroline used to think I was kiddish about those Japanese gold-fish, and I suppose you've had to hear about that."

"No," I tried to reassure him, "she hadn't. I didn't mean anything of the kind."

"Well, I am; I'm frankly childish in some ways — I've never grown up enough so as I can pretend I like people I *don't* like and so as I can take an insult like it was just a joke."

The conversation was getting bad. I offered him another drink because I didn't know what else to do.

"No, I don't want another drink — and I don't want to dance at your wedding. Maybe a wedding isn't the proper place to dance."

I broke away from his gaze, blue and blood-shot and hardening with a fury that glared through his deprecating smiles, and looked toward Caroline, who was diligently keeping away, tense with apprehension as I could see, and then toward Elizabeth Danziger, who had sat planted beside the Dewitt-Freeman group and been doing her best to get down to the level of their small-talk. She at once got up and came over.

"I think we'd better go, honey," she said. "We promised to be uptown by seven."

"All right, honeybunch," he replied, with a perceptible shade of satire. "Now that we've danced at the wedding, we must go. We must say good-by to the hostess. Well, Fritz"—he shook hands with me—"I hope you don't mind my comin'. In all sincerity I wish you luck and happiness. And now we must pay our respects to Caroline." He turned quickly and slipped on our polished floor. His collapse was instantaneous and complete. Elizabeth and I picked him up, with a hand under either arm. We walked him into the bedroom and made him lie down on the bed. He closed his eyes; he was out.

"I'll stay with him," said Elizabeth. "He'll be all right in a few minutes." She untied his necktie and sat down beside him.

I went back to the other guests. Henry and Julie at once took their leave.

"Well," said Henry — I dare say, without irony, it was the kind of thing he said — "it's been pleasant to see the modern spirit abounding in its own sense. — I had an interesting conversation with Janowitz. The expert in any field is always worth listening to. I gather that he's not as radical in his musical taste as some of you impassioned laymen."

"Jehuda," I said, smiling, "is a generation behind the times. In fact, he'd probably still be playing *Perpetual Motion* and Paganini's Variations, if his audiences would let him. He's a great violinist just the same."

With Lefanu's eclipse, Elizabeth Danziger's withdrawal, and the departure of Henry and Julie, it seemed to me that the atmosphere had relaxed. The Dewitt-Freemans and Nick and Kay and Eddie Frink and Martha Gannett had managed to get together and were now sufficiently lit so that they were laughing in unison like a chorus. But it wasn't the party I'd planned.

Miss Danziger came back to call up wherever they had been going and say that they couldn't come, and she tried to apologize and explain to Caroline. "You know how he is," she said, "when he gets carried away by one of his crazy ideas. I thought it would be better if I came with him."

"How is he?" asked Caroline.

"He's completely unconscious, I'm afraid."

Lefanu had indeed passed out, and it was difficult to bring him to even enough to get him downstairs. I poured him into a taxi with Miss Danziger, and just as I was about to shut the door, he put his hand out and grabbed me by the shoulder and said, "Fritz, you've got the woman that I love best in the world. You know that, don't you? And she knows it! But I don't harbor any grudge against you."

I detached his hand with a friendly smile and got the taxi off.

I didn't want to go out to dinner with Martha Gannett and the Dewitts and Freemans, which was what everybody else, including Caroline, wanted to do. They bored me, and I was afraid that Caroline, as a result of Lefanu's eruption, would sink herself with an evening of drinking. So we let the guests depart and had dinner sent up from below.

I remarked that Lefanu was in terrible shape.

"Elizabeth Danziger hates me," she said, "because she thinks I've been the cause of his downfall."

"He'd go to pieces anyway. They're brought up on absinthe and rich shrimp soup and nigger girls down there, and when they get to be about Lefanu's age, they squash like overripe tomatoes."

"He has awfully nice things about him," she demurred. "He used to be so gay and charming. Maybe I *was* bad for him."

"I think that Miss Danziger's got him down," I said. "He evidently resents her furiously but is powerless to get away."

"She's been hovering around for years, giving him a bad conscience. She wanted him to be a big successful lawyer. I don't know why people can't just enjoy life. People who have careers are so boring."

"That unbuilt opera house in New Orleans will always be between them," I said. "You know, after the opera burned down, they were never able to rebuild it because the only people who were rich enough were the Jews, and if they had taken their money for the opera, they would have had to let them in on the Mardi Gras — so the whole situation reached a stalemate, and the opera house was never rebuilt."

"Don't be so snobbish," she said. "I don't believe they have that opera house on their minds. I never heard Lefanu say anything about it."

"It's one of the great issues down there, though. I'm not snobbish; I'm just an observer."

"You're always worrying about social differences."

"They don't worry me, but I'm aware they exist."

"You've been worrying ever since the people left about all the problems of bringing the different ones together. I felt you were worrying all the time. I don't see why you

can't take people as they are and have a good time with
them and let them have a good time together."

"*I* take people for what they are, but they don't do that
with each other."

"All you men who go to Kendall and Yale are like that:
you have kind of a heavy social sense."

"Of course, if you're going to attack my old school!" I
retorted, being funny.

"I never noticed in New Orleans that the people were
looking askance at each other. They like to have a good
time. I lived in New Orleans for years and I never knew
that about the opera."

It was true that these considerations scarcely existed
for her. She had always — in Philadelphia and afterwards in Toronto — lived so much inside a world where
everyone belonged, and she was naturally so friendly and
sweet. She tended to think that everyone belonged: she
had learned in Toronto that certain technical breaches
constituted a man a bounder, but this was merely something she had learned, like the history that she never
could remember. She really thought that the bounders
belonged. She could see that certain people were "common," but as all kinds of people were almost always
trying to please her, she did not perceive this common-
ness often: it was only when, as happened rarely, somebody treated her with rudeness that she became aware
that the person was common. She had been liking all the
people and being sweet to them, and then Lefanu had
arrived and made her intensely uncomfortable — especially with Henry and Julie, whom she was afraid of and
who, she was sure, disapproved of her. She was suffering
from one of the twinges of bad conscience.

I told her that it showed how little idea she had about what was going on around her that she shouldn't have known about the opera house.

"All right, I'm dumb," she said. "I'm so stupid you shouldn't have married me."

But I sat down beside her on the couch and kissed her and tipped her over. I wanted the smart and bright little woman in clothes who had served the trim hors d'oeuvres and the rum cocktails, and I wanted to make her forget and to forget myself about the party. There was a warm woman with fleshy white thighs and a mat of thick hair which, though not perhaps precisely in harmony with the kind of thing at which I had been aiming, it was a relief to feel real and solid at the bottom of all that had happened. We went into the bedroom, and I pulled the shades, and she took off all her clothes, as she always preferred to do.

"Did somebody spill drinks on the bed?" she said, after she had sat down to pull off her stockings. "It's wet."

I felt it: the wetness was widespread. We stripped off the cover, and as we did so, we had a whiff of an acrid smell which identified the dampness as urine. Lefanu had forgotten himself in his stupor.

We had to change all the bedclothes and turn the mattress over. But we went on to make love just the same. We were disgusted with Lefanu and sore at him, in enjoying the exhilarating exercise of sex with our healthy and panting bodies over the mess of Lefanu's demoralization.

IV

BEDROOM CHIC

But we had a lot of fun that fall and winter.

Our partings and reunions when I made my trips West as buyer for Payne and Keller kept up a certain romance in the relationship and continually stimulated our appetite. I always took the train at night, and we always made love before I left, sometimes in a hurry when we had sat too long at dinner and it was almost time to go and the hurry heightened our gusto.

I was not tremendously interested in the drug business, but I felt that it was clean and serious, almost scientific, and though I regarded most Westerners as bohunks, I enjoyed looking out the windows at the flat snowy fields of Michigan, with their farm buildings full of cows and hogs, as we were getting into Detroit in the morning and being taken to curious speakeasies which were blinded-up private houses, where you were served very thin and foul highballs in a living-room full of stuffed arm-chairs; I enjoyed the darkness of Chicago, which was becoming almost metropolitan with modern apartment houses and big buildings lit up at night, and where I was entertained at Colosimo's, so different from our night clubs in New York, where I saw one of the most attractive women I have ever seen in this kind of thing do the Mexican towel rumba and was told that she belonged to the gangster proprietor and that to speak to her was asking for death; I enjoyed coming into Pittsburgh in the very early morning and seeing the glitter of pearl and silver of the houses on the other side of the river along the barren and gritty hillside, and the Scotch-Irish girls, pretty and thin, that ran to red hair and scrawny necks and talked snappy and had always had for me — though it might have been because I came from there — a certain sex appeal.

When I came back, it was nearly always exciting. I would clean myself up after the trip and Caroline would make me a drink and I would tell her about the early French family with obsolete dignities and elegances that was preserved like a fossil in a rock at Grosse Pointe; about my old school-friend Dick Keller, whose family had been leaders of Rock Island society and who was afraid to vote for Smith, though he drank like a fish and was opposed to Prohibition, because he said it wouldn't do in Chicago; about a dinner I had attended in Pittsburgh where the toastmaster had handed me a gardenia and said, "Pretty nasty, eh?"

I had never enjoyed these trips so much, because I had never before had anybody to whom I could really describe them — though Caroline sometimes got nervous when I made fun of the rich playboys of the provinces and broke me up by crisscross interruptions. And Caroline's soundness and bedroom chic and warm fragrance of bath salts and Chanel 5 would seem to me too good to be true after the night in Statler hotels where I had always thought about her.

And New York: what could be bleaker than those stone steps that go up so steeply and the heavy glass doors at the steps that let the cold directly in in winter? What could be more sordid than the floor of a taxi at two o'clock in the morning, with the bobby-pins and crushed cigarette-ends and dry dirt and God knows what? Yet when we would start off sometimes that autumn along Sixth or Seventh Avenue, we would see the furnace of the setting sun making molten the recurring blinding vistas that looked toward the Jersey shore, as if it were sending out just spokes of light that flashed past us as the taxi sped — the splendor and power of the center, the port, that the buildings had not managed to deaden. Could one make that effect into music?

V

THE MASKED BALL

We went one night in November to an enormous costume ball, at which everybody was supposed to represent something out of the Venetian Renaissance. The Sunday rotogravure section afterwards showed the stuffed-shirt sons of utility and oil millionaires looking blank in the robes of doges, correct debutantes and luscious young matrons posing as Titians and Giorgiones, and dog-faced night club playboys impersonating Casanova. There had also been a tableau in which Venice in the person of Harry Schauffler, apparently dressed as a gondolier, wedded the Adriatic in the person of Mrs. Eustace P. Fuller, Jr., dressed in blue velvet with diamonds. But I had thoroughly enjoyed the whole thing.

We had gone as carnival characters, which had made it possible for us to be rather vague. Caroline had a kind of red bodice that Martha Gannett had made her out of oilcloth and that stayed up without any shoulder-straps and a little short pink skirt. She wore tiny red gloves, no stockings, and her little gold high-heeled shoes that showed the toes and side of the foot. She had a mask and little clown hat that she fastened under her chin with an elastic and stuck on one side of her head. I was some kind of a buffoon and had equipped myself with a wooden sword, a fantastic rooster-tail plume, and a gigantic false nose.

Caroline asked rather anxiously whether I was going to wear the nose all the time, and I showed her that I could push it up so that it looked like a prong on my forehead.

"It looks indecent!"

I showed her that I could also push it down.

It happened that we hadn't arranged to have dinner with anybody beforehand, and we were fooling around in the apartment, inventing new touches for our costumes and intermittently consuming drinks. Caroline looked the cutest I had ever seen her. There was always about her dress something a little formal and British; and the costume brought out her nice roundness, the fairness and smoothness of her skin, and tininess of her hands and feet. When she finally put on her mask, she looked so different that I don't think I should have recognized her if I had met her without knowing her at the ball. The concealment of her straight and clear gaze, which had in it nothing of mystery or coquetry, turned into something more piquant. She was looking at herself through the mask in the big gold-framed mirror over the mantel when I came back into the living-room from the bedroom. She had just put on her lipstick, which made her mouth look smaller and fuller. I kissed her on it and told her how darling she looked; then kissed her a long time with my tongue. She responded; I put her down on a

large red-leather chair that we had on one side of the
grate, and sat on the edge with my arm around her while
with the other hand I explored the pink skirt, which had
almost nothing under it. Suddenly I substituted the reality for the false nose where I had worn it a few minutes
before. It was one of the rare moments I had known
when some actual erotic experience realizes perfectly and
completely the fantasies we have in boyhood when we
lust after pictures of chorus-girls and endow them with
the sweetness and delicacy of the ideal girls we desire. I
had to put one of her legs up on the arm of her chair, and
this symbol of triumphant *bouleversement* inflamed me
all the more. It was only not quite perfect insofar as my
feet kept slipping backwards on the floor. But I picked
her up after our flooding throbs, which the awkwardness
a little constrained, and carried her over to the gray-
covered couch, a wide daybed with many pillows, where
I proceeded without further interruption, varying and
improvising, charming her and stirring her up, as I had
when I had sat at the piano and let myself go in extem-
porizing, feeling the exhilaration of fresh combinations
and sequences which there was no one to inhibit my
making and which had never been made before; but in
improvising at the piano, I worked only with my own responses, whereas here I was working with another, who
was at once a part of the instrument and the audience. I
retarded, skipping a beat — which always proved very
exciting; speeded up to bring on a crisis from which the
artist withheld himself; banged out in different directions surprising apparently haphazard chords; then we
climbed again very slowly, so exquisitely I could hardly
bear it as we stretched toward the end of the develop-

ment, just over the end of the measure, still prolonging in another measure, still prolonging toward a further
measure, till, sweetly and thinly drawn out, the harmony
was exquisitely resolved with that strain of intense peace.

Her mask had slipped aside, but I wouldn't let her take
it off: it meant that she had to keep her eyes closed, and
I didn't like the way she tended to keep them open and
look so lucid and wide awake at the moments when she
was being made love to.

"Don't go!" she said, putting her arms around me
when I was getting up from the couch after a short span
of flushed and blurred and ecstatically satisfied peace.
But we had taken a chance the first time, and I wanted
her to do something about it now. I made her sit up and
got her off to the bathroom.

When we went out, we were rather dim. The whole
evening was dim but happy: costumes and colored lights
on a scale that made me feel sometimes, again, that I was
living in something imagined; enchanting and unknown
women by whom I was gratified to find that I was still
capable of feeling a challenge, for I found that I could
still feel desire; faces and voices I knew, drinks with
many parties, all of whom I was glad at seeing and who
were genuinely glad to see me. But by the time the
pageant came off, neither of us was seeing anything very
distinctly.

I had been thinking all the early part of the evening
that I would do it again when we got home; but when we
did, it was nearly five and we simply flopped into bed.

VI

UNCLE TEDDY

We spent Thanksgiving with Caroline's Uncle Teddy. Uncle Teddy was her father's younger brother and on that side almost her only surviving relative. He lived at Chestnut Hill in an old-fashioned yellow house with a porch that lay level with the lawn and was decorated with wrought-iron trellises and a square wooden cupola that was topped like a chessman with ornamental spikes. It looked toward the Wissahickon in a charming period landscape, dull yellow and brown and gray, in which the lines seemed to be decorously designed and the masses harmoniously distributed by some very well-established producer of nineteenth-century steel engravings.

We were admitted to a parquet hallway, beautifully polished and kept up, between a large Japanese vase and a statue of the nymph Sabrina, who was holding a rope around her marble faun in a gesture of inviolable dignity. In a room of gold mirrors, Sully portraits and old-fashioned upholstered, rather forbidding-looking furniture, we were joined by Agnes Harris, Uncle Teddy's housekeeper and companion. She was a tall, rather big-boned person, with good nature and considerable energy but absolutely no charm, who, though she came of pretty good local family, bit down, bit down on her *r*'s, as if she were crunching with her molars large lumps of soft coal. She whisked us at once into a brighter and more informal room — a kind of sun-parlor with a comfortable couch, where she evidently did her reading and sewing. The scheme of monumental elegance was, however, here still carried out by a bust of Uncle Teddy, with a wide marble brow and a curling and well-brushed amenity of middle-parted hair and mustache.

Agnes Harris was delighted to see us. She had always been good friends with Caroline, and it must have been dull for her at Teddy's. She had highballs brought at once. She explained when the butler had left — he was a frog-faced man with dropped eyelids — that there was some-thing queer about him — he didn't do things and they didn't trust him though you could never put your finger on a delinquency: they thought that he might take dope. He was to go at the end of the month. The butler they had had so many years had been devoted, but he had been murdered by robbers when Teddy was away at a cure. She had not known that the house had been bro-ken into till she came to open it up a week after the thing had happened.

"That was something!" she said.

"Where was he?" asked Caroline indistinctly.

"In the hall upstairs. He'd evidently come down from the third floor and tried to stop them. His gun was ly-

ing on the floor. They'd hit him over the head with a
blackjack."

Uncle Teddy, she said, was not so well; but he hated to
miss Thanksgiving and he had wanted to see Caroline's
new husband. When his nurse brought him down later,
he seemed, after the solid bust, almost disconcertingly
flimsy. He was a soft little man in a dinner-jacket — we
had dressed, too — with yellow hair, pale blue eyes and
a rosy-red drinker's face, full of veins and, around the
nose, horrible pimples which the medicaments had been
unable to diffuse. He had to be carried downstairs like
a child by the nurse and Agnes Harris, and, though he
managed to toddle into the room, he had to be lowered
with care into his chair. His feet on his fat little legs — he
wore ribbonless patent leather pumps — looked like the
dangling feet of the puppets in Punch-and-Judy shows,
or, better, like the atrophied tentacles on the hind ends
of hermit-crabs which have lost their function as legs, so
that they are useless for getting around and only serve to
hang on to the alien shell in which the animal lives. I
could not help wondering as I looked at him whether the
syphilis from which Henry had told me his brother had
died was not, after all, a family matter. His disease always
remained rather mysterious. Caroline, who was vague
about so many things, attributed it entirely to drinking.
Certainly he was saturated with liquor, must have been
so all his life. Now he was rationed, but drinks were doled
out to him at intervals all through the day. Tonight was a
special occasion, and he was to enjoy a special treat.

"Come!" he said, when he had finished the highball
which was supposed to be his only one. "You're not go-

ing to let us go dry! Carrie wants a drink and Fritz wants a drink — and I want a drink!"

They indulged him: I got the impression they indulged him pretty often. That is what the rich pay nurses for, and liquor must have been about the only thing that made the household tolerable for the women — the butler had his dope. Their whole life was steeped in whiskey as I don't think I had ever seen it in an equally respectable home. When Agnes and the nurse became mellow and began to feel warmly toward Teddy, they would humor him with another highball, thereby hastening his imminent demise, which they were inevitably looking forward to, anyway.

What made it peculiarly depressing was that Teddy was not very old — in the middle of his fifties, I should say. And he was an awfully nice old boy — he had the same kind of sweetness as Caroline: you saw it here without the British starching. He bowed from the waist, dropped his *g*'s and maintained the gruff and bantering tone — which for a little while covered his helplessness — of the gallant sportsman of that generation.

"I'm not married," he said, "but I wouldn't want Fritz to think that I'd never kissed a girl." He disapproved of Caroline's bobbed hair — "I've got a wig upstairs," he said.

Though he was full of old-fashioned pleasantries about never trusting women, he was always being shocked and silenced by Caroline's modern independence — going abroad alone, getting divorced on her own hook and talking quite casually, as in Teddy's time only the men had done, about "illicit" love affairs. At last she went and sat on his chair and put her arm around him, and it made her look stronger and more dominant that I had ever known her to do: her young compact and sinuous body contrasted with his thin-skinned and pulpy one, decaying in its bag of clothes.

The women couldn't help being more alive — being louder and more vigorous than the master of the house. At dinner — which was outwardly decorous — the whole thing gave me a turn. The nurse ate with us — whether because Agnes in her loneliness had made a companion of her and couldn't not include her now or because she had to be on hand in case Teddy had some kind of seizure or because in his holiday heartiness he wanted to include everybody in the dinner: on a family occasion like this, one would have preferred to have her eat by herself; and though Teddy presided and did and said all the things that a gracious host is supposed to say and do, people could not help ignoring him and talking as it were through him. His archness about the feminine sex was lost against the bluntness of the ladies; and his joke about the servants drinking the liquor, after an excellent champagne had been served, was spoiled by our knowing that the unhealthy butler never touched a drop and only seemed to bring out poor Teddy's lack of touch with the household. Suddenly, in the middle of dinner, as the highballs began to wear off and before I had been picked up by the champagne, I felt — amidst the big carved chairs, the big silver, the big carved sideboard, which abruptly seemed to have nothing to do with any of us at the table — a sinking, a horror, a conviction that it was impossible for me to establish a masculine contact with the only other man at the table. I saw him as a corpse, puffed and shreddy, drifting down to the bottom of the sea, while the three women worried him like fishes and took bites out of his damaged face.

"You're not drinking your champagne!" he said to me.

"Yes, I am," I replied. "It's wonderful."

"Well, drink it: let me see you drink it!"

When we had gone up to bed after our brandies and our after-dinner highballs and after seeing Uncle Teddy off with the nurse carrying the whiskey bottle from which he was still due to have another dose — we lay in the immense bed, a magnificently carved mahogany four-poster, and talked about Caroline's family. I asked her whether Uncle Teddy had ever done much of anything — he had complained that he was no longer able to attend to his business as he had used to.

"I don't think so," she said. "He has an office, but I don't think he does very much there."

Most of this money had come from coal, but nobody from the time of Caroline's grandfather ever seemed to have known anything about it. Caroline said that her father, when as a boy he had heard it said that somebody didn't have any more money, had asked whether he couldn't write a check — he had thought that you wrote checks to get money. Caroline herself hadn't the faintest idea how the family had come to own the coal mines or when they had acquired their money; and, in the course of her conversation, it turned out that she didn't know what coal was: she thought that it was some kind of stone that you burned. I asked her about iron and steel after I had explained; but she wouldn't hazard a guess, because she was now afraid that they might be made out of vegetation, too.

We, too, had brought up a bottle, and we kept on drinking because it was early and we had nothing else to do. I had felt somehow ever since dinner so out of key with the place that I wasn't much disposed to make love, but Caroline did evidently want to; and we did so between the big clean sheets that seemed nowadays to be slept in so seldom and which did not encourage lovers. Whoever had bred between them, they were no longer there in the house; and whoever they had been, they were not we. But I knew that she felt the need, not merely to escape as I did, but to assert her vitality against it; and for the moment it made us ourselves — not ecstatic lovers, but a pair who were something in themselves — fundamental animal beings, full of animal fats and juices and giving off animal smells, beside which the pretensions and the traditions did not for a moment seem so serious.

Yet of course it was all the more real to Caroline, and she could not forget it as easily as I could. Just as I was ready to drop off to sleep, "Who's all this going to go to?" she asked me.

I supposed that he would leave it to various people.

"He hasn't got any male heirs," she said. "There's nobody but a few scattered girls — Claire and Sophie live in Paris."

"I'm afraid," I said, "that Teddy may die before you and I have a chance to produce one."

"He will if we go on like this" — I had brought with me and had just made use of the precautionary apparatus.

I then sank into a stupefying sleep as if I were drowning in the ocean of that bed. I was waked up by a terrible shriek and then another and another shriek — so jarring and lacerating that it couldn't, I knew it, be a nightmare. I sat up in the black unfamiliar room of the unfamiliar house; Caroline was asleep, breathing deeply and roughly. I found the bed-lamp after knocking over a glass, put on my bathrobe and went out into the hall — all was silent. The family slept on the floor below. I went downstairs, remembering the butler who had been murdered by the burglars in the hall. No more screams, yet I'd certainly heard them. I didn't know where any of them slept, but I knocked at one of the doors. No answer; I knocked louder — no answer. I tried a door at the end of the hall. Movements — someone evidently getting up; Agnes came to the door, looking messy, frizzled, and gaunt. She was dressed only in her nightgown, so that she must have expected the nurse; and she held the door on a crack.

"That's just Teddy in his sleep," she said when I told her about the shrieks. "He does that sometimes in the night." She smiled, and I apologized for disturbing her.

But the incident had made me uncomfortable. I had thought I might be up against gunmen. And it was a grisly enough thought, in any case, that Teddy should have such horrors after he had been put to sleep with his drink.

VII

BURLESQUE ON SATURDAY

We saw a good deal of Nick Carter and Kay Burke. They
had been friends and allies for years — ever since just
after the War, when they had worked on a magazine
together. I felt sure they had never been lovers. Kay still
lived with her husband after a fashion. He was a little
man who sold insurance and with whom she was almost
never seen. They had no children, and she used to leave
home and stay in a hotel for weeks on the pretext that
she wanted to write. At these times, her room would be
full of friends — who drank highballs, talked show and
magazine business, and exchanged the kind of jokes they
esteemed — from lunch at about two to four o'clock the
next morning. At the end of a few weeks of this, Kay
would go to the "country" — Atlantic City or Saratoga
Springs — to get her writing done, and, after a week of
recuperation, would sit up all one night at her typewriter
and produce a monthly article on night clubs and musical shows, which her admirers would read with raptures.

One night in February we decided to go to a burlesque show. I hadn't been to one since my college days, and Caroline had never seen one at all. Nick and Kay were connoisseurs. They complained that the best of the old houses had now gone hopelessly Follies and Music Box Review, with elegant settings and a slender chorus, and that the incomparable old comedian had died, but that there was something like the old kind of show going on way over on Second Avenue.

Caroline, I could see, didn't like it when we got out in the winter mud and were confronted by the cheap and sordid entrance. She had never been in this part of town. The theater was on top of the building, and we went up in the kind of elevator that was appropriate for servicing loft-buildings. I knew that all the men we saw were the kind she would describe as "queer-looking," and in the theater itself, where the show was already on, there seemed to be nothing but men. The rest of us were tight enough to be indifferent to, even perhaps to rather enjoy, the attention we attracted as we got to our seats, the ladies in their evening cloaks; but Caroline was a little scared and chilled, and I couldn't help slightly resenting it, because going with a lady to a burlesque show is something you both have to be brazen and superior about or you can't carry it off at all.

I began by rather enjoying the act that was on when we first came in. It was in the nature of a sidewalk conversation. There were a dude and two misshapen comics. The straight man had a large square frame and a set of carnivorous teeth, which, for completeness, regularity, and whiteness, recalled the detached traplike jaws exhibited by cheap dentists; and his brutality to the comics was ferocious; he wore pressed clothes and a wide straw hat. The comics were both natural monstrosities, who could not have had to depend much on make-up. One had a dwarfed body, an enormous megalocephalic head, and the face, staring, toil-toughened and honest, of a German *Nibelung* or gnome; the other, more nonde-script and stunted still, was dressed in clothes which were disconcerting like those of a trained chimpanzee by reason of his inability to wear them in a human fashion, and revealed no human expression but only a heavy and cretinous mask, in which the closed-up slits of the eyes had the appearance of some helpless embryo aborted when the faculty of sight had scarcely had a chance to develop. The man with the teeth and the straw hat treated both with the utmost brutality.

"Say, don't look at me! Don't look at me!" he bawled at the gnome, when he was trying to play a cornet.

"I can't play when you look at me! Say, you've got the kind of face that only a mother could love! If I had a dog with a face like that, I'd shootum!"

The gnome was the principal butt: he would embark on his comic adventures with perfect good faith and solemnity, and then, when they ended in cruel disaster at the hands of the man in the straw hat or one of the cuties in bare legs and a brassière, would apostrophize the au-dience in Yiddish on a note of earnest anger and com-plaint. I suppose it was the German in me that liked it. I was aware that Caroline found it painful. Nick laughed, as he always laughed at everything; Kay said with bitter-ness, "This is terrible!"

The next was a girl number. There was a runway that ran out over the audience and that looked like a bowling-alley — though it was studded on the inside edge with a row of pink electric bulbs. The woman who sang the song and did the belly-wriggling dance would advance on us with her fat breasts, her sinewy thighs, and her muscular abdomen, and the chorus, ill-trained and stolid, would follow her with such shakings of the hips as they could manage. Some of them could merely smile; some of them did not even do much of that. But the parade had a powerful effect on the patrons. You did not notice it when the girls were there. They sat in silence and as if in indifference, without smiling and with no sign of admiration toward the glittering and thick-lashed seductresses who were standing at the level of their shoulders and addressed them with so personal a heartiness. Even when the girls had gone back on the stage, the audience did not applaud. You thought that the act had flopped. It was not until the chorus had actually gone behind the scenes and the comedians came on for the next skit that the men began to clap with an accent which was less an open tribute of enthusiasm than a summons for the girls to repeat for them a pleasure essentially furtive.

They came here, I realized, to see their erotic day-dreams made objective, and each sat there alone with his dream. They kept calling the girls back, and the number went on forever. The leading performer began to strip, and the audience watched her in silence — timidly, life-lessly recalling her when she had gone behind the wings. They finally saw her breasts, but her smile was never re-

turned. There was no final burst of excitement when she
had finally got down to her G-string, but only the same
conventional summons — to which this time she did not
respond. In one of the numbers the girls appeared with
fishing-rods and lines and dangled pretzels under the
noses of the spectators; the leading woman had a lemon.
The men did not at first react; then suddenly here and
there one would make a grab at a pretzel — like a frog
that has finally decided to strike at a piece of red flannel
or a cat that, after watching without movement, at last
pounces on a sock or a string. When they caught one,
however, they did not take it off or playfully refuse to re-
lease it, as Nick and I did: they let go at the first jerk that
the girl gave her line and relapsed into their impassivity.

Nick and Kay were carrying on a loud and ironical
commentary, in which I occasionally joined. It made itself felt, when one noticed the audience, as a desecration
of rites of Venus and as a violation of the privacy of auto-
erotic fancy; yet the whole thing amused me and reminded me of the days when Nick and I had used to go
to the Hype in New Haven together. Caroline, I knew,
was afraid of the men, who were the kind of men she felt
she couldn't trust and that she oughtn't to be among.

Even Caroline, however, was pleased by a skit about
Antony and Cleopatra. Nick and Kay were absolutely
delighted because they had already seen it and considered it a classic of burlesque. It was wonderful. Cleopatra was the woman who did the strip-tease and Antony
was a Jewish comic. Caesar, the man with the teeth, with
a tin helmet and a big cigar, walloped him over the bottom with the flat side of an enormous sword while he
was lying with Cleo on a divan, and he advanced to the

front of the stage and staggered around in a circle, groaning, "I'm dying! I'm dying!"

Caesar and Cleopatra, the red-nosed Roman soldiers, and the beautiful Egyptian slave-girls, all began to sing, "He's dying! He's dying!" and broke into a rousing shimmy.

"I hear the voices of the angels!" said Antony.

"What do they say?" asked Caesar.

"I don't know: I don't understand Polak."

When he was groggy and about to flop, he cried out, "I hear the cockroaches calling me!" and the orchestra twitched strings and growled on the drums with an effect infinitely ominous and acrid: the chant of the expectant cockroaches. He fell dead.

"Bring me the wassup!" said Cleopatra to the Nibelung, her servitor. The Nibelung knelt with a box, from which the queen took out a huge phallus. After a little rough banter on the subject with Caesar, she apostrophized it: "Come, my wassup!" applied it to her breast, and fell prone on the body of Antony, exploding a toy balloon which he had been wearing as a false chest. Caesar now produced a wreath, placed it carefully around her bottom and watered it with a watering-pot. Everybody committed suicide, and the comedy got even lewder when it came to the slave-girl and the gnome.

"That Cleopatra act," I said, as we were starting home in the taxi, "is the most colossal thing I ever saw. Isn't it?" They said it had been going on for years and that it was always a little different. "I never saw Caesar come in on a bicycle blowing a bugle before. They used to build up the entrance by all turning and looking toward the wings and blowing trumpets and things — and then he would come in on the other side and goose the last man in the row and they would all fall down like dominoes. I think that was really better."

I began to remind Nick of the "Hype rush" of 1915, in which he and I had taken such an active part. It was one of the most tremendous brawls that had ever occurred at Yale. It was the day of the Princeton game, and all the boys had turned out to see a dancer who was famous for appearing in less clothes than was customary in that primitive period. The curtain was an hour late and the audience demonstrated. At first they just stamped and sang songs, but gradually they became more bitter. Finally a man came out and announced that the star couldn't appear. A great shout of disgust arose. Then the curtain went up on an acrobat lunch-hour act, which the audience barbarously kidded. The climax was one of those elaborate formations where they all stand on each others' shoulders. Somebody shushed the audience, and then when there was comparative silence and the acrobats were just finishing their pyramid, Nick Carter, who was sitting with me in a box right up against the stage, said "Hup!" and some of the acrobats on the bottom layers mistook it for their signal to break and the whole bunch came down on their necks.

The audience, of course, was delighted and the acrobats were furious. They had to go through with their pyramid again while people yelled "Look out!" and "Hup!" When they went off, the curtain came down and there was another long wait. People began calling for Nick Carter to put on one of his popular acts. He got up, with his spectacles gleaming, full of self-confidence and beer, and went up the steps to the stage amidst terrific applause. Standing in the middle of the stage, with his hands behind his back, with his dignified debater's presence, he announced that he would do the Transformation scene from *Dr. Jekyll and Mr. Hyde.*

"But don't be alarmed," he added, "when you see me turning into Hyde, because I have arranged a new ending in which the United States Marines come in and save Dr. Jekyll from his nature." But he never got any further than his opening line: "I have r-r-ransacked London in vain for the drug that has been the cause of all muh misery!"

The curtain went up behind him and he looked round and found himself in one of those interior sets that they had for vaudeville skits which were supposed to represent the luxurious New York apartments of gay bachelors or celebrated actresses. Nick went straight to a table with a telephone, took up the transmitter and said:

"Hello, is this Police Headquarters? This is Detective O'Brien speaking" —

Before he got any further, an actor in a dress-suit came in. Nick got up and shook hands and said, "Hello, Count! Welcome to the Taft lavatory!"

Then the manager or somebody came out. Nick shook hands with him, too, and asked him when the show was going to start.

"There isn't going to be any show," said the manager, "unless you people keep quiet and act decent."

A howl went up from the front rows. Nick had been backed over to the steps and was trying to pull off a final crack in order not to make too ignominious an exit; but the manager pushed him and he fell. He was furious and got up and cursed the manager with all the savagery of the college sophomore who finds an excuse for being

nasty to an inferior. The audience went absolutely wild
and began to rush the stage, throwing the furniture
around. I didn't get up on the stage myself, but threw
down one of the chairs in the box and saw it go right
through the big drum. The management got out a hose
and turned it on the audience. The police had been
called in and arrested several students, but they didn't
succeed in stopping the riot till the theater had been
practically wrecked.

By the time we had finished these reminiscences, we
were back with some highballs at the Tavistock.

There had perhaps been a certain exhibitionism in our
revival of this exhibitionistic evening; and it did not oc-
cur to us at the time that we might not be carrying the
ladies with us. But Caroline was out of *rapport* with me
and had been uncomfortable the whole evening, and Kay
rather surprised me by definitely siding with Caroline.

"You boys must have looked wonderful," she said, "in
your big raccoon coats."

She went into the little kitchenette with Caroline, who
was making some scrambled eggs — we had stayed late
at the cocktail party and had had nothing but cocktail
hors d'oeuvre. These were so rich and elaborate, however, that for the time being they had ruined Nick's and
my appetite. Later Kay and Caroline ate in the bedroom,
continuing some personal conversation — till Nick and
I suddenly felt our talk about the rumpots and buffoons
of our college days running thin, and I summoned the
ladies back.

"We thought you were deep in Yale," said Caroline.

"What about Newhall Haines?" said Kay. "The last I heard, you were trying to locate him."

"We don't know what happened to him," said Nick.

"He was one of the most fantastic characters that was ever seen in New Haven," I asserted. "He lived at the Taft and was always tight and always recited poetry. If you said anything to him, he replied with Keats or Rossetti — didn't he, Nick?"

"*The Hound of Heaven*," Nick backed me up. "He used to terrify strangers by saying to them suddenly:

> I fled him down the nights and down the days;
>   I fled him down the arches of the years;
> I fled him down the labyrinthine ways,

and so forth. They thought he had delusions of persecution."

"He's probably a customer's man now or worse," said Kay. "And what about you chaps? Do you think you can ever be located?"

Nick took up his end; but the evening was rather sagging down, and Nick and Kay presently left.

"How did you get along with Kay?" I asked Caroline, as we finished up the last Scotch in the bottom.

"She's in a state."

"What's the matter?"

"She says she's in love. She didn't tell me not to tell, but don't repeat it. It seems she's never been unfaithful to her husband before."

"Isn't it amazing!" I said.

"She's fallen in love with some young producer, and

she thinks she oughtn't to stay with her husband. She's all harrowed up about it."

"Did you tell her the facts of life?"

"I don't believe she ought to keep on living with her husband necessarily if she's sleeping with some-body else."

"All that crowd are just incredibly provincial," I said. "It's amazing when you consider that they're known all over the country as demons of sophistication and that even in New York they're considered devastating wits. Bainbridge Wells had to go to the analyst and be treated for a year before he got up the gumption to make a pass at one of those social-working girls in the Grand Street Follies."

"I don't know, though," Caroline demurred. "I re-member how I felt when I was married to Lefanu. I hated pretending things were all right."

"She doesn't spend much time with her husband" —

"They do it once every fortnight, she says."

"I'm glad you're getting to know her — you ought to get her over some of her small-town ideas. She's really a very clever woman. Nick will never really do anything for her. He's provincial too: Yale and Bones provincial, which is the biggest kind of provincial possible — where it's impossible to know you're provincial, so that it's im-possible to escape.

"Do you know how Nick ended up that evening of the Hype riot? I forbore to remind him just now, but when I went around late to his room — he'd hurt his shoulder pretty badly when he fell and I'd lost him in the con-fusion and I wanted to see how he was — well, I found him absolutely grovelling before his room-mate, Arthur

Pound. Arthur was headed for Bones, and he wanted to take Nick along with him; Nick was sobering up and his shoulder was beginning to hurt, and Arthur was making him feel terrible. When I came in, they were sitting in Nick's bedroom and I heard Nick saying:

"'I was drunk and I know I made a damn ass of myself. When I'm drunk, I always want to play the clown; but you mustn't think, Art, that, under it all, I could be satisfied with cheap success — just with making people laugh, or that three years at Yale haven't meant more to me than drinking and parties and things like that.'

"He began telling Arthur how much he thought of him and how much his influence had meant to him and how terribly he would feel if he had done anything that would disgrace Yale. It was embarrassing, and I quietly left. That was the turning-point of Nick's career. Arthur got him to go out for track and Dwight Hall, and Nick wrote a sequence of twenty sonnets for the *Lit.* Arthur, who had an authoritative way about him that, even in those days, seemed almost official — he's in line to be secretary or dean or something now — told everybody very firmly that all the real rowdyism had been the work of the Sheff men. Nick made Bones, and he and I were never the same again. He avoided me after that: I'd egged him on that night at the Hype. Even now there's a barrier between us — though he has to try to pretend that we're all out in the great world together now."

"I never knew anybody who preyed so much on clubs and things like that," she said. "Why should you worry, when it's all so far behind you, whether you made Bones or not?"

"You mean why do these things prey on me — why

do they prey on my mind — not why do I prey on them."

"All right: I'm illiterate," she replied. "And I don't understand the subtleties of burlesque shows, and I'm just a stupid person compared with you and your friends."

She crushed a cigarette-butt in the tray with a nervous and definite gesture. "Well, I'm going to bed."

Maybe the whole evening *had* been rather adolescent, I thought as I was going to bed: the burlesque show and our college conversation. The next night, I was glad to remember, would be on a higher level. We were going to a concert of the League for New Music.

VIII

SCHOENBERG ON SUNDAY

But Caroline was still out of sympathy with me on Sunday night, and she referred to the situation of the evening before. She got very tight at dinner — which we had at a restaurant uptown — because, as I knew, she was afraid of the concert as an overwhelmingly highbrow affair; and she kept having daiquiris and cognacs. I kept up with her and drank more than I wanted to.

The concert — which was obscured for me by the drinks and which must have been somewhat distorted by my sense of the impression it was making on Caroline, who had never been to one before — seemed absolutely cockeyed and gruesome in the extreme. In the first place, the audience were queer — I had never noticed before, unaccompanied by Caroline's prettiness and taste, how deliriously queer they were. There were poltergeists with popping eyes, trolls with clammy hands and long noses, specters that had come in through the keyhole. Beside us, on Caroline's side, sat a woman in a corpse-white toque, herself as pale as a corpse, who had what seemed to be auburn sideboards. Her presence gave Caroline the creeps and drove her into an attitude of bravado, so that she kept up, throughout the first part of the concert, a sour and sulky commentary to me. From time to time the woman would turn and give her pale and awful looks, which Caroline would arrogantly ignore. On my side was a disconcerting old man, who sat all by himself on the aisle, slouched way down in his seat and with his legs crossed and one knee stuck up, like a schoolboy at a movie matinee. He was also as restless as a schoolboy and kept beating his fingers in succession in a rippling movement on his raised knee, whether in impatience or in trying to keep time to music which seemed sometimes not to have any, it was impossible to tell. Sometimes he would stop doing this and take hold of an old-fashioned gold seal on his watch, as if his attention had been arrested; sometimes he would laugh silently to himself; sometimes he would turn to me with a peculiar clear and piercing look through old-fashioned silver-rimmed spectacles — a look that seemed acutely responsive to what was going on in the music, acutely aware of me, and which always gave me the feeling that he was about to say something to me.

The first number, which we had missed through lateness, was just taking its bows when we came in, and I felt that it must look forbidding to Caroline. There were a birdlike little violinist in a boiled shirt and tails, a solid-looking man in spectacles and a prosaic sacque-suit, who played the double bass, and a harpist of the fanciest kind, who looked as if she had been dug up out of *Godey's Lady's Book* and who smiled with a beaming graciousness out of all proportion to the applause, always rather systematic and dutiful and at this early stage of the proceedings not yet stimulated by any severe sense of obligation.

The next was a kind of little tone poem by a man who had travelled in the East and brought back a large collection of Burmese temple gongs, Javanese balalaikas, Chinese wood-blocks, Ceylonese bull-roarers, Tibetan lamasery bells, and God knows what. Unfortunately, the piece itself — which was called *Nostalgie de l'Orient* — was composed of the most dreamy saccharine melodies in a German romantic mood combined with pseudo-Eastern themes of an essentially Western character in a vein that was already banal when *The Mikado* and *San Toy* were written — melodies which were rendered in the conventional way by a perfectly good piano and strings and which the battery of museum instruments only emphasized or interrupted in an annoying and melodramatic manner. I was at first afraid that Caroline would see how inferior it was, then more afraid that she might like it; so I said nothing after it was over, but looked around at the audience in the other direction, encountering the glances of the old man, in which I seemed to see something mocking and which made me conclude that he was a Philistine, some old party who liked to play Brahms and thought the concert funny for the wrong reasons: he had his arms folded as if to show he was not clapping. After all, it was worth something to have these oriental instruments brought on and the oriental systems studied: there must be other kinds of musical effects besides our Western ones, and if the composer of *Nostalgie* couldn't manage them, it was possible that someone else would.

The next number was an absolute lulu: it beat anything I had ever seen at these concerts. The composer, who was also the pianist, was a randy little man in a dinner-jacket, whose eyes were obscured by a pince-nez. The first piece he played was called *Optometry* and I suppose had something to do with his eyes: I could see that one of his lenses was terribly thick. It was as if the music were intended to alternate between the inharmonious shortsightedness in one eye and farsightedness in the other that one would get in a case of extreme astigmatism. The myopic theme was brooding and dim, the other one was clear and shrill, rapidly becoming more and more shrieking as if it was getting out of control. A period of agony ensued in which the minor theme began to shriek, too, as if it were forcibly dropped out of its existence of subterranean monotony: I assumed that the composer was being fitted with a succession of unsatisfactory glasses. At this point, at any rate, he electrified us by beginning to pound the piano with his fists and finally banging the keyboard with his forearms so as to strike simultaneously whole octaves of notes. In this way the two themes were apparently combined and the conflict between them resolved: the composition ended with the loud clank of three completed octaves, with a long interval between the second and the last, which must have represented his ultimate success in achieving a pair of glasses which brought his eyes firmly into focus. But the effect of his attack on the piano was to make the audience embarrassed, as if they had witnessed an assault or a rape — though I noticed that my neighbor was clapping.

"Good God!" I exclaimed to Caroline in order to relieve what I felt was her tension.

"He looks as if he were fighting the piano," she said.

"In the next number he uses an ax"— I followed on in the vein of Nick and Kay, though I knew I was betraying the League for New Music.

The second piece was called *Chicago Zigzag* and was composed of the same upsetting alternations. This time he produced a long piece of board, which covered more keys than his forearm, and used it for a bass accompaniment which kept recurring, always the same, and which finally got you down by sheer force of the repetition and loudness. The third piece was a little more lyrical: it sounded — it was called simply *Nocturne*— like nostalgia for an old-fashioned car-barn. At one point, he suddenly stood up, reached inside the piano and began to pluck the strings.

"I should think it would slap his face," said Caroline.

"Would you mind being silent?" said the corpselike lady in a nasal and metallic voice, which was loud enough to be widely heard and which somehow went with the music and made it worse. Caroline stopped short, became tense, sat frozen with a hand clutching her program and fixedly staring at the stage.

The intermission came next; we walked around, and I kidded with her about the people in order to make her feel a little better. We called the lady the Bride of Dracula — though of course it had been Caroline who was really in the wrong. We also saw the Grave Horse and the Marsh-King's Daughter.

"Where do they come from?" Caroline kept saying.

I vetoed going out for a drink, because I wanted to hear the Schoenberg sober. It was the song-sequence called *Pierrot Lunaire*, which I had wanted to make a point of hearing. The chief performer was not prepossessing: she was a tall and rather scrawny soprano in a long-sleeved and flowing black garment. Just as the house had become deathly still, Caroline said clearly enough to be heard by the woman on her left: "Here's the Fall of the House of Usher!" I whispered to her please not to talk, and she became tensely quiet again.

Schoenberg had always gotten me and he still did. It was partly the Wagner that was still behind it, though all reduced to moonlight and blackness, discolored and flattened out — the old thrill of the Germanic music theater, the shiver and the shudder and the longing ache. It made my blood run cold, and not merely by disconcerting dissonance and macabre connotation but by the genuine excitement of art which makes beauty of emotional shock. — I glanced at Caroline and felt that with the drop of her nerves at the wearing off of the drink the queer noise was simply affecting her like a caterwauling cat or a scraping on glass which she had to make an effort to bear.

When my attention returned to the music, it seemed to me for a moment that the Pierrot of Schoenberg was nothing but a chalk-faced homosexual in a Berlin cabaret. But no: it was the poet, robust and profound, who had spoken in *Verklärte Nacht* — sharpened as well as twisted, intensified as well as shattered. That low voice of the cello, solitary, nocturnal and ominous, that was the ground tone that still survived. I looked to see what the song was and found that it was a serenade which was supposed to be interrupted by a character called Cassander and that Pierrot was supposed to grab Cassander by the collar and fiddle on his "bald pate" — an idea which delighted me, though I reflected that the obtrusion of these grotesque notions might be making Caroline's ordeal more difficult. But wasn't it all beautifully in the key of the time — the *Gemeinheit*, as another piece was called, in which Pierrot bored a hole in Cassander's skull, stuffed him full of tobacco, and used him for a pipe? It was just like the Yiddish Nibelung and the man with the straw hat in the burlesque show the night before. And the harsh and cheap stage of Second Avenue came to life in my imagination as something artistically thrilling. The cruelty and disruption of modern life could be rendered by a music like Schoenberg's in a folk-theater like Minsky's burlesque. What a pity that a master like Schoenberg didn't have ready to his hand such a subject as the cockroaches calling — there were passages in *Pierrot Lunaire* which would have admirably served for this conception — instead of this Verlainesque *fin de siècle* Pierrot, already in its time rather sickly!

But one would have to have Stravinsky for the ensembles. You must end with a terrific jazz that will tear people out of their seats — and New York is the place for this music, the composers abroad only play with these things without having them in their bones. But *I* couldn't do anything about it — I could only imagine somebody else writing the great American ballet. One had to be a technical master to do this kind of thing. The strong orchestration of Stravinsky that builds its majestic structures out of the headlong excitement of sound! — the piercing splinters of this Schoenberg, de-

liberately chosen and accurately directed, every dissonance perfectly calculated to touch the emotions as well
as the nerves with a science so subtle that my meager
training hardly enabled me to understand it — to say
what he wants it to say. *O alter Duft aus Märchenzeit*—
that would be the old German romance again — one
never really got away from it — but very pale and far-
away — and it left one up in the air.

"Is that the end?" asked Caroline as the people began
to clap. I felt, as we were getting out of the theater, that
the whole thing had sort of paralyzed her, put her into a
rigid trance.

"Well, what shall we do now?" I asked. "I don't suppose you'd like to go to Irving and Ellis's. Phil and Claire
are going to be there, and they asked us to come in for a
drink." I somehow thought I ought to make amends to
her. We took a taxi to West Fifty-Ninth.

We found them in the usual position — that is,
grouped around the highball tray. Phil Dewitt's inspiration had evidently been flagging, and our report of the
concert was a godsend. Caroline's version was her re-
venge for the burlesque show: she dwelt particularly on
the costumes of the women on and off the platform. In
trying to explain that Schoenberg did not scratch out his
music at random, I tried to tell them about inversion and
cancrizans and that *Pierrot Lunaire* was full of "crabs,"
and this of course raised a hideous laugh — though Ellis
did not understand the joke. I had to laugh, too, but I
hastened on for Ellis's sake and my own:

"Yes: *Pierrot Lunaire* has more crabs in it than the
Great South Bay."

"The crabs wouldn't be so bad in themselves," said

Phil, whose talents had been stimulated again, "if it wasn't for the inversion."

"Schoenberg is a great composer, though," I went on insisting when the laughter was subsiding. "Jesus! He's got every one of your hangovers in this song-cycle we've just heard. The big hangover from the nineteenth century. All these throbs and shrieks he writes are what we really feel — instead of what we think we feel."

"Paul Whiteman is the master of dissonance," said Irving, who could not quite connect up with Schoenberg. "There are moments when you think that the trombone or the trumpet might be making a mistake when you hear what sounds like a sour note; but he knows every note that every instrument in that band is playing. It's wonderful to watch him rehearsing — he'll stop the whole orchestra in the middle of some terrific passage — where it seems just like stopping a locomotive — and he'll say, 'I don't hear the fourth trombone!' Then he'll make them go through it again. Or he'll say, 'Listen, pal: you tickled that triangle just a quarter of a beat too soon.' He told me that oboe-players are the hardest to get and keep. The way they blow on the reed does something to their sinuses and they go crazy if they keep it up after a certain length of time. Paul had one oboe player who was a hophead. One night he turned up all jitters because he hadn't been able to get his dose. The dope-peddler he bought it from had been pinched and Paul was in desperation because he had to open a new night club that night. I told him I'd try to raise some hop for him so I went to the phone and called up Dutch Schultz. Of course I'd never bought dope myself, but I knew that he could get it. In less than half an hour a respectable-looking man turned up with silver hair and glasses and an intellectual face. I thought at first he was a college professor who was making a study of jazz. But he asked for me and took me aside and said that Mr. Schultz had sent him and handed over the hop. Of course he was a hophead himself. He was a brilliant anthropologist who had disappeared from the academic world and it was thought that he'd committed suicide. But there he was rushing dope — Dutch Schultz's errand boy."

"And was the oboe-player OK?" asked Phil.

"He went through the evening without an error, and the place was a big success that winter. But I don't know what would have happened to Paul if I hadn't been a friend of Dutch Schultz. He offered to play anything I wanted that night, and I asked for 'Chloe,' which is my favorite song. Paul syncopated it and embroidered it with so many variations that you could hardly recognize it. But I have never heard anything like it. The musical experts say that he's one of the greatest musicians in the country."

I suppressed my impulse to explain to him about the use of the jazz orchestra for a serious composition such as I had been thinking about at the concert; and soon took Caroline home. It was one of the things that made her a little difficult that she had never lived before with a man who had to get to his office at a definite time in the morning and that she always wanted to sit up and drink. My making her leave reawakened her irritation with me and my music; and I on my side felt disgust with the turn that the evening had taken. It was partly self-disgust at my weakness in letting myself in for such people. I could not seem to keep my head above such nonsense. Last night it had been old college days with Nick. This was not the life I had contemplated. I remembered how my mother had known the Schirmers and used to go to their private concerts.

When we got back to the apartment, I sat down at the piano and tried improvising on a Charleston tune, recklessly throwing it around among Schoenbergian harmonies. I had not exchanged a word with Caroline since we had come into the door of the Tavistock, and she had gone straight to bed. I had the soft pedal down, but I couldn't annoy the neighbors and didn't want to keep Caroline awake, so I stopped, feeling thoroughly frustrated. If I only had a piano and a room to myself somewhere and leisure to fool with music!

IX

"HELLO, SUCKER!"

We dined one night in March with Julie. I was surprised
to find Jehuda Janowitz. She had also invited Kay and a
fellow named Tom Burrell, who was some sort of cousin
of Henry's and one of those easy and discreet young
though aging men who can always be asked to fill in. It
was Julie's idea of a party for us. Henry had gone to
Washington.

Kay, who was partly Irish, had a great nose for social
class and always dropped her Broadway manner and
gave a passable imitation of something else when any
breeze from Park Avenue was sniffed. Jehuda was serious
and Jewish; his Yiddish accent had a frankness and thick-
ness which made it seem rich like a national dish so that
you felt the Jewish stock was a strong one, and his smile
had a rich brown-eyed charm. Caroline, who was afraid
of Julie, got on better with her when Henry was away —
when Julie herself felt freer. Tom Burrell gave his well-
known performance, which consisted of a patter as ef-

fortless as breathing and a charm that made everything
he said sound a good deal more amusing than it was —
a performance which seemed wonderful the first time
you heard it and which, I could see, was seeming wonderful to Kay, who was delighted by a vein so different from the staged and competitive humor of herself
and Nick and the rest. Julie was dispensing the cocktails
rather more lavishly than if Henry had been present, and
there was a general relaxation in the big early nineteen-
hundreds living-room, with its piano and its Degas race-
horses and its brown carpet that covered the whole floor,
at the corner of Thirty-Fourth Street and Park.

It turned out that Henry and Julie were going to
China and Japan in the spring: Henry had never seen the
East; and Julie asked us whether we would like to spend
the summer in their house at Crolskill, on the Hudson.

"That would be very nice," said Caroline, with what
seemed to me a lack of enthusiasm. I accepted in a more
positive way; Caroline became silent.

After dinner, we talked about night clubs and it turned
out that Julie had not been to one for years. I told her
that she ought to see Dixie McCann's.

"Let's go there tonight," said Julie. "Would you
like to?"

"If you'll lend me some money," I said.

There were six of us and I saw a week's pay gone; but
I was always spending more than I intended: it seemed
to be as inevitable as drinking too much.

"Oh, this is my treat," she said, and when she came
down in her long and velvet evening wrap, with her black
almost shiny hair parted in the middle and curled back

on either side, looking, I thought, very handsome and like the countess we used to play she was, she slipped me fifty dollars.

Kay had been going to meet Nick, and she phoned him to meet us at the night club. His quick musical-comedy cracking and my arrogant German authority, which I was usually able to summon on such occasions, got us tables in a corner but right beside the floor. We ordered drinks, and Jehuda invited Julie to dance, which he did well though rather solemnly. Tom Burrell danced with Kay, and Nick and Caroline and I stayed at the table, then Nick noticed a playwright and shot over to him.

"What do you think about Crolskill this summer?" I asked Caroline.

"You've told her we'll go," she answered.

"I assumed that you'd want to."

"I know you did."

"I don't know how we could do better. It'll save us money."

"That house is expensive to run. We'll have to keep all the servants."

"Oh, Henry will have to pay them anyway. We'll be saving money on servants, too."

"I don't like living in other people's houses. I think those people up there are awfully stuffy."

"We don't have to see them."

"If you don't see them, you're being rude. I know from Canada. You have to go to dinners and you have to have them to dinner, and it all gets to be an awful chore."

The dancers came back and the show was beginning. Caroline couldn't understand, I reflected, why I wasn't willing to drop my job and go to live in her house in

Louisiana, but she didn't want to go to my sister's, which was an obvious convenience for me. She was so used to being independent that she couldn't conceive even for a summer living in someone else's house.

"Now this little girl," Dixie McCann was announcing, "isn't much of a singer — I mean, singer. She learned singing in a correspondence school and she missed a coupla letters. But she's the nicest little girl in the whole show. Now I wantcha all to give this little girl a nice great big hand."

Everybody applauded: they were compelled to. She was prodigious, Dixie McCann, dominating the compact room, among the green and red carnation panels of bogus senoritas — with her pearls, her glittering bosom, her abundant and ripply coiffure, bleached a beautiful yellow, her bear-trap of shining white teeth, the flesh of her broad back behind a grating of green velvet, and the full-blown pink peony as big as a cabbage exploding on her broad thigh. I looked to see what Julie was making of her. As I watched her in Julie's presence, I wasn't sure that I really liked her. Nothing, certainly, could be more commercialized, nothing could be more regimented, I thought as I watched her directing the show, chucking her little girls under the chin, goading them along when they seemed to be flagging, jacking up their duller moments —

"This little girl is new: give her a hand!" — forestalling possible outcry against their deficiencies — "You girls sound like Charley Schwab's backyard!" — and as a matter of fact most of them were certainly *not* talented — and at the same time commanding the audience, drilling their applause like a grounding of arms, summoning the languid to attention, dealing tactfully but authoritatively and quickly with disorderly interruptions, making short work of dissent or disapproval, driving the whole thing along through an evening of entertainment without gaiety, speed without recreation, stimulating and nagging but controlling and curbing in a race with the excitement she had roused. Yet this was what we thought we liked, and it was one of the things that had succeeded in making Caroline think that Julie's life was stuffy.

At the next intermission, there was a time when Jehuda was dancing with Caroline and Kay had gone over to talk to the Algonquin playwright, when Nick and I were alone at the table.

"You know, all this is terrible," I said. "Isn't it?"

"Joe Friganza is good," said Nick. "He'll be on in the next show."

"I mean this whole night club racket." I tried to explain what I meant. "These places are no fun any more," I concluded. "You can't have amusements that are any good," I went on, inspired by a second Scotch, "if the life of the rest of society doesn't make any sense. There isn't an idea or an ideal left in the United States. The best we've got for national heroes are a few reckless aviators. Look at this blacksmith we've just put in the White House — an illiterate engineer, who writes with his mouth full of pancakes. What have we got to offer the world except a few miracles of machinery and gigantic honky-tonk developments like this that are also mechanical triumphs."

"I know: it's not enough," said Nick, shifting into his serious vein, which never made connection with mine. "All this is not enough. That's what I'm trying to get into my play. Honest, Fritz: I've been working on a darn good play. It's Maeterlinck and Shaw — I mean it's as funny as Shaw — I want to read it to you soon — and at the same time it has the thing underneath that Shaw hasn't got. Underneath is the human soul and every one of us has got one whether we like it or not. That's what my play is about. There's this night clerk in a hotel and he sits there reading *The Last Days of Pompeii*. He seems completely indifferent to everybody, but gradually they begin to feel that he has a sort of spiritual power. First a gangster comes in who's escaping from another gangster — then a woman who's left her husband and come to the hotel with another man" —

The play sounded terrible: it was one of those things like *The Passing of the Third Floor Back*, where there is a mysterious and beautiful character who awakens the better natures of all the other characters.

"Damn it all!" said Nick, when he had finished. "They say we're materialistic, but there's something here they haven't got in Europe!"

"Where do you find it?" I asked.

"Why I find it, for example, in the man that I got the idea of this hotel clerk from — the room service man at the Algonquin. He lent Kay money once when her bill was overdue and he heard her telephoning to people trying to raise some — and he always brings me aspirin with breakfast when I order it very late — just acts of human kindness. He's one of the most wonderful little guys I've every known: There's something coming in America, Fritz — there's a new Christ coming!" His spectacles lit up with the radiance that used to come into his face when he led meetings at Dwight Hall. I was embarrassed and irritated. I had never been able to stand this side of Nick.

At this moment Ben Furstmann joined in, looking very neat in a dinner jacket. He had called up Jehuda at Julie's and found out where we were going to be. I told him that we were discussing the bankruptcy of American civilization and he took up the subject eagerly, adducing the interest of the public in a recent young violinist, who, he said, was not in Jehuda's class. Things exasperated me more and more — or rather, as I gradually got tighter, under the influence of the music, the pretty women, and the darkening of the room and the blue and purple lights, I took up a noble stand of self-dissociation from the age. I had danced with everybody and now I was not going to dance any more in that pretentious and predatory gyp-joint. I stood on my tradition of behavior and taste, a dignified if tragic figure. It seemed to me that Caroline was enjoying too much her rumba with Tom Burrell: she was always rather solemn when she danced with me, and now I saw that she was laughing and disporting herself.

The lights went on and the show resumed. This time it was Joe Friganza, who certainly was an artist. Even I in my present mood had to smile when he appeared on the dance-floor, displayed by an intensely white spotlight like a single diamond in the window at Cartier's. He took off his slightly battered top-hat and, to a long flourish of trumpets from the orchestra, bowed low in his dress suit on his sprawling legs. Then he snapped up his hat, as if he were going to catch it on his head, but it missed, and for a moment the audience was shocked by a sense of humiliation as Joe seemed to drop out of his comic character and stoop down to pick it up. Then he bowed again — another flourish, and again threw up his hat, which turned over in the air and this time fell down behind him. He turned around, quickly picked it up, and, with his back to the audience now, confronted the orchestra in what was obviously an attitude of stern indignation.

"All right!" he shouted in his taxi-driver's dialect, of which every syllable seemed intended to be plugged at some other taxi-driver, "Take it easy! Don't be noivous! and bite it off at the end!"

He turned and brandished his hat and again he salaamed low. The trumpets gave him this time a sour buzz of razz, at which the audience — laughing and yet in suspense — saw him glance aside; the flourish was bitten off so that it stopped suddenly before he had righted himself, and he straightened up in silence, for a second looked blankly at the audience, and then flipped up his hat, which, although he had apparently lost hope and ceased to pay any attention to it, landed perfectly on his head and just at the right jaunty tilt.

"Joe is himself again!" he yelled. "I t'ought I could'n do it, but Joe is himself again!" — and while the audience laughed and clapped, he went into a tumultuous song.

In a sudden inspiration, I saw that everything was based on the idea of power. Either you were funny and pathetic because you didn't have it or you were glorious because you did. And Joe Friganza was one of the most violent self-glorifiers of this era of self-glorifying performers. He would gag about the pay he was getting, compare himself with other comedians, burlesquing Harry Richman and Al Jolson. His line was different from theirs: he was exploiting his magnetic personality, but it was a magnetic personality with a flaw. He would sing about the wonderful girl who never wanted to pay the fare in his taxi and do a pantomime of waltzing with one — but somebody would cut in and take her away, leaving him alone on the dance-floor, dodging the other couples, indignant, bewildered, chagrined. He did it all with a sure sense of pantomime and a never-flagging rhythm which somehow made the whole thing exhilarating; but I saw that it was all a dramatization of the current fear of impotence, and that the current fear of impotence meant the fear of not being able to generate the self-assurance and to buy for oneself the privilege of bawling and making oneself heard above the din of an expensive night club.

During the girl-show that followed, a couple of men who were sitting against the wall behind us — one of them red faced and stocky, the other tall and with drooping lids — accompanied by what were obviously a couple of expensive tarts, began to get fresh with the chorus, and, as the girls passed through the tables, succeeded in snatching off some of the blue ostrich plumes which had been made to stick out from their rears and which were almost the only thing they wore in one of the more erotic numbers. As the night was stretching later and later, the excitement was becoming more violent: one felt all the jealousies and boastings, the fierce faces of desperations, bursting out from under the pressure that had kept them in place by day. I stared up at the central lamp, which had the look of a great closed glowing peony that joyously melted from pink through a deepening rose to orange.

Yes, I knew what I knew: the whole thing was bad and

impotent and I was lifted above it — but I felt that the big glass shade was becoming hypnotic and swollen, and I felt that I was getting drunk. I came back to the table, to my companions — but they were all talking to one another. I looked over at the ostrich-plume snatchers: the whole party was standing up. A big man in a dress-suit was talking to them. The bouncer; they were furious; they were leaving rather than take the rebuke. The bull-necked man looked sulky, the droop-lidded man depressed. They paid the check, still standing up and taking it out on the waiter. So I had once seen Dixie McCann have a drunk who was yelling bad language torn away from his party and shot out with the ruthlessness and the dispatch of a prince of the Renaissance making away with a dangerous conspirator. Would she dare to do that with one of us — when Caroline and Julie were obviously ladies? But we wouldn't behave like that. In any case, I hated the whole thing.

I sounded out Julie, and we decided to go. The fifty that Julie had given me and the fifteen I had myself were far from enough for the check, and I became, I fear, a little bit truculent in my refusal to accept contributions from Jehuda, Ben Furstmann, or Tom. Julie produced a little more, and I borrowed a few dollars from Nick Carter. The whole thing was a gyp, but you had to be magnificent.

Going home in the taxi, I made a quarrel with Caroline over what I took for her interest in Tom Burrell.

"I'm not interested in Tom Burrell," she said, flurried and stammering a little in what I thought was an admission of guilt.

"I haven't seen you so gay in ages."

"Well, why shouldn't I be gay?" she said. "Even your sister was having a good time."

"She'd never been to a place like that before."

"Well, going was your idea. And, after all, Tom Burrell's you people's friend."

"Tom Burrell is such a lightweight that he wouldn't make a dent in a feather bed."

"That has its advantages."

"What do you mean?"

"I don't mean anything. . . ."

She wouldn't talk any more. It was almost impossible to fight with her, and I sometimes missed the violent arguments and the overhaulings of one another's characters that I had had with other girls.

When we got home, she said simply, "I'm going to bed."

I was still furious and full of disapprobation of Caroline and her whole attitude that night and thought seriously of sleeping on the couch. But then I thought it was a mistake to let her have her head, and I went in and slept beside her without embracing her.

X

A SUMMER AFTERNOON

We saw a lot of Kay Burke that summer. In fact, the summer was largely given up to her.

It began late in May, when we had just moved out to Crolskill. Kay called up one Friday and asked whether she could come out for the week-end. We had invited her and Nick, and were rather surprised when she came alone. But Lyddie Burnet called up at lunch and asked us to come over for a swim. Bill Shippen, who was her brother, was there and wanted very much to see us; and when we arrived, we realized that Kay and Bill had been seeing something of each other since the night we had gone to Dixie McCann's, and that, in fact, their both weekending at Crolskill was probably preconcerted.

What we found was a typical vague afternoon. Lyddie and Bill were both rather vague, and Sam was one of those pipe-smoking fellows who doesn't say much or try to push people. But they were both in their way attractive, and this made everybody comfortable. Lyddie in

133

pink reclined at full-length in a chintz-covered chair on springs. She was slender and pretty in a thin way and had a bland patrician charm. She lay with her long legs and her long feet, in pale stockings and white summer shoes, stretched out and languidly crossed, almost as if she were in bed. She had a way of speaking very quickly that was a little like Bill's blurred drollery, but she always knew perfectly what she was doing and never was inadequate to the occasion. Sam, with a face red and swollen from a combination of drinking and sport, looked quite handsome in golf-pants. Though silent, he was unfailingly prompt at observing when anybody had finished a highball, and would immediately supply him another, wordlessly setting it beside him with his pipe between his teeth and the glass hanging down from his hand, which grasped it with all five fingers and his palm across the top. It was characteristic of the Burnets' life that, in general, you were conscious in their house of only window-seats and screens. The room that we were in was finished in some kind of dark wood, and outside was the thick grass and deep greenery that was outside all those houses; and with the vases and bowls of cut flowers rather carelessly selected and set around, the whole place gave a little the impression of a cool and spacious cave.

Kay Burke adapted herself graciously at first to the general atmosphere; but her round black eyes and her bristling black hair that had been done in what was then called a "windblown bob" so that it looked like the coat of a Scotch terrier were an alien note in the room; and I presently heard her say to Bill Shippen, beside whom she was sitting on a window-seat:

"Why didn't you call me up Thursday, you damn fool?"

Bill mumbled something about having been up the night before and lost all sense of time — "I didn't know it was Thursday, as a matter of fact — looked forward to seeing you out here."

I wondered whether they had already been sleeping together and decided they probably had. Bill Shippen was capable of anything in the way of not calling people up. They told us about a dinner they had had together at the Old Brewery on Second Avenue, when a man from North Dakota, who had come there under the impression that he was getting some kind of hot spot and was dining rather drearily alone, had entered into conversation with them and given them such a vivid description of the grasshopper plague in North Dakota that they had begun to look around them with shivers feeling that grasshoppers were landing on their shoulders and necks. They had taken him later at his own expense to a more exciting place, but they couldn't get away from the grasshoppers.

"Grasshoppers," said Kay, "was like a disease that he'd never gotten over. He could still infect other people with grasshoppers. I'd suddenly feel one on my knee and look down."

She acted it so well with her glass in her hand and her eyes that always looked surprised that everybody laughed. She and Bill worked well together, and I could see that Nick had a serious competitor. For Bill, she was like a favorite college friend — he and Sam had been to St. Paul's and Princeton — who was not only a drinking companion but a woman with whom one could go to bed: something he had never known before.

"Well," said Sam, knocking out his pipe, "are we going to play tennis?"

"Have we got to go into that again?" said Bill. "I thought we'd compromise on a swim — and then it was too cold to swim," he added.

"Dave Powell's coming over," Lyddie made one of her rare interventions, "so I'm afraid there'll be no getting out of it."

"You know, Dave Powell's tennis," said Bill, "is something there ought to be legal restrictions against. He's just like a drug addict about it. If you're a few minutes late, he fumes like a madman."

"You ought to see him at the Ledbeaters'," said Sam.

"They have a lot of old balls that make him frantic."

"Why should the Ledbeaters have bum balls?" I asked.

"They have to have them because they're so rich," said Bill.

"The same way that very rich people think they have to serve bad gin," Kay took him eagerly up, delighted and relieved, I suppose, to discover that these people were not so rich that she and they had no common attitude toward people who were very rich.

At this point Dave and Grace arrived. Dave Powell was Henry's son by the wife he had had before Julie. He was about my age and I had known him at Kendall, though he had afterwards gone to Princeton. Grace was his wife, a good-looking blond girl but otherwise terrible.

Dave refused a drink. "No thanks: not now," he said. "You better ease up on those drinks, Bill," he warned: Bill had just received a replenishment from Sam with the same smoothness with which the usher takes your ticket. "Remember, we're going to play tennis."

"But *what* tennis!" said Bill, with no sign of rejecting the drink.

"We'll beat you if you're tight," threatened Dave.

"Suppose I refuse to play."

We who had been drinking had been laughing; but Dave paid no attention.

"You really ought to play more," he argued earnestly. "You wouldn't be such a bad player"; and he went on to lecture Bill about the exasperating lackadaisical way with which he would sometimes drop the game. Dave, however, was good-natured and not really solemn, but, like Henry, he was awfully serious. Unlike Henry, he was quite spontaneous. Grace very soon broke him up.

"If Dave fails in business," she said, "he can always be a tennis pro. Really, darling, you ought to be getting money for that instead of merely boring people."

She had never been satisfied with Dave, though he was certainly one of the best guys in the world — I suppose because she had been a poor relation of a very old New York family with not much money at best and had been living in terror all her girlhood for fear she would not be able to get anybody good enough. Dave had married her with a romantic generosity quite different from his father's discretion — though I suppose it had been somewhat romantic at his age for him to have married Julie; and he was now the long-suffering victim of Grace's inappeasable misgivings lest she herself might have been victimized. He did not care about making money, but was passionately interested in forestry and used to do work for the government. This irked Grace extremely.

He had taken her on a forestry trip once, and she had complained about the discomforts of camping till, as Bill Shippen said, the howls of the coyote and cougar must have seemed mellow music, and gotten Dave in wrong at the ranches by high-hatting the people in her well-bred way.

"There's one tennis problem that can't be solved," said Bill.

"What's that?" asked Dave, indulging him.

"Why the Ledbeaters have dead balls."

"What a question!" said Kay.

Caroline and I laughed.

"And I mean in the largest sense," Bill added. "Do you think the name has anything to do with it?"

"Yes: it's a wonderful name for them, isn't it?" said Dave, acknowledging the joke with a gracious and appreciative grin but pressing on to his explanation:

"The reason is that Freddy Ledbeater doesn't like to play tennis, and that's one way he sabotages the game. Another trick he has is always to have them rolling the courts. It's silly, because he has a wonderful range and could probably be a pretty good player. When I go there now, I bring my own balls and call up first and make sure the court is all right."

"But why should poor Fred Ledbeater play tennis if he doesn't like it?" remonstrated Grace. "You think that it's a moral duty, darling, for people to like the things you do and do the things you like with you."

"Fred doesn't do anything else," said Dave, "and he might just as well be giving me practice. It's about the only thing he's good for."

"I don't see how you can say that about a person," Caroline was moved to put in. "Some people just like to enjoy life, and I don't see why people should expect them to be earnest."

"Fred Ledbeater *is* an oaf, though," I told her.

"Dave is a proselyter," said Grace, continuing under her guise of humorous wifely remonstrance. "He thinks everybody ought to be interested in forestry, as he drags people off on his trips — where they have a *perfectly wretched* time, and get robbed and bitten by spiders and get hurt chopping down trees."

"I had a terrible time," said Bill, "on that trip in the Southwest we took."

"But you were looking for Indian things, so you didn't get bored by the trees. You know Dave's a real dendrophile. He ought to be a priest of one of those cults like the Druids that get so excited about trees."

Dave had had so much of this that he was getting a little sulky under it, but he was incapable of retaliating in public.

"Well," said Sam, "are we going to play tennis? If we are, we ought to get started."

"Come on, Bill," said Dave, getting up.

"I'd just mess up the game: get Fritz."

The idea of exerting myself on a tennis-court and competing with Dave and Grace, both of whom, in their different ways, took too much satisfaction in beating you, and who usually ended angry with each other, had never been more abhorrent to me. I was afraid there was nobody else: Caroline was lazy about playing, too, and Lyddie seemed languid to a degree that nobody would have thought of suggesting it to her. But she rescued us from Dave's fell purpose when she heard me beginning to demur.

"Why don't just you and Dave play?" she said to Sam.

"Why play at all?" urged Grace, eager to frustrate Dave. "I don't think anybody really wants to. And we won't have any chance to talk to Miss Burke, who writes so marvellously about the theater."

"You know," she said, turning to Kay, "I'm one of your most devoted fans. I'm one of the people who gets *Manhattan* just to read you. I loved your article about burlesque shows — your idea that Shakespeare's *Antony and Cleopatra* would be better if it were put on by Pinsky — or Minsky."

Manhattan was not the magazine in which Kay wrote, and she had never said anything of the kind about *Antony and Cleopatra*: she had merely compared the Minsky act to an extremely bad performance of the play which had only lasted a week. Of course, Grace did this to be malicious, but she had trained herself so diligently to imitate the kind of stupidity that she must have supposed among the privileges and obligations of her position that it was not possible now to tell whether, in making Kay say something stupid, she were stupid herself or pretending.

"Oh, I'm *so* glad you liked it," said Kay, demurely flicking her eyelids.

"I'm afraid the force of inertia has set in, Dave," said Sam. In general, he liked to stay out of things. He was not enthusiastic about Dave's tennis any more than about Bill's and Kay's jokes. He was a very conservative lawyer and never stuck out his head. He did not like being beaten at things. But there was no malice of envy in him: so far as I could see, there was nothing.

"Well, I suppose I might as well have a drink then," said Dave, with a reluctant but good-natured half-laugh: it was a submission and boyish candor which had delivered him into the claws of Grace.

"I'm going to have a swim, though," he said, making a stand behind his lines of withdrawal, "whether anybody else does or not."

"I'll go with you, Dave," I said.

"I thought we were all going in," said Caroline, who didn't know them well and whom the conversation was making nervous.

"I'm afraid it's rather chilly," said Lyddie. "How was it this morning, Bill?"

"It was decidedly chill," he answered. "We ought to build up our morale before we think of going in. —Your morale isn't ready yet, is it?" he addressed himself to Kay.

"I have to get down to there"— she indicated a point on her glass.

Two fresh and clean little children came in through the front door with a nurse, babbling so that we could hear them in appealing but authoritative little voices. I could see them from where I sat, going up the 1880 stair, with its carved and light-varnished newel-posts.

"There's something," I said to Lyddie, "about these houses built at this time that's richer than the modern stuff. They're likely to be ugly, and they're inconvenient as hell, but they're always somehow romantic."

"I hadn't thought of that," she answered.

"This room," I went on, "with its dark wall and its ferns gives almost the effect of a grotto."

"The grotto in which we get blotto," said Bill.

> "There was an old man in a grotto
> Who was always disgustingly blotto.
> His fresh ferns and dark walls" —

"Wait a minute."

"And his dead tennis-balls," instantly contributed Kay.

> "His fresh ferns and dark walls
> And his dead tennis-balls" —

Bill stopped to grope for a last line.

"I must see about the children," Lyddie said quickly, getting up.

"Were as charming as something by Watteau," I suggested.

"Or Giotto," substituted Bill.

> "His dead ferns and dark walls
> And decayed tennis-balls
> Were as repellent as anything by Giotto."

"That doesn't scan," said Kay. "Besides, I thought limericks had to be dirty."

"This one is in a way," said Bill, "but I don't doubt we could make it more so."

Dave Powell, whom all this was driving crazy, began talking to Sam about cows. He took himself rather seriously and had just installed a small dairy. Sam was not really interested in this, either. Kay and Bill exchanged limerick lines in low voices that could not be heard. Grace had put on horn-rimmed glasses and was reading a magazine. Lyddie came back from above — her pink figure and long legs moving so naturally yet perfectly posing, just contained on the dark background of the stairway and framed by the high hall as if the whole thing had been fitted to her. It was pleasant sitting there with the drinks, in the consciousness of *not* playing tennis and not immediately swimming, and walking about the house, with Lyddie so slender, relaxed, and smart. There was a lovely and vague strain of music in the shadow of the high awkward hallway and the pale moving summer figure.

But you always had Grace to contend with.

"Have you seen this extraordinary advertisement?" she said, showing the magazine, while she examined the page with the slight effort which adjusting herself quickly to reading seemed to demand of her.

"Isn't that perfectly priceless?" she pressed Lyddie.

"They promise a lot, don't they?" said Lyddie, who did not get the point.

"Is this what the drug companies are coming to, Fritz?" She went on, smiling with a pretended benign fatuity. "This isn't your company, though, is it?" It was a Payne and Keller ad, and Grace knew perfectly well that I was with Payne and Keller.

"Sedatine is put out by our firm," I said, "but I'm not responsible for those ads. I think they're terrible."

The idea was that Sedatine cured heartburn and irksome belching and would cure your social embarrassment. In fact, an attempt was made, though very impersonally and discreetly, to blackmail the reader into believing that he could not really be socially acceptable unless he dosed himself regularly with Sedatine. I explained that I was opposed to the tendency that was beginning to appear in the advertising department to sell standard drugs with fancy names as if they were patent medicines."

"Don't you adore it?" said Grace, smilingly and quietly relentless; she had shown the magazine to Kay.

"It's a perfectly respectable product," I went on, "and it *does* allay the effects of bad liquor."

"Do you use it yourself?" Kay picked me up, pinning on me the familiar salesman's line.

"I hope you won't stop them altogether," said Grace, "because it's so awfully funny. There was another about a man who lost his job because he made his boss nervous by hiccoughs. It said that nothing was so fatal to the morale of offices as people who won't attend to their hiccoughs."

I felt that this was making Caroline uncomfortable: she was frightened of people like Grace; but I didn't want to move to go swimming because I didn't want to retreat from Grace. But I didn't want to be rude to Grace, so I was obliged to say something more deploring the vulgarity of our advertising. Caroline only suffered on such occasions: she had no idea of feminine combat.

"They have so many wonderful things now, don't they?" said Lyddie.

It was queer how her attractiveness evaporated when I came now to look at her closely: it was as if, though in modelling her features were feminine, all her female vitality had lapsed as soon as she had returned to her chair, and left a face that seemed devoid of sex, that might almost have been a man's or an old woman's, an absolutely neutral face. It was something that was completely bred out from a stock that had never perhaps had much to it. Caroline at least wasn't washed out like that, though I wished she had more courage. Beside Lyddie, she seemed blunt, lmost coarse; beside Grace, she seemed sensitive and human.

The afternoon had now dropped to zero. The conversation stopped or became desultory and uninterested. On our window-seats and long chairs and arm-chairs, with our cigarettes and inexhaustible highballs, with the late sun now dazzling and dazing in the windows where Bill and Kay were sitting, we were almost like the inmates of an opium den.

"Well, I'm going swimming!" said Dave, getting up and breaking through the trance. "Come on, Sam! Come on Fritz, let's take a dip! Come on, Bill!"

"I'm not sure that we can make it," said Bill. "Can we make it?" He turned to Kay.

"Well, I can't swim and I just get cold — but why don't you go in."

"We can't make it," Bill declared — he was enjoying being associated with Kay.

The ladies all decided not to go: it *was* getting rather cold. So Sam, Dave, and I, the three married men, discharged the duty imposed by our position. We brought the afternoon to a climax and gave it its justification. We dived off the springboard of the swimming-pool, which was blue-green with copper-sulphate and had a stagnant medicated taste, did short bursts of energetic crawling, climbed out, and dried ourselves.

The cold water picked me up, exhilarated me and seemed to peg the exhilaration. I took the further precaution to stabilize it, when we had returned to the living-room, by consuming another highball.

It turned out, when we were back and eating dinner, that Kay had been much struck by Lyddie.

"What is she like?" she asked.

"Just like that," I replied. "There's nothing underneath."

"I'll bet she knows exactly what she thinks, though."

"She doesn't think: she's one of the lower forms of life that simply reacts automatically to stimuli." Though I expressed myself differently from Henry, I felt, as I sat in his place, that I was taking on his attitude and tone.

"But she has a point of view — don't tell me she hasn't got a point of view!"

"Her point of view is that she's married to Sam Burnet and that she will always have what she's got and that her children will have the same things."

"I'm crazy about her: I just have to watch her sitting around and doing nothing. She makes me feel so cheap."

I laughed: "You mustn't idealize Lyddie. Really she's just blah. She's just like a sea-anemone that looks pretty when the tide's in, but if she didn't have the tide she'd be just a dull little knob of jelly."

"What are you?" said Caroline abruptly: she had brought another drink to dinner. "One of those people that studies sea-life?"

"I liked Dave, too," said Kay.

We had coffee in the pleasant living-room, which, however, looked a little bare, as Henry, before he left, had had the Monets and Renoirs put away. It was fun, I had to confess, to initiate Kay into the Crolskill world which seemed to fascinate her so.

XI

THE RATSBYS IN RESIDENCE

Things worked out, however, in a way which I wasn't altogether prepared for. What happened was that Kay and Bill spent almost every week-end with us that summer. As Bill had no job at that time — he had begun after college with archaeological expeditions, had then briefly tried a brokerage office, and was now simply living in New York in the apartment of a friend; and as there were now few new shows opening, so that Kay did not have to be in town, they sometimes stayed all through the week, too. Kay once went to visit the Burnets and was even more charmed with Lyddie; but it was easier for them at our house. Nick Carter, who was rather sexless, did not seem to be jealous of Bill, but, on the contrary, joined the combination and ecstatically rejoiced in the conviction that they were all such wonderful guys together. He was with us a good deal of the time, too.

They sat around and drank and played games. Kay taught Bill the Hiawatha-nice-girl game, and they developed this in an esoteric way: "Use a city in South America to describe Sam Shipman's plays." Then — Caroline and I played this — you drew subjects and characters out of a hat and made a speech on the subject in character. Caroline was not clever at this kind of thing: it embarrassed her to petrification to be asked to make a speech on poltergeists in the character of King Carol of Roumania; so she began to insist on staying out, and I felt that she was getting a little annoyed with it and began to drop out myself, and they went on to something else without us.

This final phase became an obsession which nearly proved fatal to our friendship. Kay had to impersonate Grace Powell and make a speech on exterminating vermin. She did it by smilingly and graciously implying that our house was overrun by all varieties, and she did it so well that Bill and Nick were delighted and kept getting her to do it again. This performance eventually turned into a character called Mrs. Ratsby, and Bill became Mr. Ratsby, who had begun as an excruciatingly boring man who wrote about modern architecture and whom one met at parties in New York: he was always expounding ideas which you were never able to grasp and there never seemed to be any beginning or end to anything he said. Bill Shippen got to imitate this with a facility that rivalled the original; and Nick assumed the role of an idiot son.

They created a whole mythology. Mr. and Mrs. Ratsby were bootleggers, poisoners, and thieves, and Nickie Ratsby was a necrophile. Mr. Ratsby held the attention of the victim by bumbling to him about functional architecture, and Nickie was always saying things that almost gave the project away in his eagerness to get at the corpses. Kay was so funny as Grace, who *was* actually horrid with her children and always telling them that they were liars and cowards in an apparently patient way, that everybody loved it at first. But Caroline got disgusted as the Ratsbys became more pathological. And it got to seem all rather queer and wrong when the Ratsbys had possession of the stage and old Karl would so sweetly and quietly be doing something in the background: it was as if it were he who was presiding. At first they would go easy on the more hideous passages when the maid came in at meals to serve things; but the thing they had imagined so mastered them that they presently paid no attention.

"I think Delia is a Catholic," said Caroline one day in an effort to restrain them.

They would try to keep the Ratsbys down when there were other people at dinner, but they would keep popping back into these characters, which were in some way now more real to them than their own. It had become difficult for them to realize that anyone could not understand and enjoy it; and Caroline's and my efforts to explain things to the guests were likely to sound ridiculous and make Caroline even more uncomfortable. One day a local lady came to lunch who was trying to be very nice to us. Though much older than Julie, she was a good friend of hers, as people say of other people that they do not really find very exciting, and played in the orchestra with her. It was evident during the meal that the Ratsbys were sizing her up as a prospect; and when we were sitting out on the porch after lunch and Caroline and Mrs. Nicolls were somewhere else, they gave vent to their stifled reflections.

It turned out that Mrs. Nicolls was just out of sight

around the house, discussing the ramblers with Caroline, and they presently stepped up on the porch. I don't know whether Mrs. Nicolls had heard — Caroline said *she* had, and had been talking flurriedly and loudly in order to direct her attention; I can't imagine she would have cared if she had: she treated us all benevolently like children. But Caroline was much upset. She disappeared and late that afternoon had drinks by herself and did not join us. I found her in her room, lying on the bed and reading.

"You made me come out here when I didn't want to" — it broke out without introduction — "and now you get me in wrong with everybody. I don't like to live in your sister's house and I don't think she wants us here — but as long as we're here you ought to control your friends so that they don't make such jackasses of themselves."

"They're at least a lot more amusing than Irving and Phil and that crowd. At least they're clever about the way they waste their time."

"They don't make fun of people to their face. Phil is always nice to old ladies."

"He has to be nice to everybody because he has to pay his way."

"Well, we evidently don't pay our way here. Mrs. Nicolls had come over to check up on the garden."

"I don't believe so," I said.

"She did. She had a long talk with the gardener, and she went around and inspected everything."

"Everything's all right, isn't it?"

"No: a lot of things seem to have gone wrong. I could handle my own garden perfectly in New Orleans, but I

didn't plant this one — I don't even know what's supposed to be in it."

I tried to reassure her. I put my arm around her and
kissed her. She was lying there in her dress without her
shoes, and I put my hand on her plump and warm thigh;
but she pulled down her little blue skirt.

"It'll be dinner-time in a minute," she said. "Your sister has dinner so early and I can't even change the hour.
Karl is like an old court chamberlain or something. I feel
as if he were telling me what to do instead of me telling
him. I don't like the way he spooks around."

Kay had known that Caroline was put out, and she became sincere and social and made all the proper apolo-
gies as soon as Caroline came down. Nick turned on the
beaming Christian fellowship that had done him so
much good with Dwight Hall and played it all over us.
They were all sure they'd been a pest, and Nick after dinner produced a bottle of Hennessy Three-Star brandy
which he had slipped out and bought that afternoon. It
appeared that they had it on their conscience that they
had been drinking so much of our liquor, and thereafter
they brought their own. I wanted to be nice about the
Ratsbys — I felt that Caroline disliked them unjustly —
and gave Kay a Ratsby cue. She declined it, but the next
day at lunch the Ratsbys broke out again. They had become practically uncontrollable. People in this situation — people who are agreed among themselves that
some hobby or pastime of theirs has been carried to a
point of perfection hitherto unimagined and that no one
else is really able to appreciate them — tend to lose the
sense of reality. They shut out the rest of the world and
become incapable of cooperating with it. It is not that

they are ill-disposed toward other people: in fact, their happiness makes them most friendly, and they try to sympathize with and interest themselves in the things that other people are doing. But it is impossible for them to take these things seriously.

I encouraged the Ratsbys, of course, by playing a role part of the time, myself, so that they thought I was entirely with them and were oblivious of the times when I was not. They thought I was Eustace, the family friend, who had once been in love with Grace Ratsby and who, conveniently being in the drug business, supplied them, i.e., legally and at list price, with poisons, aphrodisiacs, and narcotics. I was always very dignified and quick and found myself imitating Henry, but then switched it to my Uncle Felix and made him a cultivated German with heavy and elaborate manners who says banal things about the opera. I rather enjoyed this for a time, and they accepted me as a wonderful guy like themselves and assumed that things were all right. Nick and Kay might have had more sense; but Bill, who was younger than they, was still in the state of mind, rather prolonged even in his case, to be sure — the Princetonians never grow up — of the charming and charmed undergraduate who spends his vacations on visits to friends and does not need to worry about anything. Bill Shippen and I were old friends, and the fact that his sister lived at Crolskill made him feel that he belonged there. And there was also mixed up with this a certain developing cynicism which was due to the unavowed knowledge that his life was infantile and ridiculous. And Kay at that time was enraptured with Bill and found everything he did irresistible.

In any case, the summer was a blur of going back and

forth in the train beside the wide and glaring Hudson, afternoons of pretty bad tennis that made one feel fit for drinks on the terra cotta porch, love-making of which the enjoyment seemed partly dissolved in the liquor and heat, and evenings of the Ratsby fantasy, which, nagging as it seemed to me when I was out of it, became, from the moment I entered it, a sort of retreat which dispensed one from taking our real activities seriously. It was innocent, but it allowed us to satisfy our impulses of perversity and violence; it was complete and self-contained in its logic, though it did not involve the obligation of studying or making sense of the actual world; it allowed us to exercise and display our wits with the absolute certainty of applause.

But at last a certain strain behind everything began to come through into the fantasy itself. Ralph Ratsby (who was always called Rafe) was supposed to be jealous of me on account of my former interest in Grace, and he took to making invidious references to the shop-keeping character of the drug business in comparison to the role of the architect, which evidently reflected a certain antagonism on the part of Bill himself as an accomplished archaeologist who did nothing toward a friend who held down a job. There were also certain signs that Grace Ratsby was beginning to show her teeth at Ralph. Bill Shippen had been away to visit someone else and had missed his week-end in Crolskill, and she knew that he had been to the theater with another girl that week.

I had cut down on drinks one Friday night and gone to bed early with the intention of spending the next morning with the piano rather than the Ratsbys. Caroline came in from the bathroom. "I just saw Bill," she said, "coming out of Kay's room in his pyjamas. He was evidently headed for the bathroom, but when he saw me he went on down the hall to his own room."

"Well," I said, "do you think that's serious?"

"It's all right with me, but I don't think it's a good idea from the point of view of your sister's servants. I guess they've been sleeping together regularly."

"It's pretty hard to do anything about it"—I couldn't believe that those servants would say anything about it, but they seemed to conduct themselves as if they represented Henry—"You can't say anything about it to Kay, and I wouldn't know how to handle it with Bill."

"I don't see why we have to have them here every week-end."

"That's a little hard to do anything about, too. I told them to come whenever they wanted to."

The next morning I went into the music-room and locked both the doors. I wanted to improvise on some phrases that had come into my mind at the time when I had seen Lyddie Burnet on the staircase. What happened, it seemed to me, was not talentless: the pale grace in the shadow of the hallway, the careless and regular shyness of a woman coming down the stairs. Outside, there was a darkening sky and a remote menacing rumble of thunder which left the air below, as I saw it from the window, still perfectly quiet and clear—I could make the dull and the showy ripple with the clear. Now a gust blew the spray on the lawn and turned the lime-tree leaves silver-side out—while my hand in the bass wandered, I disported myself seriously in the treblelike light that lingers in water or a wind-ruffled garden before rain.

There suddenly appeared at the window a grinning bespectacled face, a babbling and wobbling head, that spoke with a kiddy voice.

"Hey, Uncle Felix," it said, "don't you want to join us in a croquet tournament?"

They had taken to playing croquet in this vein, other sports being too energetic for them.

"I think it's going to rain," I said shortly.

"Sorry, fellow," said Nick, returning to his Yale undergraduate tone. "I didn't mean to disturb you!"

"All right," I said. "I'm just fooling with some music."

I went over and shut down the window rather loudly just after he had left. But now the music all sounded like Debussy — that metallic wavering and shimmer — Lyddie Burnet coming down the stairs was simply Melisande letting down her hair. It sounded like a parody of Debussy as I played with the chords at random before I had picked it up again. I never did pick it up properly: I got to thinking that of all composers Debussy was the easiest to imitate — but it had to be the real thing or it was simply tinsel and flimsy — and I was far from the real thing. That wasn't my vein, anyway — what was my vein? I had never developed it. A real musician would have gone through a Debussy phase and before that a Wagner phase, and he would have found his own voice in the course of them — in working through those many compositions on which he had spent his early years. And now it would be nearly lunchtime and I had not gotten up very early.

It did rain, but not enough to make us sure that there was not going to be any horse show. It began to brighten up again, and we thought we could go on as we had planned. But then it got dark again, and a thick rain began to fall, just as the girls had gotten dressed. We sat in the living-room and had an unseasonable drink.

Nick asked me about my music, beginning in the "Sorry, fellow" tone, but inevitably slipping into the Ratsbys. Kay gave an exhibition of Grace being nasty about modern composers, which was really not very good because she didn't know anything about music.

"When I hear you do that, Kay," I said, "I realize there is something in you which has always wanted to be a bitch."

"So that it's perfectly clear," said Bill-Ratsby, "it's just what I've been saying for years — that the principle of the Greek vase is the principle of the diatonic scale."

"I can't see," said Kay-Ratsby, "that it has the *slightest thing* to do with it."

"Why, of course, it has everything to do with it — it's perfectly simple: you take a Greek vase — that's been made in the fourth century, say — I say, the fourth century because I consider the age of Pericles decadent — you take a Greek vase and you scrape the dirt away — the first thing is to scrape the dirt away — sometimes there are oyster-shells, too — "

"And you fill it with gin, Papa?" said Nick.

"Not yet — you scrape the encrustations away and you measure it by the sun at meridian — it's just the same principle as the sun dial" —

"You know, Bill: you ought to *be* an expert," I said. "You ought to be in the Princeton graduate school filing away Indian burial urns."

There was a sudden pause of a moment, but it was impossible to knock the wind out of Bill, and he was just about to continue when Nick, in his horrible voice, said, "And what do I want to be, Uncle Felix?"

"You want to be a case of arrested development"—I found that I was becoming savage —"You want to spend your life at a Bones reunion."

Nick and Kay went up to town that night, and Bill disappeared to his sister's. Caroline, who had been worried by the guests, was also worried by my rudeness.

I had my vacation in August, and Caroline and I drove to Canada. We drove too far in a day, stayed at too many hotels, and visited Caroline's dull relations.

XII

LIFE ALWAYS LET YOU DOWN

It was somewhere around the middle of September before we heard from Kay again. Caroline called up her hotel after we got back to town and was told that Kay was in the hospital. When she called up the hospital, Kay talked to her and asked her to come to see her — she said she had just had an appendicitis operation. Caroline paid her a visit after lunch, and I dropped in later the same day after I left the office.

I found her propped up at an angle by the raised top of the bed, looking pale and a good deal less puffy, as if she had been purified from the summer, her black hair, which needed cutting, spread out on the pillow and her bare neck coming out of her dressing-gown, in a way that made me feel her femininity in a way that one did not ordinarily feel it when she was playing her public role. She was surrounded by all sorts of objects which had been sent her or brought her by her friends: the usual flowers and books, caviare and calves'-foot jelly, together with several mechanical toys and a stuffed grebe which Nick had picked up for her at an antique store on Lexington Avenue. They thought it looked like someone they knew. They had also bought her a great deal of liquor: on the bureau there was a small bar, from which she invited me to help myself.

I asked her about Bill, and she told me that he had gone out in August for a visit to the ranch of a friend in the Southwest and had been there ever since. I saw at once that something painful had happened. She had never had a letter from him: only a couple of telegrams signed "Ratsby."

"He's not the type that writes letters," I said.

"Not to me. You know, he spent the last night he was here with some floozy. He told me he'd call me up, and I spent the whole night beside the phone. The next morning I got a wire from the train."

"Who was the girl?" I asked.

"Some model who'd been in the Follies."

"Bill is just a kid," I said. "You never ought to take him seriously."

"I know; but you can't resist that charm. Whenever I get sore at him, I tell myself that he's just a little snotty-nosed brat, and then when I see him I'm like putty in his hands."

She had a strong masochistic side — I think she was part Scandinavian — mixed in with her Irish aggressive-ness; and I was trying to head her off from self-pity. The trouble was that she had made the mistake of making demands on Bill, of accusing him and trying to check up on him. Bill was desultory and he wished to remain desultory — this in fact was one of his charms for Kay, who was purposive in a frustrated way; though appar-

ently quite aimless and drifting, he had the will to be ir-
responsible developed to a high degree. And it was furthermore unfortunate from Kay's point of view that Bill's
sex life, due to his shyness, had started rather late — only
the year before she had met him, in fact — and that,
finding it now so unexpectedly easy, he was like a child
turned loose in a candy-store. It seemed to be something
you could always get which he had deprived himself
of too long, and he resented poor Kay's complaints
and phone-calls, tenacious partings, and swollen-eyed
weeps, because they were spoiling the fun. One night he
had met the model at a costume ball in a brief leopard-
skin, a flamboyant green wig, and beautiful slender legs,
and he was so delighted with her, when he had been to
bed with her in her apartment, which really showed very
good taste, that he had forgotten about the sexual side
of Kay — always the side that had interested him least.
There was something about Kay, who was older than he,
that would have dropped her readily — I could see it as I
watched her in bed — out of the sangfroid of her Broadway character into something rather middle-class and
wifish, and Bill, who was genuinely fastidious, would
have been repelled by this. It was her lack of attention to
her hair, which Caroline said she never washed, and her
wadded and pink-flowered dressing-gown when Caroline would have had a smart bed-jacket. Poor Kay! — my
drink was warming me with sympathy — she had been a
middle-class wife too long.

"You're in love with him, aren't you?" I said finally,
trying to sound like a doctor simply diagnosing an ail-
ment. "It's an awful way to be."

"Of course: I've been crazy about him," she said, "ever

since that night at your sister's." Her eyes began to weep, and she got out a little white handkerchief. "Not," she added, "that I don't hope the son-of-a-bitch falls off his horse and breaks his neck!"

At this moment Nick came in. He was beaming as usual with his pattern of nonsense suffused with loving-kindness; but he had added a new note of heartbreak. The effect on him of Kay's passion for Bill had been to make him feel that he, too, ought to work up an unhappy passion, as he had acquired a girl from a musical show — not a chorus-girl but a girl who did bits — who had a certain raw wisecracking pungency and about whom it was his great pride to boast that, in spite of her common origins, she "came into the room like a duchess," but who always seemed to me, with her round staring eyes, to be an absolutely congenital whore. She was unfaithful to Nick, at any rate — and caused him a lot of woe, which he exploited. He was funny about his misfortunes: his play had just been turned down by some producer, and his hat had been blown off on Park Avenue and been run over by several cars; when he had got out of his taxi at Tony's, he had slipped and thrown out his knee, and inside he had found a note from his girl explaining that she couldn't meet him:

"She'd been there, with the director," he said. "I sat there and drummed on the table: I accepted the challenge of Fate! Then the people at the table opposite began to give me dirty looks — the woman would look around like this. That was the end, the bottom! 'All right!' I said. '*All right!* I'll stop. But the *day-will-come* when you people will go on your knees and *beg* me to drum on the table!'"

We roared over this.

"You didn't really do it, did you?" said Kay

"What I really did was tip Louis a dollar for bringing me the bad news and get down on all fours and crawl out — keeping as much under the tables as possible."

They all had these feelings of inferiority, I reflected, because they weren't making good in those days when money meant power and splendor and there was so much money going. It was something to have security and a business job like me, with a rising market for the products, and not to be either romantic or bitter about business.

But before Nick had finished his story, people began arriving in droves. He had his audience and forgot his sorrow; they all had their audiences in each other. Their sorrows became a necessary assumption one had to make for the right kind of humor: it was now one of the rules of the game, like the principle that the puns had to be bad in the days of *Hiawatha nice girl*. Life always let you down; everybody was frankly in pieces.

I left Kay the adored queen of the court, throning with her one drink of the day, which had already been extended to three; and I realized that now she was happy: taken care of, admired, and amused. Here she could trust them as she could not trust Bill Shippen: they conspired to guarantee her security in that world of malicious and heart-broken jokes, in which they themselves needed her. It was always the thing now to be sick, and the hospital was a new kind of party. The very prevalence of the drinks and cigarettes over the sickish medicinal smell was not only an exploitation of illness for this purpose, but almost a triumph over death.

When I leaned down and shook hands as I left, I saw that Kay was partly estranged from me. Nick and Bob Frink and the stuffed grebe and the girl with the two horns on her hat that the grebe was supposed to resemble, who had come in in the course of the conversation and who was just then a great favorite of theirs because she was always saying priceless things as to which it was impossible to tell whether she meant them to be funny or not — all this was so much more real.

When I got back to the Tavistock, I found Caroline drinking alone. I told her about my visit to Kay, and I thought she remained strangely silent.

"A touch of appendicitis," I concluded, "is just what she needs to make her happy. It satisfies her masochistic instinct; it gives her an excuse for not working; and it gets her a lot of attention."

"It isn't appendicitis," said Caroline. "She didn't tell me not to tell, but don't repeat it — she got pregnant and had to have an abortion."

"Bill Shippen?"

"Yes."

"I suppose he doesn't know about it."

"No: she hasn't told him. She's been in an awful state. She made me her confidante."

"Well, I think she likes to suffer just the same."

"Really, it was a dirty trick for Bill Shippen to go off and leave her like that. Don't be so smug: no woman enjoys being left pregnant — to have to have an abortion all alone. She had to go to some shyster doctor —"

"You say shyster *lawyer* — a doctor is a quack."

"Well, he was some kind of fly-by-night doctor up in the Bronx, and she got an infection or something, and she could only get into a hospital when things had gone wrong. Nick got her in through some Yale man that's a doctor there. She couldn't tell her husband, and she thought she was going to commit suicide."

"She never ought to have had any confidence in Bill. Isn't it incredible," I said, "that a New York wit like Kay with a great reputation for sophistication should get seduced like a small-town girl!—I noticed in the hospital when I was talking to her that she was peculiarly poisonous about children—I thought it was rather horrible—but I suppose that this was the reason. She told me that there was a little boy who was a patient across the hall and stamped up and down the hall with horseshoes—and then they operated on him and—she said with ghoulish satisfaction—everything was perfectly quiet. And she was particularly malignant about what she called Bob Frink's wife's brats."

"I wondered if she wanted children by her husband."

"I dare say she didn't," I said. "I think she was always hoping for something better."

"Is that what you're doing with me?" she said—I had had the feeling all along that there was something behind her manner.

"I didn't think you wanted a child," I said. "I thought that this wasn't the moment to have one. You had a miscarriage with Lefanu, and I thought you didn't want to take a chance."

She was silent and went on smoking in her expressionless almost masculine way, but her eyes had a fixed stare away from me as if she was looking at her thoughts and her brows were as close to being knit—there was the strain without perceptible creases—as they were capable of being. I wondered whether I ought to break the strain by speaking of something else, but I was afraid this would look like evading the subject. She broke it up herself by squashing out her cigarette with a nervous but definite gesture.

"Well, let's go out to dinner," she said.

XIII

DECEMBER 1929:

BLEEDING TO DEATH

The stock market crash at the end of October meant little or nothing to me. The drug business was not badly hit; and I had a certain satisfaction in seeing the wind knocked out of the brokers. I had listened in the years since the War to a good deal of brokers' conversation; the truth was that people in general — downtown and on the road, at the Yale Club and even at Crolskill — had been getting to talk like brokers, and I was glad to see their hopes and boasts dampened.

The deflation of these values, in fact, stimulated me to insist rather rigorously on a respect for more serious values in the first party we gave that winter. It was in the nature of a musical evening: Jehuda had agreed to play Hindemith's opus 11 for violin and piano — he graciously invited Julie to take the piano part; Eddie Frink was going to do a piano sonata which he had written during the summer — his first real attempt in years at serious composition; and I had gotten Miriam Nicolls, the angel of the League for New Music, to induce Edgar Rockland, an American composer of an older genera- tion, to perform some of his New Hampshire pastorals. I excluded not only Phil and Claire and Irving and Ellis and the rest of Caroline's friends, but also Martha Gan- nett, who cared nothing about music, and Kay and Nick Carter and Bill Shippen — who had come back from the West in the fall and was going around again with Kay. I aimed at having nobody there who would not listen se- riously to music.

Eddie Frink came to dinner with us. He had wanted to try out our piano. Though he performed at a night club every night, he was nervous about his sonata and was re- hearsing when the hotel phone rang and announced that Mr. Lefanu and Miss Danziger were downstairs. People from the provinces never understand that people always call up first in New York; in New Orleans they just drop by. It did seem a grisly fate that Lefanu always had to turn up just when we were having a party. It was Caroline who answered the phone, and she was unable to keep them off.

"Couldn't you say you were taking a bath," I asked, "and that I was getting dressed and that we were already late for some engagement?"

"I couldn't refuse to see them," she said. "I just couldn't hurt his feelings. I'm sorry, but I just can't."

She was always much too good and yielding.

But Lefanu, when he appeared, was a surprise: he had entered an entirely new phase. Miss Danziger had done a job of reform which nobody could have ever believed possible. Lefanu was steadier and stouter; he had discarded his slightly fantastic dandyism and was dressed in one of those standard blue suits that they wore downtown in New York; he even refused a drink, and it appeared that he was on the wagon. He had, in fact, become a business man — he was working in his father's cotton house. I had already observed the phenomenon of drinkers who abruptly lay off and then find they have no sober personality. Suddenly they become self-conscious, uncertain of themselves, and shy: they are groping and trying to get their bearings in a world they have never known. They have to study and watch and be careful; they feel inadequate and are almost apologetic. This was the condition of Lefanu. He had always, when in his cups, had a certain mad humor and outrageous boldness which the fluency and naturalness of his Southern manner enabled him to carry off and which gave him a sort of edge on the company — it had been, I always felt, one of the things about him that Caroline had fallen for; but now his whole tone was discreet and wholesome; his jokes were actually childish and banal; his laugh sounded stupidly hollow. Caroline said afterwards that Elizabeth had brought him round to see us to show her that Lefanu was really a perfectly good citizen with a serious and sympathetic wife and that his drinking and demoralization had all been due to Caroline; and they were certainly putting on a show.

He asked me about my business, which I dismissed in a light social way and asked about his business, a little as if he had been a salesman with whom I had started talking on a train. He assured me, like any Rotary member, that business was fundamentally sound; and I laughed at him good-humoredly and told him that he was a regular Shreveport oil man. Elizabeth at once intervened:

"We're going to save New Orleans from Shreveport," she said.

He told us about Huey Long and declared that he belonged to a group who were going to rescue Louisiana from its decadence and fight the vulgarity and corruption that Huey represented.

"Why, we're going to get that poor white out of politics and run back to the badlands where he belongs! There isn't a nigger madam in New Orleans who hasn't got higher moral principles than Huey," etc. When he got on this subject, he warmed up, and I was afraid he was going to stay indefinitely; but, after all, he wasn't drinking and Elizabeth finally summoned him to go.

"Let me tell you about Ed Rockland," I said to Eddie at dinner. "He's the only great musical original that America has ever produced. What Ryder and Eakins are to painting, Rockland is to music. He was writing polytonal and polyrhythmic stuff before Schoenberg and Stravinsky ever dreamed of it, and he arrived at it not through theory but from what you might call actual folk-sources. His father was a professional musician in New England, and he used to travel around and direct church choirs and local bands, and Ed used to travel with him. He used to hear that sometimes some of the members of a choir would get ahead of the others and that sometimes some instrument would be playing consistently off-key, and he saw that this produced some interesting effects. He decided that unconsciously they were doing it on purpose — that they were interested in the effects themselves. They were asserting their artistic personalities and giving the whole piece a new character. Well, when he went to college he began deliberately experimenting with effects of mixed rhythms and dissonance. He horrified the music teachers, but actually he was a pioneer just as much as Debussy — in fact, more. He began composing his New Hampshire with key signatures that change every bar or so."

"How is the stuff?" asked Eddie.

"Mrs. Nicolls tells me it's wonderful. I haven't heard any of it yet. She and Tony Goresan dug him up. Isn't it amazing to think of him working it all out in the heart of the New Hampshire mountains!"

"It sounds goose-flesh-making to me," said Eddie, looking out unmoved from under his drooping eyelids. "I don't like Schoenbergle with his gurgle-murgle and Igor Stravinsk of Minsk, but at least they know how to do it, and I'll bet this johnny doesn't know how to do it. The idea of a dissonance in New Hampshire is enough to unnerve me for the evening. I'm sorry you ever mentioned it. I won't play after him, I'll tell you that."

"No: you're playing before. Don't worry. It's not the kind of thing you think. The old man is a passionate artist, a fantastic character in his generation. He's a patent lawyer with a double personality."

"I'm scared of those double personalities," said Eddie. He was afraid that Edgar Rockland would eclipse his act: his own work was more frail and conventional, and I was trying to reassure him when the maid said that Nick was on the phone.

"Would you mind coming over to Kay's?" he said. "I'm

over here in Kay's apartment." I explained that we were just eating dinner and asked him whether he couldn't wait — what was it?

"I'm sorry," he said self-consciously and stammering with deliberate modesty to emphasize the seriousness of the emergency, "but it's really pretty imp — important."

I thought at first it was one of their jokes and tried to handle it on a basis of kidding; but Nick convinced me that he was in earnest. Boyscoutishly so, I thought; I concluded that Kay was down with the jitters. I left dinner with some irritation.

Kay had taken a small apartment just around the corner from us. It was a part of her attempt to be more tony, stimulated by Bill Shippen. She liked to be near Caroline, too, who had become her confidante and had had, with her inexhaustible amiability, to listen to the interminable bulletins of Kay's jealousy, adoration, and despair.

Nick opened the door. He was really shocked, subdued.

"I found Kay in the bathtub with her wrist cut," he said in a low voice.

"She's not dead?"

"No: but she's done a lot of bleeding. I put a tourniquet on her wrist, but it isn't very good."

"Have you called a doctor?"

"I called Syd Fisher, an old Bones man, but he was out to dinner and I didn't want to bother him. She won't let me call her doctor — she says she doesn't like him."

"Don't you know of somebody who would handle it right?"

The same kind of inhibition restrained me from calling Julie's doctor that had made it impossible for Nick to disturb Syd Fisher at dinner.

"Where is she? in the bathroom?" asked Caroline in her voice of the tension of crises that hardly allowed her to be articulate.

"No: I wrapped her in a blanket and put her in bed. I wish you'd go in and see her."

Caroline went into the bedroom.

"There's Brownie McGovern," I said. I had known him better than Nick because neither of us had made a senior society, but I hadn't been especially cordial to him since we had both been living in New York and had refused after my first two or three years in New York his invitations to dinner with himself and his college-girl wife; but this was not the moment to worry about such things. He was home having dinner and he came at once.

Nick knocked at the bedroom door and asked whether things were all right. Caroline came to the door and told him in a flurried whisper that Kay was still oozing blood from under the bandage; she had fainted when Nick had put it on and he didn't want to do it again, and they decided to let it go till the doctor came.

"Well, I didn't read Dan Beard for nothing!" said Nick, with a half wide-mouthed smile, as he turned back to me in the living-room — his pale and square face looking, I thought, rather skull-like. He told me that Kay had been expecting Bill to come in for a drink and take her out and that when it got to be eight o'clock and he had not even called up to explain — the engagement, she knew, had been vague and made about a week before — she had tail-spun into an awful despair — she had been

drinking all the time, of course: it was one of those pes-
simistic moments of drinking when you see the hopeless
logic of everything — and had made herself a hot bath,
climbed into the tub, and gouged her wrist with the nail-
scissors. She had, however, not been able to restrain herself from answering the buzzer when it sounded. She
had got up, wrapped a towel around her wrist, and gone
and pressed the button. Then she had got back into the
bathtub, closing the bathroom door. It was all absurd,
but she said that if it had turned out to be Bill, she was
going to get out. The truth was that she had also known
that Nick was coming that evening. She didn't answer
when he first came in and called. But when he had been
puzzled at getting no answer as well as by seeing the little
prints of bloody water left by her bare feet on the floor
and had knocked at the bathroom door she had finally
said faintly, "Hello."

He had asked whether she were all right, had gotten
no answer, and had opened the door. Then he had put
on the tourniquet, she had fainted, and this had scared
the liver out of Nick, and it had been then that he called
us up.

Brownie McGovern appeared, earnest, sympathetic,
and mild, and very glad to see Nick and me. He sealed up
and bandaged her wrist and gave her some kind of am-
monia to keep her spirits up. He said that she was perfectly all right, the loss of blood she had had wasn't serious, but he suggested that somebody ought to stay with
her. Nick was of course glad to do this, so this let Caroline and me out; but I had to stay for a minute and talk
to Brownie, since it was so long since I had seen him.

Suddenly I realized how late it was and that it was

time for our guests to be coming. The little living-room and the furniture that came with it, green-upholstered and slightly shabby, and the pictures, a fake eighteenth-century print of a lady having her hair dressed in her boudoir, and a Maxfield Parrish youth looking out at a symmetrical castle against a syrupy deep blue sky, about which Kay had some much-applauded jokes but which she was unable to replace with anything better — all this seemed peculiarly dreary. I went in to see Kay for a minute. She was lying on her back, very pale, and I a little bit got the impression that she was luxuriating in pretending to be dead. I kissed her on the cheek and took her undamaged right hand.

"I'm sorry to be such a nuisance," she said. Tears came into her eyes as she spoke to me.

"Don't give it a thought," I replied.

"You people have been so goddamn sweet to me!"

"Well, don't try to leave us. What would we do without you?"

"I'm no good to anybody," she said. "I'm too old and too cheap and too sloppy-sentimental."

"The only thing I agree to," I said, "is that you *are* a little sentimental. If I were you, I'd throw Bill out on his neck."

"He wouldn't care," said Kay, with tragic comedy.

"Throw him out and forget about him."

"I can't."

"Well, then, for Christ's sake take care of yourself — and if there's any time you feel you're not good, call us up and we'll tell you!"

It was the way you had to talk to all those people; and she really was a remarkable character: through her notices of plays and her reported *bon mots*, she was already a minor celebrity.

But this interview had held me up further; and when we got back, we were horrified to find that Rockland had already arrived. I saw at once that he was the kind of man who would come on the very moment he was invited for; but what for some reason disconcerted me more was my recognizing him as the keen-eyed old man who had sat next to me at the Schoenberg concert. I had not imagined him like that at all: I had thought he would be artistic, perhaps a little bit ham, perhaps with long hair and a resonant voice, in the manner of the older generation. But he was just like an American uncle, and his attitude toward us was avuncular. No social embarrassment was possible, because it was he, as it were, who took charge of us. Erect, with head held high, in an old-fashioned tailed coat and white tie tucked in under a low collar, he threw out his pointed beard and looked on us with his lively and shrewd black eyes.

He had also been playing uncle to Eddie, who was looking like an indignant bull terrier and who had obviously been having a horrible time. And as soon as he had received us and made us feel at home, he returned to the topic of their conversation or rather the topic, I gathered, on which he had been expatiating to Eddie.

"I've just been telling Mr. Frink," he said, "that what this country needs is more credit. We can produce right here in the United States everything that anybody could desire — we've got the greatest natural resources of any country except Russia, and they haven't got control of theirs yet. Why don't the people get the use of it? Why aren't they able to enjoy what they have? They don't even get enough to eat — they don't even have clothes and shelter — some of 'em didn't have enough even during this so-called prosperity. What's the reason? The reason is simply that though the railroads and the big corporations can get big loans from the banks any day, the *people* can't get the money to buy the products that they themselves are raising. That's the problem, and the Federal Reserve don't solve it — Hoover isn't going to solve it. The only thing that's going to solve it is to issue more money to the people. There's no reason on God's earth why we shouldn't do it except that the government is run by a lot of avaricious business men who don't care whether the citizens live or die!"

"You mean inflation?" asked Ben Furstmann, who had come in with Jehuda in the meantime and had been listening to the conversation.

"Not the ordinary kind of inflation," Rockland went on.

"What good is that going to do," said Ben — I was surprised to see his interest in economics — "when you've still got the profit system. As long as the manufacturer is taking away part of the value that is created by the worker and spending it on himself, you can't get it back to him simply by juggling the banking system a little."

At this point Henry and Julie arrived. Julie arranged her music — she was nervous at playing with Jehuda — and Jehuda turned over the score, pointing out certain things. Henry easily took up the subject being debated between Ben Furstmann and Rockland and indicated with quiet assurance the practical fallacy of remedies that depended on tampering too much with the currency.

Ben was not interested in Henry: "You simply defend the present system," he said and returned to the more theoretical and intellectually interesting argument that he was having with Edgar Rockland.

His voice began to get high and yipping, and Rockland was beginning to say to him, "Now, listen here, my friend."

To Henry, Rockland said, "Well, sir, I don't know what you mean when you talk about 'sound financial policy.' I don't know how a policy can be sound which allows these investment trusts to issue people bonds for money that doesn't exist to the tune of millions of dollars."

"I agree," said Henry reasonably, "that we need legislation to make any repetition of this impossible —"

But Rockland, not interested, swept on: "I find that the word *sound* usually means *obsolete*. When people begin talking about things being 'sound,' it usually means they're ripe to collapse. It's so in music — it's so in physics — it's so in teratology."

Henry smiled as he replied. Rockland's lecture was delivered with so much good-humor and sweetness that nobody could have possibly resented it; he had adopted toward Henry, too, his semi-avuncular attitude.

Miriam Nicolls and Tony Goresan now came and were followed by some of our friends and by a number of musical people whom Miriam and Tony had invited and whom we did not know or know well. They were the kind of people one saw at the League for New Music concerts, and I found them rather hard to talk to. Eddie

Frink, I could see, was scared to death. The lady with the red sideboards was talking to him about "indigenous American folk-music" — by which she meant Kentucky mountain ballads — and thought that they would provide the material for serious composition as Russian folk-music had done for Moussorgsky. I reflected that Eddie's songs and the rather subtle changes that the jazz orchestras could wring on a blues did represent a technical sophistication of native American material, and I wondered why it came out so differently from the lightest song by Moussorgsky. Was our public inevitably so vulgar that not even the well-trained composers were able to do anything distinguished? — since there was really no other language for them to talk. When they talked the musical language of Europe, was it as if our poets and novelists should write their books in German and French? Perhaps Eddie Frink's sonata would show us that something *could* be done — perhaps Rockland had already shown it.

Eddie was looking up sidelong at the lady from under his drooping lids, and he at once turned away to me: "Let's get started and get the damn thing over," he said. "Oh, God! it's going to be hideous. They expect me to do Erik Satyr and *les Six* and *tutte quante*: *tutti frutti*."

I stood by the piano and announced: "If people will sit down," I said, "Mr. Janowitz and Mrs. Powell are going to play Hindemith's sonata for violin and piano — Hindemith's opus 11."

Jehuda, of course, played it exquisitely, but I can't say I found it very exciting. The old romantic dissonant music was subsiding into something more classical, and, it seemed to me, just a touch dreary. But parts of it were charming, and the applause was as loud as thirty or so people could make. Only Rockland, I noticed, seemed polite rather than earnestly positive.

I next announced Eddie, explaining that the sonata was his first serious composition. I was afraid even before I had finished that he would feel I sounded patronizing, but it was too late to do anything about it. At any rate, when I was turning the pages for him, his nervousness communicated itself to me, and I became so nervous watching the notes that I wasn't able to do justice to the sonata — which, however, seemed to me more commonplace than I had hoped. I had a depressing feeling that when Eddie's musical ideas were stripped of their perhaps superficial wit, what was left was rather banal and sentimental. The audience, it seemed to me, applauded less, and I felt unpleasantly embarrassed in relation to both Eddie and them.

The maid called me; I looked around; there was somebody on the phone. I told her to tell them to call back in an hour; but just as Rockland was coming to the piano, received with tremendous applause, she returned and explained that it was Nick Carter and Kay, who were downstairs and wanted to know whether they could come up.

I couldn't refuse, on account of Kay. "Meet them at the door," I told the maid, "and tell them to be quiet till the music is over."

I started to turn Rockland's pages full of irritation and apprehension, and Rockland's music and his way of dealing with it soon got me down completely. The first of the New Hampshire pastorals, which represented a thunderstorm in the mountains, consisted of a series of spasms where the tempo was abruptly increased and which seemed to be completely atonal. The first spasm left me behind and Rockland turned the page himself, violently twitching it over as, marking the rhythm with his head and the energetic movement of his body, he entered into the spirit of the storm; and thereafter he continued to turn for himself, as if he could not expect anything of me and it did not bother him anyway. His playing, though absolutely daimonic, was as informal as everything else about him; and I soon didn't know whether to keep on turning or to abandon the whole matter to him. I compromised by doing the quieter parts and letting him attend to the more tempestuous.

The second piece, *Sabbath Morning*, was certainly relatively placid, and Nick and Kay arrived right in the middle of it. I glanced around and saw them standing in the living-room door and saw that Brownie and Bill Shippen were with them. At that minute, to my great surprise, though I had heard he used such themes in his music, the tune of "Onward, Christian Soldiers" suddenly sang out from the piano. It was not exactly caricatured— though there were several sour chords and a mimicking of the voices of a village choir marching up and down the steps of the stage in a lackadaisical Sunday morning way: the hymn had been given an authentic value by being reflected in the mind of the composer, who made it all a part of the New England landscape. Or had he only tried to do this, leaving the hymn-tune still as unassimilated to serious symphonic music by Rockland's home-made sophistications as the jazz themes of Eddie's sonata had been by the conventional echoes of Ravel? I can't help thinking that to Nick and

Kay the whole thing must sound awfully funny, and I was almost afraid that they would be unable to resist joining in and singing "Onward, Christian Soldiers."

I signalled them at the end of this piece to sit down before he had started the next. This last, I could hear them thinking, was a honey. It was called *Saturday Night in Nashua*. It included "How Dry I Am," a few bars of what, from the directions on the score, I could see was intended to be movie-music, and a final passage of spooning in a hammock with moonlight that owed something to Beethoven but also involved "By the Light of the Silvery Moon." It got, of course, a just ovation, but I couldn't be sure whether it meant anything. Now that I had heard the great Rockland, I found that my faith in him was shaken. Did I really believe in American music?

And now we had highballs and punch. I took a highball over to Kay, who looked pale but very pretty with her lipstick. It seemed that Bill had felt uneasily while dining with someone else that he had had some sort of engagement with Kay and had finally called her up. He had not been told what had happened; she had put on a dress with long sleeves which concealed her bandaged wrist. And she had been so delighted to see him that she seemed to him unusually gay. They had decided to look for amusement and, having gathered that we were having a party, naturally tried us first. Brownie McGovern had eagerly fallen in with their plans, as it was very exciting to him to find himself in this world of wit and glamor. He was prematurely bald, with a little rather fuzzy hair that was parted over his brows; and he was trying to live up to the company by making inept jokes.

Henry and Julie melted early away; I don't think

Henry liked the look of the people. Rockland, whom I rather wanted to talk to about music, got back into his argument with Ben Furstmann: he was smiling and shaking his head and explaining with a self-assurance which had never admitted a doubt that the whole economic situation could be expressed in an algebraic equation, and that all you had to do to straighten things out was to extend the amount of credit represented by X. I wondered uncomfortably whether his system of harmony had anything in common with his currency scheme. He had crushed Eddie and made him furiously indignant by saying to him:

"Listen, my boy — you can't creep up on Inspiration — you can't put salt on its tail! If it hits you, it hits you Wham! If it doesn't, you're not elected. There were some very pretty little things in that piece, and you oughtn't to be afraid to be pretty. It's something to be pretty and there aren't many people who can really do it. Did you ever think of writing any popular music?"

Eddie left, and most of the New Music contingent left: they were not late-stayers-up or drinkers. But Nick and Kay were, and Rockland, though he hardly drank, was a long-distance talker who liked nothing better than to talk — you would have said, in fact, that he was a bore if his vitality and his enthusiasm and his pungent way of putting things had not held you as you listened to him. He got to talking to Bill Shippen about New Mexico, and of course he had his own ideas about the origin of the Indians. It was mixed up with Indian myths, which he tended to take rather seriously as explanations of what had actually happened; and as Bill and Kay listened, it seemed to me that the Ratsbys were getting ready for a festival with Mr. Rockland's theories. Kay's black and bright eyes were beginning to sparkle with amusement and malice: she would see it as common ground upon which she and Bill could reestablish their understanding.

It was Brownie McGovern's idea of showing his appreciation of music to say to Rockland:

"I suppose you know the songs of Hugo Wolf. Of course, I'm not a musician, but I regard him as a greater song-writer than either Schubert or Schumann"; and the line that this started with Rockland was that Wolf's going insane was a disaster that might have been averted. The best treatment for that kind of insanity was hypnotism, and the therapeutic failures of hypnotism had been due merely to the fact that the hypnotist had not been a great enough person. The hypnotist who would have cured Wolf would have had to be a man who could appreciate Wolf and who at the same time had the strength of personality to give Wolf command of himself.

"Are you a hypnotist, Mr. Rockland?" asked Bill.

"Only in an amateur way," said Rockland.

"Could you hypnotize somebody now?" asked Kay, with an intention I knew was ironic.

"I could hypnotize you," he replied, looking at her with his sharp and flashing eye which had something of the Ancient Mariner about it and which did seem a little hypnotic.

"You'd be a very good subject," he said. "You're trusting and suggestible, and you're lacking in confidence in yourself." If anybody else had said this, I might have thought it was ridiculously stupid, that Kay was opposite of that; but there was something about him that inspired respect, no matter how wildly he seemed to be talking, and in a moment I felt it was true. Kay herself was startled and taken aback and her reply was not up to her line of retorts:

"You read me like a book," she said. "Don't hypnotize me, though: I couldn't take it tonight!"

"Do you think you could hypnotize me?" asked Caroline: it was the feminine and silly side of her.

He looked at her: "Yes, you could be hypnotized, I guess."

"It's too late for hypnotism tonight," I murmured.

"I hypnotized my secretary with this," he said, holding up a large gold seal on his old-fashioned watch-chain that stretched across his vest. "She lay rigid on the desk, and we were able to pick her up that way."

Bill Shippen was slightly smiling, obviously thinking of the ribald possibilities of hypnotizing one's secretary in the office.

"Let me see," demanded Kay, as if fascinated. "Hold it up and let me see how it works."

Rockland detached the seal and held it up in front of Kay's eyes. "Now just watch it," he said. "Don't think. Just see how bright it is! — a very bright thing. Just a seal from my watch-chain, but a very bright thing — a very bright round thing." He paused; she was staring at it.

"If you look at this seal long enough," he went on, his voice dropping slowly down and making spaces between the words, "if you look — at this seal — long enough, it will — make you — very sleepy. You are — sleepy, and — it will — make you — sleepy. It will — make you — sleepy — and put you to sleep." Kay's eyes were actually drooping. "We will — make your — eyes droop — and will — put you — to sleep." Her eyes were closed now.

I disapproved: I thought that, after what had happened, she shouldn't be hypnotized. Bill and Nick were grinning; but we all sat silent and watched.

"You will sleep — and you will sleep." He paused. "Can you lift your right hand?" She did so. "Put it down. And now your left. Put it down. And now get up." She got up. "Sit down at the piano." She did so — still with her eyes closed. "Play something." She played a little waltz, which was the only thing she knew.

"I wouldn't have her do too much," I said in a low voice to Rockland. "She's in rather bad shape tonight." He nodded.

"Come back here," he said. She got up and walked back to her chair. "Now sit down — and when I count ten, wake up."

He counted ten, very slowly and deliberately, but at the end Kay did not wake up. For a moment I was frightened, then I wondered whether Kay might not be doing it on purpose: I had already had the idea that the whole thing had been kidding on her part.

"Wake up when I count five." He counted this time more loudly and with emphasis that became imperative. But at five Kay failed to wake. "This young man will now count five," he tried, nodding to Bill Shippen — "and this time you will awake, because you want to do what he says. You will wake up when he comes to five."

Bill counted, but would not lend himself to the portentous hypnotic manner. Kay opened her bright round black eyes. "Mama's getting sleepy," she said. "Will you boys take me home?"

"Don't you want another drink first?" I suggested, getting up to get her one.

"No: I've had too many," she said. "I drink too much." And when I looked at her again, she was crying. "You people never ought to have gotten me out of the bathtub," she said, half joking, half pathetic. "You've done a wonderful job on my wrist, doctor," she said to Edgar Rockland, "and if there's still any bleeding"— she laughed —"it isn't your fault."

"Listen, Kay," I said, trying to break in on her daze. "Take a drink and you'll feel better. We're just here sitting around after the music."

"I'm a mess tonight," she said. "I better go home." Rockland explained to her what had happened. "I *would* get myself hypnotized tonight!" she said. "—And play the piano with an audience of experts!"

"What's the matter with your wrist?" I heard Bill ask her when we had shifted the conversation to take the weight off Kay.

"Oh, nothing: I just cut it." The tears started into her eyes again, and she said, "I must go: take me home."

"We're all bleeding to death," said Rockland. "What you were in"— to Kay —"was the same place we're all inhabiting: we're bled of our emotion and we're bled of our money — and our music is bleeding away. What violated the wholeness of our organism? How do we know? It may be something from outside. But every man and every woman has got to hold on to him- or herself in order to staunch the flow. We've got to check it with vigils and prayer — and every man's got to do it for himself."

NOTES

The references to Wilson's notebooks are identified by Roman numerals (his own numbering system), the year of the entry, and their location in his published journals.

PRELUDE: JUNE 1928

Wilson's plan for this chapter was well thought-out in his earliest notes and in his proposal for *The Story of the Three Wishes*. When he began a first draft of *The Higher Jazz*, after a lapse of two years, he simply followed his outline for the Prelude, building most of it around the experiences of an unnamed narrator who resembled himself. His own life in Manhattan, the train trip to New Jersey, and his family in its nineteenth-century house became background for the story of transformation, as he buttressed his memory from his notebooks. In his second and last draft, he deemphasized the autobiographical elements by shortening the narrator's stay in Manhattan and considerably enlarging the narrator's description of the man and woman he sees on the train.

2. **my grasp of the subject:** To Wilson, the Ziegfeld Follies, which he described and reviewed for the *New Republic*, were the symbol of an era. When he assembled his articles dealing with the 1920s for the first section of *The American Earthquake*, he entitled them "The Follies (1923–1928)."

2. **On the brandies, I called up Lucille:** In the first draft Wilson gives much more space to the interlude with Lucille. There he noted marginally, "Peggy To[m]pkins, VI-78" (1926; *Twenties* 289–290), a reference to the model who was the mistress of his good friend John Amen. The scene in the novel echoes another notebook entry, in which Wilson describes how Amen had to wait until Peggy's "rich and elderly protector" had left before he could "enjoy her sumptuous apartment" and "drink the liqueurs and whiskeys"

with which it was "abundantly supplied" (V, 1924; *Twenties* 195–196).

2. **Monmouthbury:** Red Bank, New Jersey, where Wilson's family lived, is in Monmouth County.

2. **in those days bottled in bond:** Whiskey from a bonded warehouse was prized during Prohibition. Except for a visit to the speakeasy in this chapter and the nightclub in Chapter IX, the characters in the novel drink at home rather than in public places.

3. **of American popular music:** The narrator displays the susceptibility to popular music that rings through Wilson's other novels and his notebooks. In his first draft Wilson included a list of song titles similar to the lists he kept in his notebooks: "Tea for Two," "Lady, Be Good," "All Alone with [by] the Telephone," and "some Harlem numbers"— "Red Hot Mamma, Turn Your Damper Down" and "You Gotta Love Mamma Every Night or You Can't Love Mamma at All."

3. **rank befouled green wilderness:** Wilson frequently recorded his distaste for the depressing landscape between the Hudson River tunnel and Newark, which he described as a "country forever tarnished with a dingy haze of dampness and smoke" (IV, 1919; *Twenties* 21–23).

5. *hypnogogic:* The narrator is susceptible to obsession and compulsion in this drowsy state between sleeping and waking, a kind of self-hypnosis.

6. **a big square old house:** The four-square American house of the 1870s and 1880s constantly recurs in Wilson's writings, including the poem "A House of the Eighties" (1935) and the play *The Little Blue Light* (1950). He describes the prototype in Red Bank in the autobiographical essay "The Author at Sixty" (*A Piece of My Mind* 1956), where he discusses the relationship between his parents, echoed here, as well as his father's investment in Florida real estate.

8. **I had a cousin:** Elly, twenty-six, a second cousin once removed, with an alcoholic painter for a father and "red hair

and a round body," suggests Wilson's cousin Helen Augur, whom he mentions in the notes for another episode of the "Red Bank and Moscow Novel."

12. **You did not simply seem to mirror the other person:** In the Coney Island episode of *I Thought of Daisy*, the narrator goes through the first "symptoms" of transformation. He finds himself looking at a strange man, who turns out to be an image of himself in a mirror.

12. **The train passed beside a high green privet hedge:** A note at the end of the chapter refers to "XII-80" (1932; *Thirties* 193): "*Going down to Red Bank on the train* when the orchards were in bloom — the green country through a lace of pink and white."

12. **the border of maribou:** A soft, downy material popular in the 1920s.

13. **I had the sensation again, and even more completely than before:** In the earliest notes, for the "Red Bank and Moscow Novel," the narrator does not get off the train at this decisive moment but merely gets up to buy a newspaper.

15. **the station platform with MAYPORT:** Mayport, with its scene at the broad Navesink (or North Shrewsbury) River, is, like Monmouthbury, a fictionalized Red Bank.

CHAPTER I. A WEEKEND AT THE SHORE

When Wilson began this chapter, from the viewpoint of his new character, he had little to go on. His earliest notes for the 1920s section of his projected three-part novel had consisted only of "Swimming, love-making, gin." In his formal proposal he was more explicit, although the summary of his hero's experiences was still spare: "He is now actually the other man. Rapidly his former past fades into vagueness, vanishes; other memories are there instead." The new man and the woman, a divorcée, "spend the week-end at a summer hotel on the shore." In his first draft of this chapter of *The Higher Jazz*, Wilson developed his notes and outline into a story that could have been his own: the "Swimming, love-making," and drinking are accompanied by the woman's fear of being seen and the couple's hopes of marriage. He fed his memories with frequent entries from his notebooks of scenes at Sea Bright. His intimate descriptions of Caroline came from an assortment of notes on Margaret Canby.

When he came back to this chapter for the second draft, he knew how he wished to shape the character of Fritz Dietrich and direct the plot of *The Higher Jazz*. His imagination was in control as he incorporated his earlier marginalia and false starts. Fritz's Germanic background becomes clear; he talks about his musical tastes and theories. Fritz and Caroline have a past, a juvenile attachment from before the War.

17. **Archie Graves . . . was killed in the War:** Newt Graves is the name of a classmate killed in the war in "Reunion," Wilson's short story of 1927 (*New Republic* 27 April: 275–276; *American Earthquake* 145–151).

18. **large plutocratic estates:** The affluent community of Rumson separates Red Bank from Sea Bright, a small resort town that lies across the Shrewsbury River on a sandbar facing the Atlantic.

19. **it was right next-door to the hotel:** On loose sheets for 1929–1930, Wilson recorded a stay with Margaret in Sea Bright at the Peninsula House, a rambling galleried hotel of the 1880s destroyed by fire in 1986: "Arrived early in season before there was anybody to speak of in hotel — a drink in the corner room and went in the water" (*Thirties* 13).

20. **after almost exactly twelve years:** In his second draft, Wilson added the recollections of Fritz (still unnamed) of the intervening years between 1916 and 1928.

21. **a flapper of 1916:** Although "flapper" is commonly associated with the boyish silhouette and bobbed hair of the 1920s, the term was in use in the United States by 1910 for a "young and somewhat foolish girl" (H. L. Mencken, *The American Language*, Supplement I, Knopf, 1945, 515).

21. **I embraced her, still nude:** On the title page of his manuscript, Wilson has the note, "description of C. standing naked." In notes for the late spring of 1930, just before he and Margaret were married, Wilson wrote of her: "Margaret standing up with her clothes off in the sitting room at 12th Street — her round soft bosom (white skin). . . . Short little figure, when I'd embraced her without her shoes, standing up nude, fat hips and big soft breasts and big torso and tiny little feet she was standing on. . . ." (*Thirties* 6).

22. **that I thought at first was a boy:** This archetypal flapper, 1920s style, came from Wilson's notebook of 1926: "the girl on the sand whom I took at first for a boy — she had glossy black hair, boyish-bobbed, and wore a white shirt tucked inside a pair of black trunks like a boy" (VI; *Twenties* 311).

22. **I saw us as a most attractive couple:** Wilson inserted this paragraph in his second draft. Fritz reveals his vision of a gracious, sophisticated married life, in which he, "as a cultivated man," condescends toward the snobbish "smart people" around him. Although Wilson himself might have hoped for (but never achieved, either with Margaret or Mary McCarthy) the social success his character imagines, the vanity and sense of cultural superiority shown here belong to Fritz, and raise some problems for him in the course of the novel, particularly in his relations with Caroline.

24. *Ça empêche un peu:* That hinders a little, slows things up.

24. **we met with a contretemps:** In his second draft of this chapter Wilson added a major element when he introduced Nick Carter, Kay Burke, and others from a group resembling the wits who met for lunch at the Round Table at the Hotel Algonquin.

24. **Nick Carter:** Nick Carter, apparently named for the hero of more than a thousand dime-novels, is the bright but fatuous friend of Kay, the Dorothy Parker character; Wilson incorporates in him the qualities of Robert Benchley and an evangelical Yale man. In the margin Wilson referred to "Bench-

ley's Lindbergh joke," a cable to a friend in Paris asking whether the flyer had arrived on his famous flight (VIII, 1927; *Twenties* 367).

25. **the iron laws of life at Yale:** Nick deserted Fritz to become "a big man at college" by going out for Dwight Hall (the Yale YMCA) and the track team, as a consequence being "tapped" for Skull and Bones, the senior honor society.

25. **the exploiter of a trained seal:** Benchley began as a writer — a humorist and theater critic — but during the 1920s developed a career as a monologuist on the stage and in a number of short films. His subjects included sea lions, penguins, pigeons, and newts.

26. **We heard somebody playing the piano:** Wilson was recalling a night in Sea Bright in 1925, at dinner with John and Marion Amen. While they were eating clam chowder and fish, they "heard a woman playing a piano in the next room, which did not open into ours, a playing which began with jazz, then became troubled and desultory, finally lapsing altogether, till it commenced again in a soft strain of contented revery: MacDowell's 'From an Indian Wigwam'" (IV; *Twenties* 218). In his second draft Wilson added Fritz's aspiration to compose an American music to take the place of MacDowell's "flimsy nostalgic stuff."

27. **the bells in *Parsifal* or the bird in *Siegfried*:** In *Parsifal* (1882), real bells are rung offstage, accompanied by percussion instruments; in *Siegfried* (1876) the bird motif is represented by oboe, flute, and clarinet.

28. **because I had a German name:** Unlike Fritz, Wilson did go to a training camp and served in France in the medical corps, and later, in intelligence and at general headquarters. Writing at the time of the U.S. entrance into World War II, to which he was decidedly unsympathetic, he gives Fritz the opportunity to comment on the anti-German propaganda of World War I. This discussion was added in the second draft.

29. **Syd Lefanu:** Caroline's dissolute first husband, from New Orleans, suggests Jim Canby, Margaret's hard-drinking ex-

husband, and possibly Ted Paramore, Wilson's carousing friend who had been a suitor of Margaret. Syd's rather unusual name also belongs to Joseph Sheridan Le Fanu (1814–1873), Anglo-Irish author of mystery stories.

31. **About every ten yards we were confronted by a dead animal:** To reinforce Caroline's sense of vulnerability while on a weekend "escapade" among the imposing houses of wealthy acquaintances, Wilson combined two grotesque images from his notebooks: a passage on "run-over birds V, 89": "Birds killed and run over and over by motors on concrete motor roads until they are flattened into black inorganic patches on the black surface of the road" (1924; *Twenties* 191); and "*A cat run over by an automobile* on the Oceanic road (concrete with a stripe of tar down the middle and flattened out like a tiger-rug of fur and blood, in which only (*sic*) recognizable feature was a small series of ribs)" (VII, 1926; *Twenties* 321).

32. **Honest, I'm writing a darn good play, Fritz:** This is the first mention of Fritz's name in the text. Nick's intent to combine the dreamlike qualities of the Belgian dramatist Maurice Maeterlinck and the rationality of Shaw is patently ridiculous.

32. **There's going to be a new Christ:** Here Nick is given one of Donald Ogden Stewart's facetious lines: "there's a new Christ coming in America!" (VII, 1926; *The Twenties* 330). Stewart, a long-time acquaintance, was a member of the Algonquin circle who made Skull and Bones at Yale. He wrote *A Parody Outline of History* (George H. Duran, 1921), a number of screenplays, and an autobiography, *By a Stroke of Luck!* (Paddington Press, 1975).

33. **Well, shall we go back:** At the beginning of this paragraph, Wilson wrote in the margin: "He must think that if it weren't for their situation, they might be having fun with D. Parker, etc."

34. **Kay's Hiawatha:** More than ten years after writing this chapter, Wilson quoted Dorothy Parker's "Hiawatha" pun

in a retrospective comment in his notebooks of the 1920s (*Twenties* 45).

34. **She had already learned:** Margaret "followed my turns in bed all night" (Loose notes, 1930; *Thirties* 41); "she [was] always turning with me, no matter when or how many times I had wanted to turn." ("Death of Margaret," *Thirties* 241).

36. **New York is where we will live:** In his second draft Wilson added the conversation that deals with the qualities of Caroline's family and friends, potential issues between the couple.

36. *dolce far niente:* Sweetly doing nothing.

36-37. **Her father had never done anything:** Margaret "Had never known any men that worked before she married me — her father, Jim Canby [her husband], her uncles" ("Death of Margaret," *Thirties* 260).

37. **the Scotch Presbyterian of her mother's family:** Almost word-for-word from the notebooks (VIII, 1927; *Twenties* 366).

CHAPTER II. AN ESTATE ON THE HUDSON

Writing this chapter in his first draft, Wilson, who had run out of hints from his outlines, now conceived the character of Fritz. He provided his protagonist with a "German patrician" background, an enthusiasm for modern music, and a sister and brother-in-law with an estate on the Hudson. In the second draft, he developed an intergenerational debate between Fritz and his brother-in-law (twenty-three years his senior), of the kind he had shown a fondness for in his play *The Crime in the Whistler Room* (1924) and his dialogue between "A Professor of Fifty and a Journalist of Twenty-five" (*Atlantic Monthly* February 1926: 235-242).

The estate of Fritz's brother-in-law, at "Crolskill," was created out of Wilson's visit to his college friend Bill Osborn at Garrison, New York, in July 1936 (XVI; *Thirties* 625-636). Beginning with his first draft, Wilson worked the details of his extensive account into Fritz's description of the houses and grounds.

40. **Mary Cassatt:** The American impressionist (1845–1926) was noted for her paintings of mothers with their children.

40. **My brother-in-law Henry:** Wilson based the character of the cultured, civic-minded Henry ("Corliss" in his first draft) largely on William Church Osborn, Bill's father, whom he described in *A Prelude* (1967) as "almost too perfect" and "completely confident . . . in any situation," conveying his wisdom "without pomposity and with a certain bland ironic humor" (48).

40. **William Travers Jerome:** Jerome was the prosecutor of Harry K. Thaw for the murder of Stanford White, the lover of Thaw's wife, Evelyn Nesbit, in 1906.

41. **It was pleasant on the porch:** Henry's and Julie's house is described in images from Forest Farm, Bill Osborn's residence, among them "green summer chairs, two earth-colored bowls of white flowers set on a stone wall," a "triple arch," and the "variegated green finches," which bring to Fritz's mind the birdlike appearance of his sister (XVI; *Thirties* 625).

41. **Mrs. Al Smith's reply to . . . Queen Marie of Roumania:** Fritz is struck, in this exchange, by Henry's lack of snobbery toward Al Smith, Governor of New York and candidate for the Presidency in 1928. Smith's Irish Catholicism, New York accent, brown derby, and unfashionable wife made him the easy butt of upper-class condescension. Queen Marie of Roumania, the English-speaking granddaughter of Queen Victoria, toured the United States in 1926 to great fanfare. In *Enough Rope* (1927), Dorothy Parker had written that "love is a thing that can never go wrong; / And I am Marie of Roumania."

42. **I looked out over the smooth lawn:** This passage is adapted from Wilson's notebook, where the lawn "heaves so easily and daringly into a hillside" and the "gravel path" runs up the hill to the garden and tennis court (XVI; *Thirties* 625).

43. **The dark old hollow house:** Wilson is describing another house based on his family's home in Red Bank. Fritz's early

life in Pittsburgh supplies an American side to his character. Like Dos Passos (in *USA*), Wilson regarded Pittsburgh as one of the cities at the heart of industrial America. It was the home of his first wife, Mary Blair, who, like the young women of the 1920s in *I Thought of Daisy*, *The Crime in the Whistler Room*, and *This Room and This Gin and These Sandwiches* (1937), had come from Pittsburgh to make her way in New York.

43. **what kind of job Fred Lagrange has been doing:** Fred Lagrange is a "Village drunkard" in Wilson's notebook: "if you shaved him and cleaned him up, you could pass him off for a foreign nobleman — evidently had some very good French blood." Henry's comments on the Dutch migration are taken from Wilson's observations in a subsequent passage (XVI; *Thirties* 632).

44. **I gazed up the wooded hill:** Wilson noted that Bill Osborn's grandfather, the founder of the estate, had "built for himself, on the top of a wooded hill, a sort of castle with a pointed red tower and a long gingerbread-house roof"; one window was shining "as brightly as a lighthouse" against the clouds (XVI; *Thirties* 625, 634). In his first draft he made a comparison to a scene by Maxfield Parrish (1870–1966), the American painter of popular dreamlike landscapes.

45. **Already I was seeing myself:** Wilson added Fritz's dream of himself as a "patron of tolerated musicians" and a composer in the second draft.

47. **Poor Julie, through only three years:** Julie, born in 1894, would have "come out" before the war, in a world much different from Fritz's.

48. **the most somnambulistic place in the world:** Henry's comment on Fred Lagrange playing tenpins in the mountains, presumably with Hendrick Hudson and his crew, as in Washington Irving's "Rip Van Winkle," comes from Wilson's notebook reference to the Hudson Valley as "the most 'somnambulistic place' — unmistakably the origin of the Rip Van Winkle and the Sleepy Hollow stories" (XVI; *Thirties* 632).

49. **At dinner we talked about music:** In his second draft Wilson considerably expanded a brief discussion of Beethoven and Schoenberg into a platform for Fritz's theories.

49. **League for New Music:** A fusion of the International Composers' Guild and the League of Composers. In 1925 and 1926 Wilson reviewed the concerts of both groups, which were dedicated to giving a hearing to modern composers.

49. **what the moderns were up to:** Fritz explains to Julie the initial resistance to Debussy and Richard Strauss and the evolution from their music to Schoenberg's atonalism. Strauss's tone poem *Ein Heldenleben* (1898) was attacked for its autobiographical nature. Fritz finds the bitonality in *Also Sprach Zarathustra* (1896) and *Salomé* (1905) to be a source of Schoenberg's progression to atonality. Bitonalism was explored extensively in the 1920s, in the music of Stravinsky and the French composers. Fritz is accurate on the influence of Schoenberg as a teacher and theoretician.

50. *Wenn man A sagt, man müss B sagen:* If you accept A, B must follow.

51. **But Schoenberg *is* beautiful:** *Verklärte Nacht* (*Transfigured Night;* 1899) is a Romantic symphonic poem. Fritz's comments on Schoenberg's "later work" anticipate his reaction in Chapter VIII to *Pierrot Lunaire* (*Moonstruck Pierrot*). Here Wilson wrote in the margin: "The diatonic scale a law of nature," perhaps to remind himself of the extent of Schoenberg's innovations.

51. **attempted to read Spengler:** Fritz is attracted to the ideas of Oswald Spengler's *Des Untergang des Abendlandes* (*Decline of the West*), published in 1918–1922, just after Germany's defeat. He later defends Spengler's account of the decline of Western civilization in a discussion with Henry. The narrator of *Memoirs of Hecate County* has a strange dream after he falls asleep reading Spengler.

51. *sans ambages:* Without equivocation.

52. **Fred Stokes was a great man about town:** Fred was Caroline's uncle, Pete her father. Wilson gave Caroline's uncle

some of the history of Margaret's father, who had left her mother and married his mistress Daisy Green, a singer and dancer in the **Floradora Sextette** of the 1890s (VIII, 1927; *Twenties* 365). By the time they were married, he "had had softening of the brain" (IX, 1928; *Twenties* 434).

54. **She even cooks her own meals sometimes** and **to camp out:** Fritz's use of these expressions reveals that it is not so easy for him to break free from Henry's world of Edwardian affluence as he thinks.

57. **to buy the Impressionist painters:** To Fritz, the paintings of the French Impressionists, like Henry's suit and his mustache, are the visible signs of his refined *fin de siècle* tastes. Fritz does not consider Monet (1840–1926), with his "splatter of light paint," the equal of Renoir (1841–1919); he seems to be confusing Claude Monet with Edouard Manet (1832–1883), when he says that "Monet had been Renoir's master."

CHAPTER III. THE FIRST PARTY

From Chapter III on, Wilson had no early draft to work from. The manuscript shows many marginal reminders, comments, and revisions; he seems to have read back over his manuscript, but not consistently. In this chapter Fritz and Caroline embark on the social and cultural regime he envisioned as he was lying on the beach at Sea Bright.

59. **an old Kendall boy:** Nick is taking off on the old-school tie in the rambling burlesque style of Benchley.

59. **for two weeks to Florida:** Wilson's marginal notes indicate that he thought "Nassau or Bermuda" might be more appropriate. Fritz had expressed his distaste for Florida in Chapter I.

60. **an apartment on lower Fifth Avenue:** Perhaps intentionally, Wilson is evoking the living quarters of an earlier generation, with the carpeted stairways, high ceilings, and "elevators run by quiet Negroes." According to Elizabeth Hawes in *New York, New York* (Knopf, 1993), by the 1920s apart-

ment-hotels of this kind had been replaced on lower Fifth Avenue by commercial buildings.

61. **Eddie Frink:** A character derived from Cole Porter.

64. **Mary Stopes:** Phil can't get quite right the name of Marie C. Stopes (1880–1958), the English birth control advocate and author of the best-selling marriage manual *Married Love* (1918), that at one time was banned from the United States as obscene. Condoms were a subject that only the smart set would discuss in mixed company in the 1920s.

67. **Mrs. Moskowitz:** To Henry's irritation, Irving drops the name of Belle Moskowitz (1877–1933), social worker, reformer, and confidante of Al Smith.

68. **These two elements of New York gaiety:** One was Fritz's friends, Nick's circle of wits, the other Phil and the "cocktail set," Caroline's friends.

68. *cabotin:* A strolling player, a lowgrade actor, a mere mummer.

69. **Paroxysm marvellous city** and **Embezzle woman in the world:** From Wilson's conversation with Dorothy Parker in 1926: "Paroxysmarvellous city. Embezzle woman in the world! . . . Dorothy thought they were not right unless the word began the sentence" (VII; *Twenties* 344).

69. **Irvin S. Cobb:** Widely known and admired as a raconteur, he was an American humorist (1876–1944) born in Kentucky, author of innumerable short stories and other works.

69. **Jehuda Janowitz:** Although he is a virtuoso rather than a composer, Janowitz, the young Russian Jewish violinist, lives in the womanizing high style of his contemporary George Gershwin. In his essay "The Problem of the Higher Jazz," Wilson commented on Gershwin's efforts to place jazz in the setting of Italian opera. Wilson encountered an artist named Janowitz in Chicago in 1932 (XII; *Thirties* 294–295).

70. *cénacle:* A coterie.

70–71. **like one of those puny and tender and almost transparent tree-toads:** On the manuscript, Wilson had written: "Cole Porter like a tree toad." Like Frink, Porter (who would have been a few years ahead of Fritz at Yale) wrote the scores for musical comedies and hobnobbed with the international set, but on one hand he was not a cabaret performer, and on the other had no ambition to make his mark as a classical composer. Porter's social life and verbal wit are satirized in the portrait of Frink, through his "chic of the Riviera" and the philistine irreverence he shows towards "Schoenbergle and Stravinsk."

71. *assommant*: Wearisome, tiresome.

71. **Auric and Honegger:** George Auric (1899–1983) and Arthur Honegger (1892–1955), members of *Les Six*, a French group of anti-Romantic composers who gave concerts together from 1917 to the early 1920s.

73. **They take them down there on a special train:** Lefanu's description of his encounter, on a trip to Florida, with the evangelical real estate salesman was adapted from a story that had amused Wilson when he visited Louisiana in the spring of 1926. He absorbed this anecdote into the time frame of the novel, as he did many other events, although his notes show that he knew the Florida real estate boom was "down" by then.

> *Florida real estate.* They took prospective buyers on a special train out to a barren waste where it was proposed to sell them lots. Hastily thrown-together headquarters — indifferent lunch. But, after lunch, sudden eruption into room of real estate evangelist: he said there were three cardinal sins — fear, caution and delay — and gave them a sermon on those three heads. "And if Jesus Christ were alive today, he'd buy a lot right here!" — Inspirational effect on audience — several bought lots then and there. — When everybody else had gone, the promoter complimented the evangelist, who was mopping his brow like Billy Sunday: "That's a great line of bunk you've got there!"
>
> Evangelist: "Yes, it is. And I don't get paid half enough." (VI; *Twenties* 259)

76–77. **It is not long the singing and the laughter — Hope and desire and hate:** Lefanu is quoting "Vita summa brevis . . . ," the world-weary lines of the English poet Ernest Dowson (1867–1900).

78. *Perpetual Motion:* Mendelssohn's opus 119.

80. **they squash like overripe tomatoes:** Wilson returned to an anecdote about Lefanu that he did not develop, when he wrote in the margin, "What was it about the goldfish? — I see what you had to put up with."

80. **People who have careers are so boring:** This is Caroline's problem; if Margaret Canby felt this way, she was not so explicit.

80. **they would have had to let them in on the Mardi Gras:** Until the 1970s, Jews were generally excluded from the "krewes" of leading citizens who entered floats in the Mardi Gras parade (Calvin Trillin, "New Orleans Unmasked," *New Yorker* 2 Feb. 1998: 38–42).

81. **constituted a man a bounder:** Wilson's definition of a "bounder" is indicated by a reference to Dick Knight, a notorious ne'er-do-well of the 1920s from Dallas, who was a friend of Fitzgerald and John Amen (VIII; *Twenties* 355).

CHAPTER IV. BEDROOM CHIC

Having married off Fritz and Caroline and launched them socially, Wilson hoped to establish the intimacy of their life together before they began to grate on one another. He did not flesh out the next two chapters, probably because he could not find enough material for this idyll in the irregular regime of his life with Margaret. During their two and one-half years of marriage, they were frequently separated: Wilson would be writing in the East or exploring industrial tensions in the South or Midwest, while she was living with her young son in California. In Chapter IV Wilson drew upon notes from his trips to the Midwest in the 1930s, before and after Margaret's death, to broaden the novel's setting. He was trying to show Fritz's sensitivity to a region of the country from which he had grown apart and contrast his reactions with his responses to New York. These efforts were frustrated by the passages Wilson used, which depict the bleakness of the Depression and were incompatible with the early chapters of *The Higher Jazz*.

83. **Payne and Keller:** Wilson has found a job for Fritz, as a buyer for a drug company ("pain-killer") involved in the business culture of the Coolidge years. Although he is further from the center of the Boom Era than the stockbroker the author envisioned for the first part of *The Three Wishes*, Fritz's work is more conventional than that of the Greenwich Village writer of *I Thought of Daisy* or the art critic of *Memoirs of Hecate County*.

83. **bohunks:** Working-class people of immigrant stock, crude and uncultured, from "Bohemians."

83. **Chicago, which was becoming almost metropolitan:** In his notebook, "a big metropolis, as Chicago is now becoming" (XVI, 1936; *Thirties* 664); in a marginal note, "lumpy/hardhitting."

84. **Colosimo's:** "*Chicago.* . . . Colosimo's: girl with slightly Negroid cast of features, bright amiable as-if-intelligent brown eyes . . . did Mexican towel dance." (XII, 1931; *Thirties* 145–146).

84. **I enjoyed coming into Pittsburgh:** Wilson combined notebook entries from two trips to visit his ex-wife Mary Blair in the hospital. He labeled one of them with a marginal note, "XVI-58": "*Pittsburgh, September '37* . . . arriving early morning, the glitter of pearl and silver (in pearl light?) of the houses on the other side of the river on that barren and gritty hillside" (*Thirties* 694). He wrote, "Iron city — the signs," next to a passage taken from an entry of December 1936: "Those pretty and thin and sometimes little scrawny-necked Scotch-Irish-looking women — to which the West (Pittsburgh) had added sex appeal" (XVI; *Thirties* 664).

84. **my old school-friend Dick Keller:** Was he related to Fritz's employers?

84. **was opposed to Prohibition:** In the 1928 election, Smith was running as a "Wet," in favor of the repeal of Prohibition.

85. **the furnace of the setting sun:** Wilson wrote and crossed out, "like a steel furnace disgorging on the Jersey shore," an intestinal image for blast furnaces that had fascinated him so much that he copied it from one set of journals into another (V, 1922; *Twenties* 130; *Thirties* 76–77).

CHAPTER V. THE MASKED BALL

Wilson enlarged upon his notes and memories of Margaret for the description of the masked ball, a social apogee of the 1920s, and the sexual interlude, which becomes, for Fritz, a musical composition.

86. **The Sunday rotogravure section:** During the 1920s and 1930s, when color reproduction was rare, the Sunday newspapers included sections of pictures of noteworthy people and events, printed from a rotary press in sepia tones. ("You'll find that you're / In the rotogravure"— Irving Berlin, "Easter Parade," 1933.)

86. **wedded the Adriatic:** A play on the annual ceremony, when a ring was thrown into the sea. ("In Venice where the Doges used to wed the sea with rings"— Browning, "A Toccata of Galuppi's," 1855.)

88. **I had to put one of her legs up on the arm of her chair:** Wilson had written in "The Death of Margaret": "How she had looked at the Beaux-Arts ball: tiny red gloves and shoes so pretty, little strawberry girl, I made love to her in her costume in the gray armchair" (XII; *Thirties* 241).

88. *bouleversement:* Overturning.

89. **the way she tended to keep them open:** "She would lie with her sharp (bright) clear eyes open while I was making love to her" ("Death of Margaret," *Thirties* 252).

89. **I made her sit up:** Wilson is exorcising his guilt by repeating his own actions through Fritz. He wrote in "The Death of Margaret": "She said that I ought to have engraved

on my tombstone, You'd better go in and fix yourself up"
(*Thirties* 252) and "I have since wanted children but I evidently didn't . . . want any by her at that time, since I worried
about her not taking a douche" (*Thirties* 244).

CHAPTER VI. UNCLE TEDDY

The visit of Fritz and Caroline to Uncle Teddy was inspired
by Wilson's and Margaret's visit to her cousin Toby Waterman
("Cousin Watty") at Chestnut Hill, a fashionable section of
Philadelphia, in May 1930, shortly after they were married. For
this bizarre household, which suggests the family created by
the *New Yorker* cartoonist Charles Addams, Wilson elaborated
upon brief entries on the loose sheets he kept in 1929–1930 and
slipped into the pages of a nearly empty notebook.

90. **He lived at Chestnut Hill:** "*Chestnut Hill*. Gray stuccoish
    wall of piazza at right angle with the yellow floor that was
    level with the lawn, and wrought-iron cornice and trellises
    (or whatever they'd be called). . . . The house from outside:
    shiny yellow, new-painted . . . square cupola with fancy
    spikes like the tops of chessmen" (*Thirties* 9–10).
90. **the nymph Sabrina:** Nymph of the River Severn, who saves
    the Lady from the pagan god Comus in Milton's masque
    (1637).
90. **Sully portraits:** Thomas Sully (1783–1872) was a prolific
    English-born American painter, the creator of the famous
    cliché *Washington Crossing the Delaware*. Teddy's tastes, like
    Henry's, are an index to his age and personality. Sabrina, a
    Sully portrait, and (very briefly) a bust appear in Wilson's
    journals (*Thirties* 10).
91. **Agnes Harris, Uncle Teddy's housekeeper and compan-
    ion:** In looking back over the chapter, Wilson wrote on the
    first page: "a little more of Agnes!" He was tempted to ex-
    plore further the character, and possibly the intrigues, of
    this guardian of the hapless roué. In his list of characters, he
    called her Teddy's "girl-friend."

91. **bit down on her r's:** In his notes Wilson commented on the "hard Pennsylvania accent: r's" of "Edith," apparently a friend or relative at dinner in Cousin Watty's house (*Thirties* 10). He added the "lumps of soft coal."

91. **the butler . . . was a frog-faced man:** All Wilson had written in his notes was "butler, sinister, about to be fired" (*Thirties* 9).

92. **He was a soft little man in a dinner-jacket:** "Dinner jacket, ribbonless pumps on little feeble short legs in piazza chair" (*Thirties* 9). Short legs, like Caroline's (and Margaret's) ran in the family.

92. **patent leather pumps:** The "pattened-leather pumps" in Wilson's manuscript suggest that he confused "patent" with "pattens," which are shoes with wooden or metal soles.

92. **the syphilis from which Henry had told me his brother had died:** In Chapter II Henry had related the history of Teddy's brothers, both dead: syphilitic Fred (Caroline's uncle) and alcoholic Pete (her father). After introducing the heavy-drinking Cousin Teddy (from Toby Waterman), Wilson had thought he might combine him with Fred, and went back to make a marginal note next to Henry's account of Fred in Chapter II: "Change to fit Uncle Teddy, C's father's youngest brother./ Princeton?" As it stands, without the change, Uncle Teddy is the third and surviving brother of Caroline's father and uncle.

92. **Now he was rationed:** In the margin Wilson had written "keeping Teddy policed," echoing a note: "take up whiskey to room — kept Toby policed" (*Thirties* 9).

93. **He bowed from the waist:** "What it meant to have French manners — bow low from the waist . . . Cousin Watty as a beau of the nineties — Crowninshield — dropped his *g*'s" (*Thirties* 9–10). Frank Crowninshield was Wilson's editor at *Vanity Fair* in the early 1920s (*Twenties* 32–44, 49–50).

93. **"I'm not married," he said:** Wilson drew most of the next two paragraphs from his loose notes. They include: "He wasn't married but he didn't want Mr. Wilson to think that

he'd never kissed a girl — didn't like Margaret's bobbed hair: 'I've got a wig upstairs' . . . His pleasantries about trusting women . . . Men could do things that were winked at, but if women did them, the other women would talk about them. . . . Margaret's solid sinuous woman's young body, as she sat on the arm of his chair on the porch, contrasting with his pulpy thin-skinned decaying flimsiness — she kissed him, put her arm around him" (*Thirties* 11).

95. **I saw him as a corpse:** "My vision at dinner of Cousin Watty as a drowned body drifting to the bottom while three women worried him and took bites out of his face, which was rose-red with drinking and broken out" (*Thirties* 9–10).

95. **Most of this money had come from coal:** "*Margaret.* Her father had come from Philadelphia; her grandfather had made money in coal (which, for Margaret, was now giving out)" (IX, 1928; *Twenties* 434).

96. **He will if we go on like this:** Caroline continues to resent, as Margaret did, her husband's reluctance to have children.

97. **I was waked up by a terrible shriek:** Wilson successfully conveys the sense of "His blood-curdling shrieks when he had nightmares at night" (*Thirties* 11).

CHAPTER VII. BURLESQUE ON SATURDAY

Wilson originally juxtaposed, in a single chapter that I have divided into two, Fritz's visits on successive nights to a burlesque show and an avant garde concert. These experiences reinforce his awareness of the common qualities of popular and genteel culture.

98. **They had been friends and allies for years:** This is an accurate portrait of Dorothy Parker's relationship with Robert Benchley, a major source for the character of Nick. Parker and Benchley were still close but platonic friends in the period in which *The Higher Jazz* is set, but by then Benchley had begun to drink heavily and was acquiring a series of mistresses (*Twenties* 46–47; VII, 1926, 345; VIII, 1927, 402).

98. **Kay still lived with her husband:** Wilson is again using a situation from an earlier time: Parker and her husband, Edward, a stockbroker, were married in 1917, separated in 1924, and divorced in 1928.

98. **They had no children:** Kay Burke's personal regime and literary assignments are adapted, with a few changes, from Dorothy Parker's. Parker wrote drama criticism and from 1927 served as Constant Reader, the *New Yorker's* book reviewer. The hotel was the Algonquin, mentioned by name in Chapter IX. Wilson favorably reviewed a collection of Parker's poems for the *New Republic* in 1927 (19 Jan.: 256). In 1944, in "A Toast and a Tear for Dorothy Parker," among other things he compared her prose to Ring Lardner's (*New Yorker* 20 May: 75–76; *Classics and Commercials* 168–171).

99. **we decided to go to a burlesque show:** Wilson mined Fritz's description and comments from his reviews in the *New Republic* in 1925 and 1926. He must have reread the manuscript of this chapter before he prepared "Burlesque Shows" for *The Shores of Light* (274–281), since that essay includes revisions he had made for the text of the novel.

99. **Nick and Kay were connoisseurs:** Wilson assigns to Nick and Kay his own published opinions on the general decline of the old burlesque houses ("the present taste for . . . slim legs and shallow breasts") and the death of the Yiddish comedian Jack Shargel, whose likeness was drawn for the *Dial* (January 1920) by E. E. Cummings (*New Republic* 8 July 1925: 181; *Shores of Light* 276–277).

99. **The theater was on top of the building:** Wilson is thinking of the National Winter Garden, the locale for one of the burlesque shows he merged in this chapter.

99. **the act that was on when we first came in:** Wilson adapted the raucous comedy and the chorus line from an account of "Burlesque in its primitive form" at the Olympic theater on Fourteenth Street (*New Republic* 18 Aug. 1926: 365–366; notes in *The Twenties* 303–305). He took directly from his article the three characters in the first act: the "leader" with

"a Straw hat . . . a large square frame and . . . a wide set of strong white teeth" and "the other two, the low comedians," one with "the staring, honest, toil-toughened face of a German gnome or nibelung" and the other with "no human expression at all, but only a heavy and cretinous mask." He added a few details ("the cuties") and Fritz's personal comments ("I suppose it was the German in me that liked it").

101. **The next was a girl number:** The chorus line and the reaction of the audience are elaborated from the same article. The striptease is an addition. Nick's and Kay's "loud and ironical commentary," which follows, is drawn from his own comments.

102. **the Hype:** The Hype (Hyperion) was a theater in New Haven.

102. **a skit about Antony and Cleopatra:** This skit, "a curious piece of folk-drama," is from Wilson's review of "the Minsky Brothers' Follies" at the National Winter Garden (*New Republic* 8 July 1925: 181). Here he connects it with the earlier material by having "the man with the teeth" play the part of Caesar and the "Nibelung" be a servant of Cleopatra.

104. **the "Hype rush" of 1915:** Wilson adapted the riot at the Hyperion theater from the short story "After the Game (Princeton and Yale Ten Years Ago)" in the *New Republic* (45, 25 Nov. 1925: 16–17; *American Earthquake* 139–144). In the story, a Princeton man visiting New Haven for the Yale-Princeton game observes the undergraduate horseplay and dedicated piety at Yale. The struggle between these two impulses is acted out by a Yale junior; in the novel, Wilson replaces him with Nick, first in the riot and then in remorse. To Fritz, these actions explain the separation of Nick and himself, according to "the iron laws of life at Yale."

105. **the Transformation scene:** Plays derived from *Dr. Jekyll and Mr. Hyde* were popular in the late nineteenth and early twentieth century.

105. **the Taft lavatory:** The Taft Hotel, near Yale, was a New Haven landmark.

106. **Caroline was out of *rapport* with me:** When Wilson looked back over the manuscript, he felt that he had been too slow to develop the discord between Fritz and Caroline. He made this note at the head of the chapter: "Begin more from the point of view of F[ritz] and C[aroline]'s relation! / They must start off on the wrong foot that evening; she must be miffed about something."

106. **we had stayed late at the cocktail party:** Presumably a party before the visit to the burlesque show.

107. ***The Hound of Heaven:*** Nick recites the opening lines of this romantic confession (1891) by Francis Thompson (1859–1907), a Roman Catholic poet addicted to opium who enjoyed considerable popularity in the late Victorian period. Wilson admired Thompson, although he thought the writer's "religious emotion" was too "gushing" for his friend W. H. Auden (*The Sixties*, 1993, 262).

107. **a customer's man:** Often a term of ridicule in the 1920s for a stock or bond salesman (Mencken, *The American Language*, Supplement I, 1945, 577).

107. **She says she's in love:** Wilson changed this lover from the "young producer" of this chapter to the "Algonquin playwright" of Chapter IX, to the amateur archaeologist and stockbroker who appears in Chapters X–XIII.

108. **All that crowd are just incredibly provincial:** Wilson restated Fritz's opinion in the 1950s. In a retrospective section of *The Twenties* he characterized the Algonquin Round Table as "people from the suburbs and 'provinces,'" with a tone set "mainly by Benchley," who "were now able to mock from a level of New York sophistication" the provincial gentility in which they had grown up" (45).

108. **the Grand Street Follies:** In Fritz's view, the women in the cast of this satirical revue of the mid-1920s would be more intelligent and perhaps less available sexually than the chorus girls in the Ziegfeld Follies.

108. **Do you know how Nick ended up that evening:** Wilson continued the satire of Yale from "After the Game," in Fritz's

account of Nick humbling himself to his scholarly, high-minded roommate, than being tapped for the honor society.

109. **the Sheff men:** Students at the Sheffield Scientific School, where Yale undergraduates could get a bachelor's degree without classical languages, were looked down upon.

CHAPTER VIII. SCHOENBERG ON SUNDAY

Wilson found the inspiration for this scene at a concert of the International Composers' Guild on March 1, 1925. In the *New Republic* he contrasted the "unmistakable impression of bankruptcy . . . in spite of their courage and skill," he got from four "characteristic moderns"— Edgar Varèse (1883–1965), Henry Eichheim (1870–1942), Erik Satie (1866–1925), and Arnold Schoenberg (1874–1951)— to the natural way in which Stravinsky, the main subject of his essay, "energized and syncopated" Russian folk songs into "something analogous to jazz" (1 April 1925: 156–157; *American Earthquake* 104–108). Writing this chapter almost twenty years later, Wilson reconstructs the recital, omitting Varèse and Satie, adding Henry Cowell (1897–1965), and changing the compositions of Eichheim and Schoenberg. Schoenberg is the only figure he does not satirize.

111. **a woman in a corpse-white toque:** Wilson had used this description in another article in the *New Republic*: "At the concerts of modern music, the ladies wear auburn sideboards [literally "sidewhiskers"] and corpse-white toques" (17 March 1926: 105; *American Earthquake* 122).

112. **a disconcerting old man:** Wilson enriches the occasion with the anonymous presence of Edgar Rockland, the eccentric composer based on Charles Ives (1874–1954), who comes into his own in Chapter XIII. Although Ives was noted among his friends for his jaunty manner, by the 1920s he studiously avoided most musical performances. Wilson is probably enlarging upon physical descriptions from others; it is unlikely that he ever met Ives.

112. ***Godey's Lady's Book*:** The nineteenth-century magazine

that was the epitome of Victorian gentility. The musicians who have already played the first number provide a static caricature of concert performers.

113. **a man who had travelled in the East:** Eichheim, a neighbor of Margaret in Montecito (near Santa Barbara), had travelled to Asia and composed Oriental music. Wilson had commented on his use of "Chinese music instruments — series of gongs and bells, drums" and described his romantic temperament and tastes ("Death of Margaret," *Thirties* 253–254). The Javanese balalaika is an unlikely instrument.

113. *The Mikado* **and** *San Toy*: *The Mikado* was produced in 1885; *San Toy* (1899) was an operetta by Sidney Jones (1861–1946), British composer of *The Geisha* (1896), a work that enjoyed enormous success.

114. **The composer, who was also the pianist:** His techniques are those of Henry Cowell, who in his piano recitals struck clusters of notes with fists, forearms, and boards and plucked the strings. Cowell was an admirer and follower of Ives, whom he met in 1927. When the elderly man modeled on Ives (who himself used tone clusters) claps at this performance, Fritz, who had thought of him as "some old party who liked to play Brahms," is surprised.

116. **It was the song-sequence called** *Pierrot Lunaire*: *Pierrot Lunaire* (1912) is an atonal adaptation in *Sprechstimme* (speaking voice) by Schoenberg of twenty-one poems, translated into German from the French lyrics of the Belgian symbolist Albert Giraud (1860–1929). In "Moonstruck Pierrot" the lovesick young man, a late addition to the *commedia dell'arte* troupe, torments Cassander or Pantaloon, the father-figure of the *commedia* tradition.

116. **a Berlin cabaret:** Fritz is thinking of the Berlin cabarets of the Weimar Republic; Schoenberg had composed songs for Berlin cabarets of a much earlier time, in 1901.

116. *Verklärte Nacht*: The theme of *Verklärte Nacht* (*Transfigured Night*, 1899) is love and forgiveness.

116. **twisted, intensified as well as shattered:** Wilson wrote in

the margin, "squawking, hollow?" and had trouble deciding between "viola" or "cello"; "mysterious" or "nocturnal"; and "ruminative" or "ominous." Speaking through Fritz, Wilson does not deal with Schoenberg's Romantic compositions, which he had called a "sifting of ashes" in his 1925 review, but turns to *Pierrot Lunaire*, a subject of his continuing interest. In the *Baltimore Sun* (19 June 1923: II, 19) he had written that Schoenberg's later work revealed "the man of unusual state driven at last himself to snarling and rasping by the hideousness of the modern world," and observed that Schoenberg "should have written a musical setting" for *The Waste Land*, "which his own work closely resembles." In later years he was to write about Schoenberg in the *New Yorker* (14 April 1951: 129–134) and in "Every Man His Own Eckermann" (*New York Review of Books*, Spring 1963, 1–4; *The Bit Between My Teeth*, 1965, 76–97).

116. **I looked to see what the song was:** The dissonance and the cruel, eccentric behavior of Pierrot in *Pierrot Lunaire* remind Fritz of a scene in the burlesque show — the bullying of the dwarf by the straight man in the straw hat.

117. ***Gemeinheit:*** Mean trick.

117. **Minsky's burlesque:** Wilson had not used this name in the previous chapter, although the Antony and Cleopatra skit ("the cockroaches calling") was taken from his review of a Minsky show.

117. **this Verlainesque *fin de siècle* Pierrot:** Wilson had discussed Paul Verlaine's torments at the hands of Arthur Rimbaud in *Axel's Castle* (1931) 272–275.

117. **But one would have to have Stravinsky:** In the 1925 essay that incorporated his review of the four moderns, Wilson praised Stravinsky's dynamic rhythms, which seemed to have been "heard first in the composer's own head," and observes that *Le Sacre du Printemps*, which "presents a fertility rite of prehistoric Russia," has "stimulated its hearers to talk about both jazz and machinery."

117. **writing the great American ballet:** In 1924 Wilson himself

had written the libretto for *Cronkhite's Clocks*, a ballet for Charlie Chaplin, to music by Leo Ornstein (1892–   ), a "futurist" composer, friend of Varèse and Paul Rosenfeld. The Chaplin character, "Sensitive Casper," is an office boy driven to distraction by his working-place. The boss, Mr. Cronkhite ("sickness") has "a time-clock dial for a face and time-clock indicators for hands." Frustrated and despairing, Casper is brought to life by the mellifluous jazz rhythms of a dance led by a Negro porter; soon the entire clock-headed staff join the party, which swells into a "bacchanalia, a bursting-out of regimented souls." The dance rises to a frenzy, and ends when everyone falls to the floor "exhausted and burnt out," and Casper collapses and dies. Wilson wrote John Peale Bishop that the ballet was scored for "full orchestra, movie machine, typewriters, radio, phonograph, riveter, electromagnet, alarm clocks, telephone bells, and jazz band" (*Letters on Literature and Politics*, 1977, 117). But this ballet was never produced. Despite a trip to California, financed by the Swedish Ballet, Wilson was unable to recruit Chaplin for the part. He later noticed that Chaplin had used a similar idea in *Modern Times* (1936; *The Twenties* 153–154, 158–159). Wilson printed the libretto in the collection *Discordant Encounters* (1926).

118. ***O alter Duft aus Märchenzeit*:** Oh, ancient scent from fabled times! The last line of *Pierrot Lunaire*.

118. **inversion and cancrizans and . . . "crabs":** An inversion is the use of a theme upside-down; a cancrizan or crab is the use of a theme backwards. Both of these devices of atonal music were used as early as the Middle Ages and Renaissance.

118. **I had to laugh, too:** Wilson must have recalled his experience of 1929: "Discovery on Christmas Eve of crabs — shaved myself and spent evening removing them" (Loose notes; *Twenties* 535).

119. **Paul Whiteman:** Irving reveals his vanity and the thinness of his musical tastes when he tries to demonstrate his inside knowledge of Paul Whiteman, the prominent dance-band

leader misnamed the "King of Jazz." In a review of a 1926 concert at Carnegie Hall, included in his essay "The Problem of the Higher Jazz," Wilson observed that Whiteman's music, so pretentiously described by Irving, lost all its dance-hall vitality in a concert setting. In the 1925 essay that evoked the recital in this chapter, Wilson said that Whiteman lacked the "rousing and elliptic effect" that Stravinsky obtained from Russian folk songs.

119. **Dutch Schultz:** The professional name of Arthur Flegenheimer, the New York gangster who controlled the rackets in "numbers" gambling and bootleg liquor during Prohibition. He was murdered in 1935.

120. **Chloe:** Wilson wrote "Swanee River," then changed Irving's choice to the sultry popular song of 1927, "Chloe," the "Song of the Swamp."

121. **the Schirmers:** The prominent family of music publishers.

121. **improvising on a Charleston tune:** The notion of combining "a Charleston tune" with atonal "Schoenbergian harmonies" might seem far-fetched but it is at the heart of Fritz's preoccupation.

CHAPTER IX. "HELLO, SUCKER!"

Fritz meditates upon power and impotence in the present age, as seen in the microcosm of the nightclub. He is becoming disillusioned: "There isn't an idea or an ideal left in the United States. . . ." He becomes seriously angry with Caroline for the first time in his jealousy over Tom Burrell, who had begun the chapter as an amiable character whom Kay found attractive. When he reread the chapter, Wilson reminded himself, "Tom. B. ought to be brought out a little more. This ought to be preceded by a touch of his business life," but he chose instead to drop him from the novel.

122. **Kay, who was partly Irish:** Wilson may have been thinking of Mary McCarthy, although the rest of the description here is of Dorothy Parker.

123. **at the corner of Thirty-Fourth Street and Park:** In the conservatively fashionable section known as Murray Hill. The Degas was another sign of Henry's turn-of-the-century taste.

123. **what seemed to me a lack of enthusiasm:** Wilson had set this up at the beginning of the chapter, when he made the note, "Caroline doesn't want to spend summer in Julie's house." Caroline was uncomfortable with Julie, who was slow to approve of her.

123. **she ought to see Dixie McCann's:** Dixie McCann's is the Texas Guinan Club. Mary Louise Cecelia Guinan, known as Texas Guinan (1889–1933), a chorus girl from Waco, is generally credited with opening and popularizing the nightclub in New York during the Prohibition Era. She was known for her customary greeting of "Hello, sucker!" (*New York Times* 6 Nov. 1933: 19). After "Dixie McCann's," Wilson had written but decided not to include, "and Durante, Clayton and Jackson." The comedian Jimmy Durante had a popular nightclub act with Lou Clayton and Eddie Jackson in the 1920s.

123. **If you'll lend me some money:** Fritz's salary was not equal to his social position; though Wilson had a small inheritance, he was always likely to be borrowing.

124. **my arrogant German authority:** Fritz's surprisingly blunt self-appraisal is revealing of Wilson's view of the German character, with perhaps the shadow of his feeling that he himself was given to autocratic behavior.

124. **then Nick noticed a playwright and shot over to him:** Wilson inserted this line and changed "producer," from Caroline's description of Kay's lover in Chapter VII, to "playwright," an echo of Charles MacArthur, with whom Dorothy Parker had an affair in 1922. Later, Fritz refers to this character as an "Algonquin playwright"; MacArthur was on the fringe of the Algonquin circle.

125. **Now this little girl:** As he wrote the next two paragraphs, Wilson was looking at the Texas Guinan section of his article on "Night Clubs" in the *New Republic* of 1925 (9 Sept.: 71).

He made minor changes in the wording, adding Fritz's personal reactions ("Nothing, certainly, could be more commercialized, nothing could be more regimented").

125. **Charley Schwab's backyard:** An entire city block surrounding the massive chateaulike mansion of the industrialist Charles M. Schwab (1862–1939), at Riverside Drive and West Seventy-Third Street.

126. **a few reckless aviators:** Fritz is referring to Lindbergh and Richard Byrd, the Antarctic explorer, whom he called "audacious sportsmen" (*Shores of Light* 338, 432).

126. **this blacksmith we've just put in the White House:** A slur on the engineer Herbert Hoover, who was inaugurated on March 4, 1929.

127. **I've been working on a darn good play:** Nick's enthusiasm for his play and his evangelical bent, the result of his conversion at Yale, become even more embarrassing than they were when he collared Fritz in Chapter I with many of the same lofty clichés. The idealistic play was Nick's own response to the gaudiness of the Boom.

127. *The Last Days of Pompeii:* This 1834 novel by Edward Bulwer-Lytton (1803–1873) portrays the decadent life of the Roman empire before the city is destroyed by the eruption of Vesuvius.

127. *The Passing of the Third Floor Back:* A sentimental, moralistic play of 1908 by Jerome K. Jerome (1859–1927).

128. **pretentious and predatory gyp-joint:** Wilson's change from "vulgar" to "predatory" brought his vision of the nightclub into sharper focus.

128. **Joe Friganza:** Wilson has invented an act inspired by what he calls the "Dadaist" or nonsense humor of the comedian Joe Cook (1890–1959). In a review of Gilbert Seldes's *The Seven Lively Arts* (1924), he explained that Cook's kind of humor expresses "the bewildering confusion of the modern city and the enfeeblement of the faculty of attention" (*Dial*, September 1924: 244–250; revised in *Shores of Light* 156–164). Wilson's enthusiasm for the comedians of the 1920s,

from Charlie Chaplin to Will Rogers, is demonstrated in the "Follies" section of *The American Earthquake*.

128. **Cartier's:** The luxurious jewelry store still housed in a mansion at Fifth Avenue and Fifty-Second Street.

129. **Harry Richman and Al Jolson:** Al Jolson, the star of *The Jazz Singer* (1927), the first sound film, and Harry Richman were essentially singers rather than comedians.

130. **a pantomime of waltzing:** Wilson extracted from his article on "Night Clubs" the description of a "dance with an invisible girl" by Johnny Hudgins, "the Negro jazz dancer and pantomimist" at the Club Alabam: "nothing he does is better than the bad few moments he passes when he has been cut in on and has lost her, and is left alone on the dance-floor dodging imaginary couples — disappointed, bewildered, gaping."

130. **As the night was stretching later and later:** Wilson enlarged upon further short passages from his account of Texas Guinan's: "As the night is stretched later and later, the excitement becomes more and more violent"; "the great closed glowing peony melts, . . . swollen and hypnotic to drunken eyes"; "the brawlers are summarily torn up by the roots and put through into the street with the ruthlessness and dispatch of a Renaissance prince making away with a conspirator."

130–131. **Yes, I knew what I knew: . . . and I was lifted above it:** Wilson inserted this observation into the text to emphasize Fritz's sense of superiority to the impotence of the frantic, empty revelry going on around him.

CHAPTER X. A SUMMER AFTERNOON

When Wilson wrote this chapter (in the spring of 1942, as one of his notesheets shows), he seems to have decided on the final shape of his novel. He had settled on the final names for most of his characters. He seemed to be speeding toward a conclusion as he combined a sequence of events concerning Kay Burke into a single disjointed chapter, which I have divided into three.

The author brings the Algonquin set to a visit on the Hudson with some friends of Scott Fitzgerald. The house of the Burnets (near Henry's and Julie's), where this chapter takes place, is in fact, as Wilson wrote in the margin, "Scott's house at Baltimore." The details are derived from a 1933 visit to Fitzgerald, who was then writing *Tender Is the Night*. In *The Higher Jazz*, Sam and Lyddie Burnet are the hosts. For Scott, Wilson substitutes a pipe-smoking Princeton man who complaisantly serves drinks and "like[s] to stay out of things"; but Lyddie resembles Zelda, as Wilson remembered her in his notebook, "subdued, a plaintive note in her voice" (XIII; *Thirties* 323). (Andrew Turnbull recalls her as "a boyish wraith of a woman" at this time; *Scott Fitzgerald*, Scribner's, 1962, 230.) To Fritz, Lyddie is an ephemeral spirit, a "sea-anemone" that turns into "a dull little knob of jelly" when the tide is out. Wilson adds the outdoorsy, tennis-playing Dave Powell and his wife, the snobbish, acerbic Grace (in the mold of Brownie l'Engle, an acquaintance from Cape Cod whose malice rings through Wilson's journals). Kay Burke moves toward the center of the story as a self-conscious, neurotic, but nonetheless appealing intellectual. She is overwhelmed by the empty grace of Lyddie Burnet, as Dorothy Parker was by the Fitzgeralds and Gerald and Sara Murphy. The host and hostess, the Burnets, inherit the social presence of the Murphys, described by Wilson on pages adjacent to the notes on the Fitzgeralds (*Thirties* 323, 324).

133. **Bill Shippen, who was her brother:** Kay's lover makes his first appearance by name, after his obscure beginnings as "a young producer" in Chapter VII and "an Algonquin playwright" in Chapter IX ("that night we had gone to Dixie McCann's"). For the rest of the novel, he is Lyddie's brother, a self-absorbed Princeton man without professional commitment, who, as it turns out, finds an avocation in archaeology after a stint in a brokerage office. As Wilson telescopes a number of Dorothy Parker's experiences into Kay's adventures, he uses John Garrett, the Wall Street type who didn't

love back, as the model for Bill. In 1933 he had described John Garrett as "Dorothy Parker's infatuation" and thought of "merging" him "in a character," with a "young man in Chicago who thought Hoover had done a good job" (XIII; *Thirties* 327).

133–134. **Lyddie in pink:** Fritz's image of Lyddie suggests Zelda, and there is the shadow of Nick Caraway's impression of Daisy Buchanan and Jordan Baker reclining on an "enormous couch" when he first encounters them in *The Great Gatsby*.

134. **but her round black eyes . . . in the room:** Wilson inserted in the margin this description, which fits Dorothy Parker.

136. **these people were not so rich:** Kay, like Dorothy Parker — and, of course, Fitzgerald — was fascinated with the rich. Wilson thought the Burnets were over-extending themselves, like the Fitzgeralds. He wrote in a note, "They must live on Park Ave. and this uses up a lot of their income."

136. **a good-looking blond girl but otherwise terrible:** Wilson wrote "terrific" here, but in view of the "but" and the character of Grace that emerges, he evidently meant to write "terrible."

138. **rolling the courts:** In the 1920s and 1930s, private tennis courts were usually clay.

139. **that trip in the Southwest we took:** Wilson and Margaret had visited New Mexico in 1931 (*Thirties* 91–110). At the end of *Memoirs of Hecate County* the narrator escapes from the sterility of the New York suburbs to the Southwest with Jo Gates, the second, lesser Margaret.

141. **the 1880 stair, with its carved and light-varnished newel-posts:** In *Scott Fitzgerald* (209–210) Turnbull describes "La Paix," the "dim" and "cavernous" house near Baltimore built by his grandfather in 1885; Fitzgerald rented it from Turnbull's parents, who lived in another house on the grounds. Wilson's visit in the spring of 1933 came six months after Margaret's death. In the margins of his manuscript, he copied some of his notes: "XIII-82/1886/newelposts — and

fancy bulbed railings and big landing/perforated cut-out piece of woodwork, above it, that corresponded to the balustrades, making out of the whole thing a light-brown woodwork jigsaw lace — the clock set into the woodwork below, with, in gothic, Our Times, etc. = Look out at an old stable? — see XIII, 83." His memory was also sparked by other notes, such as his observations of Fitzgerald's daughter Scottie, the "little girl" who played on the "big landing," and his comments on the "richness and confusion of houses of this period" (XIII; *Thirties* 322–323).

143. **cure your social embarrassment:** Advertising in the 1920s and 1930s frequently emphasized social acceptance — the avoidance of halitosis (bad breath) and "B.O." (body odor). Wilson jotted down advertising slogans in his notebooks.

146. **to peg the exhilaration:** In the sense of "to pin down" or "to check."

CHAPTER XI. THE RATSBYS IN RESIDENCE

In the summer before the Crash, Wilson continues to parade the self-destructiveness of the wits of the Boom Era and their friends, this time at the house where Fritz and Caroline are staying while Henry and Julie are away. Fritz is caught up in a wicked variation of the puns, word-games, and charades that were popular among the Algonquin set on summer weekends amidst drinking, swimming, tennis, and croquet. The participants impersonate a "Ratsby" family, with identities "in some way now more real to them than their own," which allowed them to "display [their] wits with the absolute certainty of applause." Although this world was "complete and self-contained in its logic," a "certain strain behind everything began to come through into the fantasy itself."

148. **As Bill had no job at that time:** On a sheet of note paper clipped to his manuscript, Wilson wrote an idea for this chapter: "*Difference between Bill Shippen and Fritz*: Fritz

thinks that, whereas Bill has never even had the real impetus to take anything seriously — his archaeology —*he* has at least had his music. He thinks this before he begins to work at the piano the morning that Nick interrupts him."

148. **the Hiawatha-nice-girl game:** See note on **Kay's Hiawatha**, Chapter I.

149. **poltergeists in the character of King Carol of Roumania:** Carol II was a playboy king, son of Queen Marie, who in 1929 was living in exile with his mistress Magda Lupescu.

149. **a character called Mrs. Ratsby, and Bill became Mr. Ratsby:** In the note clipped to the beginning of the chapter, Wilson wrote: "Ratsbys talk about poisoning birds." In the manuscript, Wilson added "bootleggers" and "thieves" to "poisoners." In addition to the hint of Fitzgerald's *Gatsby*, the name reflects in an unexpected way Wilson's peculiar interest in rats. In his satiric "Rat Letters" (*Sixties* 895–901) and his poem "The Rats of Rutland Grange" (*Night Thoughts*, 1961, 252–261), both from later years, he finds the rats more attractive than most human beings, let alone the insidious Ratsbys.

152. **Christian fellowship:** Wilson changed this from "friendliness" to emphasize Fritz's frustration at Nick's evangelical bent.

153. **Eustace** and **Uncle Felix:** Fritz switches between roles that exploit sides of his own identity of which he is not particularly proud: the man in the drug business and the "cultivated German."

156. **Melisande letting down her hair:** From the opera *Pelléas et Mélisande* (1902), adapted by Debussy from the play by Maeterlinck.

CHAPTER XII. LIFE ALWAYS LET YOU DOWN

This is the last section of the rambling chapter that I have divided into three parts. On the brink of the Crash, it is clear to Fritz that Kay and Nick are getting nothing out of the age of prosperity: "they weren't making good in those days when money meant power and splendor and there was so much money going . . . everybody was frankly in pieces."

159. **I found her propped up:** Whatever the cause of her hospital stays — appendectomy, abortion, or suicide attempt — Dorothy Parker, propped up in bed, turned her friends' visits into cocktail parties (Marion Meade, *Dorothy Parker*, Random House, 1988, 160–161). Fritz's description comes from a series of notes Wilson made about Parker and the Round Table group in 1926. When Wilson visited her in the hospital (after a suicide attempt, although he does not say so), "She [had] got thin; her intelligence and sensibility came back into her eyes" (VII; *Twenties* 344–347).

160. **to head her off from self-pity:** The actress Margalo Gilmore called Parker a "weeping spaniel" (*The Ten-Year Lunch: The Wit and Wisdom of the Algonquin Round Table*, ed. Donna Marino, Aviva Films, 1987, 55 min.).

161–162. **ever since that night at your sister's:** Wilson is thinking of the dinner at Julie's before the visit to the nightclub (Ch. IX), evidently confusing Bill with Tom Burrell, whom he had once thought of as a possible love interest for Kay.

162. **she "came into the room like a duchess":** Wilson wrote in a notebook for 1926: Benchley "would say, 'She enters the room like a duchess.'" He also reported Parker's view: "his girl an awful little whore, unfaithful to him" (VII; *Twenties* 345).

162. **I sat there and drummed on the table:** Nick's humiliating adventures resemble Joe Friganza's act in Chapter IX; in his review of Seldes's *The Seven Lively Arts*, Wilson had compared Benchley's nonsense humor with that of Joe Cook, the inspiration for Friganza. He described Benchley's antics in his notebook: "Drumming with fingers on table at Tony's — he stopped when people at opposite table indicated disapproval. 'All right, then: I'll stop' he said that he said to him-

self. '*But the day will come* when you'll come to me on your knees and *ask* me to drum!!!'" (VII, 1926; *Twenties* 346–347).

163. **almost a triumph over death:** At this point Wilson considered introducing other characters before Fritz left the hospital ("other people: man with red face") but decided not to expand the scene.

164. **It isn't appendicitis:** Dorothy Parker had an abortion in 1922 as a result of an affair with Charles MacArthur; in 1928 she c d have an appendectomy.

165. **a little boy who was a patient across the hall:** In his notebook for 1926, Wilson wrote of Parker: "she told me . . . when I went to see her in the hospital" about "the little boy who marched up and down the halls with horseshoes, and then they operated on him and nothing more was heard" (VII; *Twenties* 346).

CHAPTER XIII. DECEMBER 1929: BLEEDING TO DEATH

Wilson was determined to end the novel with an exposé of the falsity of American life in the 1920s, epitomized by the Crash. In his original plan for *The Story of the Three Wishes*, the stockbroker-protagonist would have been disillusioned and converted to Communism. Although Fritz in *The Higher Jazz* is primarily an onlooker, he too is disillusioned: his musical disappointments and domestic frustrations coincide with the economic collapse.

The author hoped to set the stage for these culminating disasters with an introduction to the chapter on the results of the Crash. In the first half, Wilson slipped out of Fritz's persona into his own, pointing out that the Crash was the culmination of the "general deflation" that had already taken place in American life. In politics, the "darkness of political night" had closed down on the Republican Party. In literature the "perfectly blank . . . intellectual landscape" had been dominated by the New Humanism of Irving Babbitt and Paul Elmer More. In music a "sterile . . . retrenchment" was underway: Stravinsky was returning to Bach and the Germans were ignoring Schoenberg. In the second half of his essay, Wilson reverted to Fritz's narrative, taking up the stories of three individuals "convulsed by crisis" after the Crash: a "little man" in his office who discovered that his mistress was a call-girl; then Fritz's Aunt Sophie's husband, who went bankrupt in Europe; and Martha Gannett, a friend of Caroline's (introduced in Ch. III), whose antiques business and personal life were in a bad way.

The next stage of Wilson's plans for the last chapter was a one-page outline, to which he stayed fairly close until a new conclusion unfolded in his mind.

167. **The stock market crash at the end of October:** Wilson preserved only this paragraph from his original introduction to the chapter. Fritz is speaking with the same gratification at the collapse of the Boom that Wilson was to take in "Literary Consequences of the Crash" (*Shores of Light* 492–499).

167. **Eddie Frink was going to do a piano sonata:** This satirical counterpart of Cole Porter had talked about his classical aspirations in Chapter III. Wilson is preparing to contrast implicitly the cabaret rhymer who aspires to compose serious music with the classical composer who uses popular tunes in his works.

170. **He told us about Huey Long:** Huey Long, who came from a town near Shreveport, in the Protestant "redneck" part of Louisiana, was elected governor in 1928; in 1932 he resigned and was appointed to the Senate. He was assassinated in 1935.

170. **Let me tell you about Ed Rockland:** In this paragraph on Rockland's background, Wilson is faithful to the music and career of Charles Ives. Throughout his outline for the chapter, he refers to "Ives," rather than Rockland: "He explains to Eddie about Ives. . . . Little concert to do something for American music." Ives, like the artists Albert Pinkham **Ryder** (1847–1917) and Thomas **Eakins** (1844–1916), ignored European masters in his attempts to capture the essence of American life: he was "polytonal and polyrhythmic" before Schoenberg and Stravinsky. Wilson portrays directly the in-

fluence and techniques of Ives's father, leader of the town band in Danbury, Connecticut, and Ives's own ability to discomfit his teachers; he composed his *First Symphony* (1898) while he was a student at Yale. (In this description, the only fictional change is from Connecticut to New Hampshire, i.e., "Rock-land".) Wilson had almost certainly learned about Ives from Rosenfeld and Copland and had heard his music at the composers' groups in the 1920s. At the time this chapter was written, in 1942, Ives's compositions were widely played. Since that time Ives has been the subject of a number of biographies and monographs as well as an unpublished novel reported in Vivian Perlis's *Charles Ives Remembered* (Yale UP, 1974, 168–169).

171. **a patent lawyer with a double personality:** Ives earned a substantial living, not as a patent lawyer, but as a manager of the Mutual Insurance Company in New York City. In the margin Wilson added: "must try to make him sound like a fantastic and Proustian character."

172. **I found Kay in the bathtub with her wrist cut:** In the outline, Nick found a note in Kay's apartment. The text here is closer to Dorothy Parker's suicide attempt in January 1923, a month after her abortion. She cut her wrists and was found in the bathroom when a restaurant delivered a meal she had ordered (Meade 106–107). She made other attempts: in 1926 (with Veronal, like Hazel in her story "Big Blonde"), when Wilson visited her in the hospital, and in 1932 (barbiturates).

173. **Dan Beard:** Dan Beard (1850–1941), founder of the Boy Scouts of America, was the author of the *Boy Scout Handbook*.

176. **Rockland had already arrived:** Wilson exaggerates Ives's eccentricities (the tailed coat) in re-creating him as Edgar Rockland, although he stays close to Ives's "avuncular" yet curmudgeonly demeanor. Ives regarded musical societies as European and "sissified," even though such groups were the first to play his works.

176. **what this country needs is more credit:** In his outline

Wilson had written, "talks about currency scheme," and in the margin, "I[ves]. It stands to reason, don't it?" presumably an example of his advocacy. Wilson makes Rockland a proponent of the economic theory of Social Credit, originating in England in the 1920s, by which citizens are paid "dividends" for the productivity of their society. Ives was disturbed by the unequal distribution of wealth in the United States and in one of his tracts argued for a limit on personal income, but most of the time he proselytized, at his own expense, for world government and for government by referendum along lines later advocated by Ross Perot.

178. **which allows these investment trusts:** Rockland is referring to conventional financing, based on what he regards as an absence of tangible assets, as opposed to Social Credit.

178. **teratology:** The study of monstrosities.

179. **Erik Satyr and *les Six* and *tutte quante*: *tutti frutti*:** This time Eddie plays on the name of Erik Satie. Eddie turns *tutte quante* ("full quantity") into a joke: "tutti frutti," an ice cream flavor.

179. **Hindemith's sonata for violin and piano:** A neo-classical sonata composed in the early 1920s.

180. **Meet them at the door:** Wilson had planned, in his outline, to have Kay keep Fritz away from the performance: "Just before Ives number, Fritz has to go downstairs about Kay," and "When he gets back Ives has finished playing and goes back to boring people about currency." Had it been written this way, Fritz would not have heard Rockland's music.

180. **New Hampshire pastorals:** Rockland's compositions resemble those of Ives in oversimplified form, almost in parody.

181. ***Sabbath Morning*:** Wilson may be thinking broadly of *The Camp Meeting*, Ives's *Third Symphony* (1904), in which he quotes several hymns (but not "Onward Christian Soldiers," which appears elsewhere) and the "Children's Day Parade."

182. ***Saturday Night in Nashua*:** This piece suggests the secular

side of Ives's *Second Symphony* (1902), which he later re-garded as a "joke." Ives quotes "Columbia! the gem of the ocean," along with "Bringing in the Sheaves" and "Turkey in the Straw." In Wilson's notebook for 1965 (his only writ-ten reference to Ives outside of this novel), he comments on the symphony's "successful" mixture of "semi-sacred music originally composed for the organ, alternating with the comic and the rowdy," including "motifs from Beethoven and Brahms" (*Sixties* 471).

183. **Eddie left, and most of the New Music contingent left:** In his outline, Wilson had planned to have Ives [Rockland] leave as well, in which case the ending would have been different.

183. **He got to talking to Bill Shippen about New Mexico:** In the margin Wilson added, "?? The Zuñi Creation Myth — F.H. Cushing." Wilson was acquainted with the writing of Frank Hamilton Cushing (1857–1900) on the Zuñis before he used them in his account of the Zuñi Pueblo in New Mexico in 1947 (*New Yorker* 9 April 1949: 62, 65–73, 16 April 1949: 80–94; *Red, Black, Blond and Olive*, 1956). The earliest version of this visit is printed in *The Forties*.

184. **Hugo Wolf:** A composer (1860–1903) of dark Romantic songs. Brownie reveals the naïveté of his taste.

187. **We're all bleeding to death:** Rejected ideas in the last two lines of Wilson's outline further reveal how, as he wrote the chapter, he changed the ending. "Fritz delivers his lecture about people cracking up" shows that he had thought of having Fritz, rather than Rockland, sum up the Boom Era. (In one of the notes on the manuscript, Wilson referred to "Fritz's speech about the times.") In the very last line, "Feels for the first time the impulse to strangle Caroline," Wilson continued to remind himself that the tension between Fritz and Caroline needed to come to a head. He could not carry through this plan, perhaps because he identified Caroline so closely with Margaret.

THE GENESIS OF THE NOVEL

SOME CORRECTIONS

Edmund Wilson's plans for *The Story of the Three Wishes*, the genesis of this novel, have been printed in his journals of *The Forties*, edited by Leon Edel (Farrar Straus, 1983, 11–24). They consist primarily of his early notes for a "Red Bank and Moscow Novel" and his proposal in 1939 for what he planned to call *The Story of the Three Wishes*. (Most of the original material is in the Wilson collection in the Beinecke Library at Yale.)

Edel gives the impression that the formal proposal (11–17) was a "preliminary general statement," and that the summary of a "Red Bank and Moscow Novel" (19–24) was a "scenario" (xxiii) that came later. It turns out that the reverse is true. The notes for the "Red Bank and Moscow Novel" came first. Wilson wrote them in the back of his notebook XVI for 1935–1943. They are fresh from his head, with specific references to people and places, based on his own recent experiences in Russia and at Provincetown. Wilson revised his raw notes, but Edel's transcription follows the original version, with all the jottings and inconsistencies that the writer later corrected. The brief notes for the "First Episode," from the 1920s, out of which *The Higher Jazz* developed, are intact in *The Forties*. But in the "Second Episode," in which the American hero is transformed into a Russian bureaucrat, Edel's text includes an irrelevant anecdote about a Russian monk and a glass eye, which Wilson had removed; and he garbles Wilson's musings on Pushkin's premonition of death, Пара, мой друк, пара ("It's time, my friend, it's time"), into meaningless Latin letters which are not a transliteration (22). In commenting on the plan for the "Third Episode," where Wilson freely draws upon his impressions of Cape Cod and his friends there, Edel misidentifies Mary ("Bubs") Hackett, the wife of Chauncey Hackett, as Mary McCarthy (21). Sentences and paragraphs are out of order in the text of this "Red Bank and Moscow" summary.

Wilson's typescript for his later, more formal proposal is accurately reproduced in *The Forties* (11–17). However, Edel prints, between the two outlines (17–19), material that belongs to a later period, when Wilson had abandoned his original plans and was working on *The Higher Jazz*. The scrap that the editor uses as another example of Wilson's search for a Mary McCarthy character in the *Three Wishes* (19) belongs to the new novel, where it is an attempt to incorporate certain qualities of McCarthy into Kay Burke ("Caroline" is mentioned). More important, the list of "Names for Characters" (17–18) that Edel reproduces has nothing to do with Wilson's plans for *The Story of the Three Wishes*. It contains the names he was using in *The Higher Jazz* at about the time he was finishing his work on the manuscript. Some names have been misread from Wilson's notes: "Bill Chippen" for Bill Shippen, "Joe Frijanza" for Joe Friganza, "Monmontaburg" for "Monmouthbury."

A NOTE ON THE NAMES

Wilson was fascinated with names; he made lists for many purposes in his notebooks and on random scraps of paper. From a list containing such oddities as "Pussy Willow" and "Navesink Jones," he picked two names for his novel: "Fred Stokes," Caroline's uncle, and "Newhall Haines," the bond salesman who had gone around as an undergraduate reciting poetry. He picked "Crolskill," the estate of Henry and Julie, from a list of such Dutch-sounding possibilities as "Wittskill," "Hookskill," and "Poolskill." He chose names in a variety of ways. "Dixie McCann" was close enough to Texas Guinan; "Eddie Frink" sounded silly enough for the character with that name. Charles Ives becomes "Rockland," the composer from rocky New Hampshire. I have discussed others, such as "Nick Carter" and "Janowitz," in the notes.

Wilson stayed with the names of most of his major characters through the novel, but he did not go back to make the names of lesser people consistent. Of the friends of Caroline from the "cocktail set," it takes a number of chapters before "Phil Davis," "Phil Stewart," and "Stuart Leigh" come together as "Phil Dewitt"; his wife is "Loretta," "Clover," and finally "Claire." In some cases Wilson may have simply slipped (he alternated between "Katherine" and "Elizabeth Danziger," and used "Nicolls" for two different women). In most instances, however, he was striving for a suitable name. This is conspicuous in the case of Kay Burke, the major character whose name gave the author the most trouble. She first appears as "Betty Frick," then becomes in turn "Myra Frost," "Myra Fisk," "Myra Burke," and finally "Kay Burke." Wilson showed much less uncertainty about Caroline: in a few places in his text and notes he flirted with "Carrie" and the maiden name of "Glover," rather than "Stokes." Among place names, he began with "Hitchcock" as Fritz's school; after trying "Hillcrest" (after his own Hill School), he declared, "School should be

Kendall," and adopted that name from his short story "After the Game."

Throughout the text I have used the names that Wilson used at the end of the novel. In almost every case, he decided on the final names by the time he wrote Chapter X. Most of these names appear in the list of characters he made when he was concluding his work on the novel (*Forties* 17–18).

"THE PROBLEM
OF THE HIGHER JAZZ"

Editor's Note: This essay on the difficulty of fusing jazz and classical music, which gives *The Higher Jazz* its title, was published in the *New Republic* in 1926 (13 Jan.: 217–229). Wilson supplied the current title of the essay when he returned to it in 1958, printing it in *The American Earthquake* (112–115) in the company of two reviews of Stravinsky (104–111). (See the first note to Chapter VIII.) In "The Problem of the Higher Jazz" Wilson compares the use of popular materials by Louis Gruenberg (1884–1964) and Arthur Honegger to the other side of this process — the attempts by George Gershwin and Paul Whiteman to put popular music in a classical setting. Gruenberg's *Jazzberries*, Honegger's piano concerto, and Aaron Copland's *Music for the Theater* (a work in which Wilson finds a successful synthesis) had been performed in late 1925 at recitals of the kind Wilson satirizes in Chapter VIII. Gershwin's opera *135th Street* (originally called *Blue Monday*) and Whiteman's arrangements were performed twice at Carnegie Hall near the end of the year. Deems Taylor (1885–1966), whose *Circus Days* was played at the same concerts, was a member of the Algonquin Round Table group and one of the lovers of Dorothy Parker. (He had written an earlier tone poem based on the romance *Jurgen*, 1919, by James Branch Cabell, 1879–1958.)

The efforts of popular jazz and serious musical art to effect a junction and a marriage continue unabated. In fact, the struggle has furnished the chief source of interest of the new music of the season.

On one hand the *Jazzberries* of Louis Gruenberg and the piano concerto of Arthur Honegger, both played under the auspices of the League of Composers, apply to the rhythms of popular music the fastidious selective formula of modern impressionism, and in splitting them up and shaving them down, largely rob them of their power. On the other hand, Mr. George Gershwin, parallel with his regular business of turning out musical comedies, has proceeded with his assault on the concert hall from the direction of Broadway. The present writer was unable to hear Gershwin's new piano concerto played by the New York Symphony Society (it has been discussed elsewhere in the *New Republic*); but his one-act Negro opera, *135th Street*, was one of the most interesting features of Paul Whiteman's recent concert in Carnegie Hall. This opera was first produced three years ago in George White's *Scandals* and its origin probably explains the disappointment we feel in it as a drama when we see it on a more pretentious stage. It is impossible to tell whether *135th Street* is to be taken as tragedy or burlesque. The scene is a Negro joint in Harlem: one of the girls is in love with a professional gambler; the latter announces to the proprietor, though not in the presence of his sweetheart, that he is going to visit his dear old mammy, whom he has not seen in many years. The café fills with people; the girl and her lover are together; the latter suddenly receives a telegram and leaves the room, refusing to divulge its contents to his jealous companion; interested parties induce her to believe that the telegram is from another woman and when her lover returns, she immediately shoots him. He dies; but not before he has had an opportunity to hand her the telegram in self-justification; it says, "It is no use to come. Your mammy has been dead three years." Mr. Gershwin's music, however, evidently aims at a certain dignity; a prologue imitated from *Pagliacci* introduces a score of which most of the setting of the action speaks with the conventional tragic accents of modern Italian opera. This setting cements together separate "numbers" in a vein of sophisticated jazz — a mammy song, a love song and a "blues." And here again the attempt to combine jazz with more respectable music idiom seems mechanical and unsatisfactory. In the case of the composers mentioned above, their invincibly alien spirit and technique had the effect of blighting the jazz spirit and rendering it uninteresting. In the case of Gershwin, the jazz

itself, which is his natural vehicle of expression, does not lack
vivacity or color; in *135th Street* it is admirable — especially in
such passages as the prelude, where he elicits sinister and disturbing effects from the characteristic voices of the jazz orchestra. But it gives the impression of emerging in blocks from a
background of conventional opera which has nothing in common with it and which, beside the vulgar vitality of the jazz,
tends to take on the aspect of an imposture.

More artistically satisfactory than any of these compositions
was Aaron Copland's *Music for the Theater* played at one of the
League of Composers' concerts. There are traces of Stravinsky
in Mr. Copland; but he is not an imitator of Stravinsky —
rather, he has a similar gift for conveying the excitement, the
emotion, of the time, which has its popular expression in jazz,
in a distinguished musical form. His vitality is as spontaneous
as his culture is genuine. And there is probably more musical
drama in his untitled and unannotated *Music for the Theater*
than in the whole of Gershwin's opera.

The career of Mr. Paul Whiteman, at whose concerts in Carnegie Hall the Gershwin opera was sung, is another interesting
episode in the artistic development of jazz. Mr. Whiteman, as
everybody knows, was formerly the leader of the most popular
hotel dance orchestra in the United States. Now he occupies a
different position: he appears in vaudeville and gives concerts;
his orchestra has become an entertainment, an artistic performance, in itself. In listening to a whole evening of Paul Whiteman, we cannot always rid ourselves of the feeling — which
obtrudes itself also, and to a greater degree, in the case of Vin-
cent Lopez — that we should enjoy the music more if we were
eating and talking while we listened to it. But, on the other
hand, Paul Whiteman's orchestra nowadays would never do in
a hotel; and I do not know whether it is any use for dancing.
No modern French composer could have robbed the Charleston music more completely of the qualities which make people
dance the Charleston to it than, by reducing it to its abstract

pattern, Mr. Whiteman has. He has refined and disciplined his orchestra to a point of individuality and distinction where it would be likely to embarrass dancers and diners. Not that it is free from a virtuosity rather curious than distinguished. Among the features of Mr. Whiteman's recent concerts were a pair of pianists who played the same compositions at the same time on two different pianos in exact synchronization and with the effect of automatic piano players; and a man who performed a duet on a cornet and a clarinet, played *Pop Goes the Weasel* on a violin held in sixty-five different positions and finally rendered *Hiawatha* on an old bicycle pump. But Whiteman has drilled his musicians to better artistic purpose. When he makes a speech, as he did at Carnegie Hall, we realize how much his orchestra owes its peculiar excellence to its conductor, how far he has succeeded in investing it with his own characteristics. Whiteman's voice has precisely the qualities of one of his own muted trombones; he speaks with a hard Western *r*, but his phrases have a precision and economy, a sharp edge and a metallic resonance. And this is the character that his instruments take on when they depart furthest from their function of playing for other people to dance and come closest, apparently, to Mr. Whiteman's heart; a little dry, a little deliberate, a little lacking in lyric ecstasy, but very fastidious and elegant and stamped with the ideal of perfection.

Mr. Deems Taylor has hitherto been rather conspicuous for his avoidance of the universal fashion. He has, however, in *Circus Day*, which was played at the Whiteman concerts, made use of jazz material. Nevertheless, he still stands outside the developments I have discussed above. It is as plain from his own compositions as it was from his musical criticism that the problems and the struggles of contemporary music do not interest him. I did not care much for his *Jurgen*, a symphonic poem played earlier in the season by the New York Symphony Society. It seemed rather syrupy and insipid. These are qualities, to be sure, of which Mr. Cabell himself is by no means guiltless; but there are also to be found in his novel a genuine note of natural magic and a sinister malaise. That Mr. Taylor desired to capture at least the second of these elements his program notes show; but, to this author at least, he failed to evoke either Mother Sereda or Koschchei the Deathless. He seems too easygoing, too amiable, too smooth, to be deeply troubled by the unknown quantities which these symbols represent; he leaves out the disturbing elements of *Jurgen*, as he did those of *Through the Looking-Glass*.

But in *Circus Day* he has a subject as amiable as possible and he makes of it as charming as possible a piece of descriptive music. With great ingenuity at finding musical equivalents for roaring lions, jugglers, clowns, and the other features of the old-fashioned circus, he combines a taste which always restrains him from overdoing his efforts and sacrificing music to cleverness. *Circus Day* was perhaps the happiest number of the Whiteman concerts.